Schooled
by the
Bastard

ANNABELLE
ANDERS

IN FOR
A PENNY

MAYFAIR, LONDON IN THE
SPRING OF 1815

*L*ady Augusta Primm eyed the bustling backside of her maid, who'd gotten quite far ahead of her as she chatted eagerly with an old friend. Augusta slowed her own pace as she strolled along the path that crossed this section of Hyde Park.

Before she arrived in London a fortnight before, Augusta hadn't appreciated the level of independence she'd been allowed at home. Because here, her father proved even more overbearing, insisting she only go out with a companion, thusly ending the solitude she'd taken for granted walking along the cliffs overlooking the sea near Starbridge Manor.

But spring was in the air, and she was on the cusp of beginning her life.

Her heart ought to be lighter. There ought to be no time so special in a young woman's life as when she was but seven and ten. Especially when that young woman was the daughter of a wealthy marquess and she was finally making her much-awaited come-out.

Augusta's heart, however, remained heavy with disappointment.

Only two days prior, her father had informed her that he'd made an agreement with the Duke of Malum—promising her to his old friend's son—a boy she'd met only once. That had been over a decade before, and all she remembered of him were his overbearing demeanor and cruel eyes. He'd failed to leave her with a good impression.

Two young men she recognized from a garden party the day before glanced toward her from across the lawn, but then turned away, hurriedly marching in the opposite direction. News of her betrothal had spread quickly throughout the *ton* and the decently-sized pool of suitors she'd accumulated had immediately dried up.

"Hello there! Have you seen a young man with dark blond hair running about? Dressed in ridiculous finery?"

A low voice cut through her melancholy, stirring an odd sensation in the depths of her being. She was certain she'd never heard the man before, and yet her heart skipped a beat.

Holding her breath, she pivoted slowly.

The sensation of almost recognition spread through her again. She had not imagined it.

Him, the wind seemed to whisper as her gaze landed on the young man who'd spoken to her.

He met her gaze, stepping forward. "I seem to have lost track of my brother. Addison looks younger than his age, which is four and ten, and he's... well, he's eluding me this afternoon."

This young man's most prominent feature was his hair, which was black and curly and longer than it ought to be. But then his eyes caught and held her attention, so dark as to almost be black, and a shiver rolled through her.

Him.

He stilled, staring back at her, and even from several yards away, she could see his throat move. Did he feel it too?

He resumed walking toward her, and Augusta immediately

shook herself. Even as a little girl, she had never been the sort of child to give in to flights of fancy. With the Marquess of Starbridge for a father, she knew better than to believe in fairy tales.

"I—" she began. He'd asked her a question. Oh, yes. "I haven't seen such a boy." Though she truly wished that she could help him.

Her answer did nothing to deter his approach, and Augusta glanced around to see if anyone was watching them. Luckily, this part of the park didn't attract many visitors. The abundance of trees didn't lend itself to showing off a lady's ensemble as well as the clearings near the lake.

The young man smiled, and white teeth contrasted against his not-quite-bronze skin. He was the most handsome boy she'd ever seen. No, not a boy, but not a grown man either. He was tall with a slim physique that would likely fill out over the next few years.

Augusta guessed him to be a few years older than her.

He stopped but two yards away, and as though their meeting had been scripted for a play, neither looked anywhere but at the other.

Leaves rustled in the wind, a few billowy clouds floated across the sky, and yet time stood still.

If Augusta was breathing, she was not aware of it.

It was he who broke the spell. "Mr. Rowan Stewart, at your service." He bowed low, performing the gesture with more grace than she'd ever seen.

Rowan Stewart.

Following his lead, Augusta executed what she hoped was an equally elegant curtsey. "Lady Augusta Primm," she provided, pleased that her voice sounded normal.

It was not at all acceptable to introduce oneself in this manner, without a proper introduction, but at that moment, she felt as though higher powers were at work—giving him her name was merely the formality to a beginning.

To a glorious beginning.

He cleared his throat, his gaze locked onto her. "It's a beautiful day, is it not?" he asked.

This made her smile. Taking in the quality of his clothing, sturdy tan breeches, a perfectly tailored coat, and elegantly tied cravat, he ought to appear similar to other gentlemen of the *ton*. But Augusta immediately sensed that he was nothing like them. Not because of the color of his skin or the impropriety of their introduction, but because of the look in his eyes.

Familiar while proving utterly unreadable.

And yet, like other young men had done over the past few weeks, he'd commented on the weather.

She tore her stare away just long enough to glance toward the sky which, although mostly blue, held dark clouds gathered in the west. "But not for long."

Something life-altering was happening to both of them, and here they were discussing the weather. Butterflies zinged around her belly and her bodice felt tighter than usual.

"We're lucky to have come this morning, then," he answered. He took another step toward her, cutting the distance between them in half. If she reached her hand out, she could almost touch his chest.

This close, he appeared even taller and might seem imposing if not for his expression—a little stunned. Was it a mirror of her own?

"We are." Augusta gripped her elbows to ward off a shiver. With the sun already bright and warm, she could only attribute the shaking inside to his nearness.

"Have we met before?" He cocked his head sideways. "You seem familiar."

Because he was, and yet Augusta would have remembered meeting him. "I don't think so."

One of the nearby trees shook, drawing both of their attention.

Then the tree spoke.

"Row!"

And suddenly the two of them were grinning at one another. "I think we have discovered the whereabouts of your brother," Augusta said.

After a moment's hesitation, Mr. Rowan Stewart strolled across to the suddenly-animated tree and tilted his head to look up. "Get your arse down here, Addison." But he spoke the words lovingly.

Augusta bit her lip. She ought to bid him farewell and catch up with Martha.

But she wasn't ready.

"I hate him," the tree answered.

Mr. Stewart's grimace was sympathetic rather than disapproving.

"I know, Add. He's a beast, but he's... Father."

"All I did was ask about going to Eton, like you did."

"I'll try talking to him, but you know how he is..." Another heavy sigh. Mr. Stewart glanced over his shoulder, back to Augusta, looking apologetic. "Our father refuses to send Addison off to school. He insists Addison, instead, learn from England's finest tutors."

"Who are you talking to?" the voice in the tree demanded.

"A lady, Addison." This time, Mr. Stewart's glance included a wink, which reignited all those butterflies. "Come down here, Addison, please, so I can make the proper introductions."

The tree shook rather violently, for a tree, as black boots and then a pair of legs dangled before landing on one of the lower branches. Next appeared the tails of a fine powder-blue coat and a boy's head, his not-quite-blond hair decorated with leaves and twigs.

A thud sounded as the young man landed solidly on the ground.

Mr. Stewart gripped the boy's shoulders and turned him in Augusta's direction. "My lady, may I present you to my brother, Lord Addison Briarton, Earl of Samson, Marquess of St. Alastair. Future Duke of Bedwell. Addison, Lady Augusta Primm."

Augusta blinked and then stared at Rowan's *younger brother*, who, most exceptionally, was the future Duke of Bedwell. She dropped into another curtsey. "My lord," she said.

Lord St. Alastair was the heir... She glanced back to Mr. Stewart, who looked nothing like the boy. She'd heard the stories. Her elegant and charming young man, the man she'd practically woven into the hero of a fairy tale, was the duke's bastard son.

He had the bearing of a duke himself and more. Before the silence grew too long, Augusta turned to stare up at the tree. "I imagine you had quite a good view from up there." Augusta knew the lure of a good climbing tree. She'd given in to it often enough, although not since arriving in Mayfair.

"Splendid, really," Lord St. Alastair responded with a grin, but it just as quickly jerked into a frown. "I'd never come down if it was up to me."

That was when she spied the cut just below the young man's eye. Opening her reticule, she removed one of her mono-grammed handkerchiefs and stepped forward. "Looks like one of the branches caught you." The young man tensed, and she paused before dabbing at the spot. Some of the blood around the cut had dried, but blood still oozed out of the wound—not a long surface scratch, but a deep tear, and around it, a disturbingly familiar red mark.

In the shape of a hand.

"Do you mind?"

"I'll tend to it," Mr. Stewart moved directly behind her and took the linen from her hand. He then dropped to one knee. "Have a seat, Addison. You're lucky none got on your coat."

"I'm not a child," the future duke said but did as his brother requested just the same.

"I know, Add." Mr. Stewart dabbed at the cut efficiently, and the boy tilted his head and brushed a leaf out of his hair. Mr. Stewart froze, his eyes turning serious. "Where's your ring? You know you aren't supposed to take it off."

The boy's eyes opened wide, but then he jumped up and glanced over at the tree. "I left it up there."

"In the tree?"

"Hooked on one of the smaller branches."

His older brother scrubbed a hand down his face. "I'll fetch it."

"No. You wouldn't be able to find it, whereas I know exactly where it is."

"Be quick about it, then," the older brother said.

"And do be careful," Augusta added.

She really ought to take her leave of these two, and yet her desire to draw out the meeting as long as possible compelled her to stay.

"I'm sorry about that," Mr. Stewart turned back to her when his brother once again disappeared into the thick branches.

"I've a few younger brothers myself," she said. In fact, she had five of them. "They're always getting into some sort of trouble or another."

"But you'll do anything for them, won't you?"

Augusta laughed. "Indeed, Mr. Stewart. Even when they don't deserve it." But then she frowned. "Why won't your father allow him to go away for school? Eton is more than respectable."

"Because he will eventually be Bedwell."

But of course. The duke must be controlling, like her father.

"That's a shame," Augusta said. "Not that he will one day

inherit a dukedom but that he must miss out on learning with other boys." And then she sighed. "I enjoyed my time away at school. Did you?"

Rather than answer, he gave her a vague smile, which flustered her. As the pause stretched on, she hurried to fill the silence.

"I wouldn't mind becoming a teacher someday." Not that that would be possible—not if she was married.

But if she was going to have a dream, she might as well make it a good one. She slid Mr. Stewart a sideways glance. "I'd mind even less running my own school." Was she rambling?

She laughed, but he did not. He simply studied her.

"Will you call me Rowan?"

"I should not," Augusta answered.

His black eyes practically twinkled at that. "But you will?"

Oh, he was not only magnificent to look at but disarming as well.

Augusta contemplated his request and then nodded. "Only in private. My brothers call me Auggie."

"I like Augusta." His voice, speaking her name, felt like a caress. "It suits you."

She laughed out loud at this. Because she doubted she could ever live up to the meaning behind her name: great, magnificent.

Without thinking, she asked, "Will you be at the Willoughby Ball tomorrow night?"

He frowned and then rubbed his chin. "I hadn't planned on attending. However, I hadn't met you yet."

"And now that you have?" Augusta had never been so bold.

"How can I not? But I have one stipulation."

"What is that?" A thrill shot down her spine.

"That you save a dance for me."

"Yes." She'd barely gotten her answer out before steps

sounded on the path, followed by her maid's exclamation of relief.

"There you are!" Martha caught sight of Mr. Stewart and then turned a narrowed gaze back on Augusta. "If your father sacks me, you'll be stuck with Mrs. Bitters, you know. See if she lets you dilly-dally behind her like a lost pup the same way I do. Now come along. It's already ten minutes past the hour, and you need to change for this afternoon's *At Home.*" She slapped herself on the head. "I should know better than to leave you alone for too long…"

Augusta found herself being dragged away just as Rowan's little brother dropped out of the tree.

"Martha." Augusta could not formally introduce her maid to Lord St. Alastair nor Mr. Stewart, and yet she needed the woman to realize she was in the presence of nobility. She gestured toward the two brothers. "These gentlemen are the Duke of Bedwell's sons."

Martha merely lifted her chin, not at all impressed. "Oh, I know who they are, alright." She addressed Rowan specifically. "You, sir, should know better than to come sniffing around an unchaperoned debutante."

And then her remarkably strong maid tugged so hard, Augusta thought her arm would break off.

"Goodbye, my lord, Mr. Stewart," Augusta called, waving as she was pulled away.

Neither answered, but Rowan's gaze twinkled. And that was the expression she held on to, the image she stored away, as she and Martha left the park and turned toward her father's town-house, Rosewood Hall.

Yes, she was betrothed to Malum's son, but this… extraordinary meeting today with Rowan Stewart transcended such worldly matters as betrothals.

And for the first time in her life, she wondered if her father's iron will could be thwarted—by fate.

"He's a bastard, you know," Martha spoke up from beside her. Rosewood Hall was just across the street, and they'd paused to wait for a high-flyer and a vendor's wagon to roll past.

"Of a duke," Augusta pointed out. "He's attending the Willoughby Ball tomorrow." In exchange for a dance.

With her!

There was nothing she could do to tamp down her excitement at the thought. Even if her conscience warned her to, because knowing her father, she ought to be wary.

But suddenly, she experienced all the anticipation of any other debutante.

Rowan Stewart.

"But you know how your father is," Martha reminded her.

Her maid made a valid point. When it came to the proprieties of the *ton*, of society in general, the Marquess of Starbridge controlled his family with a heavy hand. And her mother always went along with his decrees.

And yet, all Augusta could dwell on was the light of promise in Rowan's eyes. What would it feel like to dance with him? To hold his hand? To perhaps go walking in the garden alone with him?

She could not marry the Duke of Malum's son. She could not!

The thought made her want to die.

As impossible as it seemed, she contemplated going to her father and telling him she'd met the Duke of Bedwell's heir today. She would casually mention Mr. Stewart. Before making her come-out, Augusta had studied all the books on lineage. The Bedwell ducal line was twice as old as Malum's—the sort of thing her father cared about. And if she was correct, the Bedwell line was abundantly more prosperous.

"I want to wear my new rose silk tomorrow night," Augusta said. "With my silver slippers."

"I thought you were saving that one for the Dunkirks' Ball. Isn't it your favorite?"

"It is." Augusta sent Martha a meaningful smile. "He's asked that I save a dance for him."

Martha had just lifted her hand to push the door open but stilled.

"Oh, but, my lady, you cannot. He's well-dressed and fine to look at, I'll give you that. And, yes, he was raised in a ducal household, but he's a bastard, and that's all your father will care about. Don't test his lordship, I beg of you. You'll only regret it."

"You're being a tad melodramatic, don't you think, Martha?" Augusta ignored the warning twinge low in her belly. "He's a gentleman through and through. You ought to have seen how sweet he was to his brother. Piers and Liam could learn a thing or two from Mr. Stewart."

All of her brothers would do well to be more like the gentleman who'd caused her world to tilt. But they spent more time competing with one another than providing any brotherly support.

They were her father's sons, after all.

"No, my lady." Martha took Augusta by the shoulders and turned her so she had no choice but to look into the maid's eyes. "Mr. Stewart can be the smartest, kindest, most charming gentleman in all of Mayfair, but he's a bastard. And nothing can ever change that. I beg of you, don't play with fire like this. You have more than most ladies can ever hope for. You'll do good to remember that." And then she added, "Mark my words, if you persist in this nonsense, you'll be sorry."

Augusta rolled her eyes toward the sky. Martha was always worried about something and hardly anything ever came from any of it.

Unfortunately, this was one of the times she'd been right.

MISS PRIMM'S SEMINARY FOR
THE REFINEMENT OF LADIES

WINTER 1831

*M*iss Augusta Primm, founder and headmistress of one of England's most renowned schools for girls, closed the office door behind her and locked it.

In the midst of the winter holiday, the temperature in the little room was frigid. But rather than strike a flint to the wood in the hearth, she crossed over to her desk.

She then dropped into her chair and exhaled a shaky breath.

After a very uncomfortable visit home, where she and her brothers had made arrangements for her mother, who was ill, and her father, who was… ill in another way, she'd returned to the school to face other, more pressing troubles.

Her world—this school she'd carefully constructed since establishing her independence at the age of ten and eight—was suddenly closing in on her.

She choked on a harsh laugh. No, it wasn't just closing in on her, it was falling down around her—both literally and figuratively.

At least she was home again—away from her father and the tension he brought out in her younger brothers.

Removing her spectacles, she rubbed her eyes, forcing herself to breathe normally. *"I can do this. I've handled worse."*

Or had she?

After working for nearly two decades to maintain the school's near-spotless reputation, the tides had seemed to shift against her. The more prominent the school became, the more intense the scrutiny it came under.

Her graduating students had done exceptionally well for themselves—a few, perhaps too well.

And this scrutiny was of the worst kind—from members of the *ton*.

And that was the very last thing the school needed. Because, although Primm ensured her girls learned the skills society expected of them, they were exposed to other, more meaningful subjects—subjects many didn't consider appropriate for young ladies.

It was best to keep the nature of some of the classes vague, best to dismiss them as mere tokens to the proper lady's education.

The wrong kind of criticism from the right person could ruin her. It could ruin the school.

A year ago last autumn, Augusta had been forced to fire a perfectly good teacher when a handful of parents had discovered the young woman's questionable family background. They'd gone so far as to sign a petition, threatening to withdraw their students if the young woman remained on staff. Augusta abhorred such snobbery, and if she'd been financially solvent at the time, she would have taken a stand rather than succumb to that sort of pressure.

Unfortunately, Augusta and the school had not been solvent, and after studying the account books from all angles, she and her assistant headmistress, Miss Victoria Shipley, had agreed they couldn't afford to take such a risk.

When English society got involved, the losses could not be predicted.

Augusta's guilt over the firing would have persisted if that teacher, Miss Collette Jones, hadn't landed a husband shortly after, the brother of one of her students as well as a distant acquaintance from the past—the Duke of Bedwell.

Trouble had been averted.

But here Augusta was, a little over a year later, facing yet another scandal. This time, the threat came from within. Miss Shipley, who not only assisted with administrative duties and fundraising but also taught the etiquette classes, had been caught in a most compromising situation—with Augusta's own brother! *Her favorite brother*, as a matter of fact.

The couple had been stranded at the school over the holidays together—alone—and when one of their students returned early, they'd been caught in a most compromising situation.

Augusta closed her eyes. Dear God. *What had they been thinking?*

The trouble was, the student who'd witnessed it was not just any student, but rebellious, spoiled, and manipulative Allison Meadowbrook. Allison had, of course, decided to use the information to her full advantage.

She'd blackmailed Augusta into contemplating an impossible scheme.

And since Augusta's top priority was keeping the school running, she once again found herself walking a fine line between practicing her ethics and stomping them into the ground.

A knock sounded, interrupting her spiraling thoughts.

With most of her teachers not yet returned from holiday break, it was likely Victoria. Augusta dabbed at the corners of her eyes and then adjusted her spectacles on the bridge of her nose before rising to unlock the door.

She was Miss Primm, headmistress and businesswoman. Now was not the time to show weakness.

Augusta and Victoria had worked together for years, but Augusta had always kept a professional distance. But since Victoria was newly married to Augusta's brother, the other woman was her sister-in-law now and not her employee.

However, just as she expected, Victoria stood at the open door waiting patiently with a forced smile.

Augusta hated that the other woman's newfound happiness was tempered by guilt.

"I thought I might find you here," Victoria said, but after glancing at the hearth, she paused. "It's freezing! Are you... well?"

Augusta straightened her shoulders and returned to the seat behind her desk—a place where she'd always managed to find her balance—to find her calm.

She knotted her shawl so it wouldn't slip. "I'm perfectly fine. I'm just making a list of tasks to complete before the students begin returning."

Victoria hugged her arms in front of her and feigned a shiver. "You'll catch your death working in the cold like this."

"Yes... well..." Augusta ignored Victoria's concern and methodically straightened the papers on her desk. When she was satisfied with those efforts, she then fixed her favorite quill so it sat parallel to the stack. "I hadn't noticed."

Fussing more than usual, Victoria crouched in front of the hearth and, after a few failed attempts, set a flame to the kindling that had been prepared earlier. With nothing else to distract her, she returned to sit in the chair opposite Augusta.

"It's because you work too hard." After a short pause, Victoria cleared her throat. "Anyway, I wanted to talk with you. I know I won't be able to do any teaching next session, but if you've a few moments, I'd love to share the ideas I have to expand our curriculum."

Definitely a more tentative Victoria than Augusta was accustomed to.

Under normal circumstances, Augusta would have greatly appreciated discussing the subjects that ought to be at the forefront of her thoughts.

Unfortunately, these were not normal circumstances.

"I'll be happy to," Augusta said. "As soon as we've dealt with the Allison Meadowbrook situation."

Augusta flipped to a new page in her journal and wrote the girl's name. How was it possible that one manipulative little girl of seven and ten could cause her so much trouble?

"Miss Fellowes is leaning toward agreeing to the scheme," Victoria said. "I would do it if I could. Oh, Primm. I'm so terribly sorry."

"Miss Fellowes is the only teacher who looks young enough to pose as Allison. Besides, I doubt my brother would appreciate you acting as another's betrothed so soon after your nuptials." Augusta very nearly found humor in the irony.

"No, I don't suppose he would, which reminds me. He intends to go ahead with the purchase of Longbow Castle. I'll only be living a few miles from the school and can still help you on a part-time basis." And then she added, "If that's something you might be open to."

"Let's wait and see, shall we?" Augusta couldn't make any promises yet, no matter how much she valued Victoria's assistance. "I hope Piers knows what he's getting into. That castle looks as though a stiff wind will blow it over."

"It's not that bad. He's sent for an architect—one of the best in all of England according to him. It's going to be beautiful when it's finished. But that reminds me." Victoria reached into her sleeve and removed a folded note written in Piers' familiar handwriting. "He asked me to give this to you."

. . .

AUGGIE,

I'm expecting to meet with a renowned architect to head up the renovations at Longbow Castle. After I've secured his services, I'll show him to the school so he can meet with you and examine the damages to the school's foundation. Send word if you need anything else.

Your favorite brother,

P

MY FAVORITE BROTHER, *ha!*

This offer was a gesture, no doubt, to make up for his part in the potential disgrace currently hovering over the school. More than likely, he'd try to pay for the repairs as well. But Augusta couldn't allow that. Not unless she had no choice.

She had accumulated some savings for maintenance, and the school was her responsibility. What had begun as a means to independence had come to serve a much greater purpose.

"I'll tell him if you aren't interested," Victoria said. "Or if you've already secured someone to address the damages."

"No. That's fine." Augusta struggled to summon a small amount of enthusiasm. "Tell my *favorite* brother that I will consider the services of his expert."

Hopefully the damages, which had begun appearing last autumn and consisted of several sections that had seemingly eroded for no reason at all, wouldn't require extensive work. The thought added weight to her shoulders, however.

Such optimism was often in vain.

The foundation—the literal foundation of the school—was disintegrating in spots. And no matter how many times her groundskeeper repaired the breaks, the material that made up the footing seemed to be crumbling left and right.

"I only wish there was more we could do." Victoria looked as though she might burst into tears. Even ashamed and obviously uncomfortable, the other woman was a beauty. When Piers had arrived at the school in the middle of a snowstorm to find Victoria alone and damsel-like, he hadn't stood a chance.

Augusta pinched her mouth together. Victoria and Piers were partly at fault, but Augusta ought not to have left Victoria alone. The very last thing she wanted was for her brother's wife to be upset. Victoria was a newlywed and ought to spend this time caught up in the euphoria of being in love.

Because eventually some trouble or another would come along and rob the lovers of their newfound happiness. Passion could bring great satisfaction but could also leave one's life in ashes.

Augusta only hoped that Piers and Victoria's marriage might be the exception.

She most definitely did not want shame to taint their marriage—especially not because of her. Their initial guilt was temporary, but shame was a heavy burden to bear. It made one weary.

And cynical.

If she were a more demonstrative person, Augusta would have reached across the desk and taken Victoria's hands in hers. Instead, she merely stared into the other woman's eyes and forced a smile. "These things happen," she said. "Please stop blaming yourself."

Improprieties transpired all too easily, and Augusta had no business judging her brother and Victoria. "And despite Miss Meadowbrook's insistence that Miss Fellowes end her engagement for her, I am thrilled that you and Piers have found one another. I was beginning to think he'd never settle down." Augusta winced. "Besides, I'm the one who left you alone in the first place."

Victoria smiled and, for a moment, looked almost dreamy. "We are so very happy, and although I would rather matters had been settled with more decorum, I couldn't wish things didn't turn out as they have."

And Augusta was truly, genuinely pleased to see these two people find contentment together.

That empty part in her own heart pricked at her, but Augusta ignored it. She'd learned long ago not to compare other people's lives to her own circumstances.

Because Augusta's life was filled with a reasonable amount of satisfaction and success.

Aside from a few hiccups.

THAT SAME DAY, ON THE ROAD TO LONGBOW CASTLE

"Why would an earl, a man who stands to inherit half a dozen estates already, wish to purchase another one—one that's, from what I understand, all but gone to ruin?" John Rhys, Rowan Stewart's foreman and right-hand man, pondered out loud as the spires of what must surely be Longbow Castle reached toward the sky in the distant treetops.

"No idea," Rowan answered, running his hand over his head, which, but for a few scars, slid smoothly beneath his palm. For practical purposes, he preferred keeping his hair short and shaved it every fortnight or so.

"It's my understanding most nobs struggle to fund what they already have," Rhys continued his train of thought.

"Rosewood's different, though. Word is that he's been lucky with investments. Manufacturing and whatnot. I've given up trying to understand the workings of the aristocracy." He might have been raised in an aristocratic household but blood won out. And when push came to shove, he'd realized he'd never been one of them.

Amongst the English elite, there was no room for a man like himself, one who was not only a bastard, but half-Barbadian.

And he didn't care.

Besides, he was happiest as a tradesman. Designing and building gave him purpose, something most nobs lacked.

This job, however, as Rhys pointed out, was something of a conundrum.

When Rowan had first received the letter from Piers Primm, the Earl of Rosewood, he'd immediately believed that it was an ill-conceived joke—or worse.

Because Rosewood was heir to the *Marquess of Starbridge*. A man who, seventeen years prior, had made his opinion of Rowan perfectly clear. Starbridge had left no doubt that he wanted no ties with the likes of him.

As had his daughter.

Quite.

Clear.

Rowan rubbed at the long-faded scar on his chin that had been left as a reminder. He hadn't stood a chance against Starbridge's ruffians. Back then, Rowan had been wiry enough, but the thugs were more beasts than men, each outweighing him by nearly half a dozen stone.

Rowan only remembered the first half of the beating. He'd been unconscious for the second half.

So when, a few weeks ago, he'd opened the letter from Augusta's brother, he'd been skeptical, to say the least.

Following further correspondence with the earl, however, and after doing some checking around London, he'd decided it was not a joke.

More of an ironic coincidence.

The earl was considering purchasing Longbow Castle from the Earl of Hardwood, who, Rowan had learned, was in dire need of funds.

And the infamous Longbow Castle, it was rumored, was in dire need of renovations.

Rosewood had insisted Rowan was his first choice to head

up the repairs—for no other reason than Rowan's reputation as an architect and builder. Without being boastful, Rowan conceded the earl's reasoning was sound.

But as he and Rhys neared the castle, Rowan tensed.

Not because he'd maintained any fear of Rosewood's father, the old marquess, or because he held ill will toward Rosewood himself, but because Piers Primm, the Earl of Rosewood, was one of Lady Augusta Primm's younger brothers. And Lady Augusta was Miss Primm now, headmistress of her own school.

Miss Primm's Seminary for the Refinement of Ladies just happened to be less than five miles down the road from Longbow Castle. And Rowan never wanted to see that woman again.

Rowan leaned forward, patting Whisky's neck at the same time he stretched the muscles in his back.

Having recently completed a rather impressive project in the heart of Mayfair, Rowan's coffers were full. He was in no way short of funds. He'd had other offers on the table, but the idea of returning Longbow Castle to its former glory was too intriguing to resist.

If not for his half-sister, Fiona, he could avoid the school altogether. Fee was enrolled at Miss Primm's, however, and if she learned that he was in the area, she'd expect him to visit.

Miss Primm.

No doubt she'd changed in the seventeen years since he'd last seen her. The years would have left their mark on her, in the form of wrinkles, gray hair, and perhaps extra pounds. But he wasn't at all curious...

Augusta.

She had been Lady Augusta to the *ton*, Augusta to Rowan.

Her family had called her Auggie—a name he'd never felt right calling her.

Images he'd failed to erase flooded his memory—images of

a girl with milk and honey skin, intelligent eyes, and mahogany hair that, when unpinned, fell past her waist. Rowan's fingers had never forgotten the sensation of being tangled in those silken strands.

Focusing on one of the castle spires, Rowan exhaled a heavy sigh. In the short month they'd been acquainted, Augusta had transformed from a less-than-confident girl into a passionate woman. He'd intended to make her his wife but had never been allowed the honor.

Rowan's father had treated him like a son, more so than his actual heir, causing him to greatly underestimate the rigidity of society. His father had been the bloody Duke of Bedwell, by God. At nine and ten, Rowan had believed that meant something.

Thanks to the Marquess of Starbridge, by the time Rowan left London, he'd learned differently. His perception amongst his father's peers had all been an illusion.

He'd painfully learned the full extent of his disadvantage as a bastard.

"Did you say you've met the earl before?" Rhys asked.

"I've a prior acquaintance with the family," Stewart answered. *Unfortunately.* "But I've never met Rosewood."

When they'd been together, Augusta had presented him to her parents, the Marquess and Marchioness of Starbridge, as well as Lord Eli, the initial heir, who was since deceased.

Starbridge's wife, after presenting him with Augusta, had gone on to provide her husband with an abundance of spares.

Judging from his correspondence with Rosewood, however, the earl was nothing like his father.

Rowan remembered that single meeting, though. He ought to have trusted the doubts he'd had about the marquess. He ought to have believed his first impression that the man hated him—that his lordship would see Rowan die before marrying his daughter.

But Rowan had been too besotted at the time.

"One of my sisters attended Miss Primm's Seminary," Rhys said. All of John Rhys's sisters were ladies, daughters of a baron. Rhys himself, however, held no claim to his father's title. Because, like Rowan, the foreman had been born on the wrong side of the blanket.

"Miss Primm's is in the area. From what I remember," Rhys added.

"It is." Rowan stiffened, and Whisky's normally even steps faltered for a fraction of a second.

Rhys glanced over curiously, and Rowan forced himself to relax.

Seventeen years had passed since he'd known Augusta Primm. Rowan had been young and foolish.

Both men turned the corner, and as the trees gave way to chaotic lawns and gardens, they simultaneously drew their mounts to a halt.

"Oh, hell," Rhys said.

The castle, which resembled a medieval fortress, towered above the property. Of the spires shooting up, only two appeared intact. Half the walls crumbled from erosion, and the massive structure listed to one side.

And yet, it was… It could be… "Magnificent," Rowan said.

With the first impression out of the way, they urged their mounts forward, resuming their approach.

Rhys stood in his stirrups. "Is that supposed to be a roof?"

"A few centuries ago," Rowan answered.

"It's going to need a new foundation."

While Rhys listed the potential snags that could kill the project from the outset, Rowan made his own assessment. Longbow Castle wasn't just a renovation, it was a massive rebuild. It would require years to complete. And after that, regular maintenance.

He'd barely finished that thought when an imposing but

friendly-looking fellow appeared on the threshold of the main entrance and skipped down the front steps.

"Mr. Stewart?" the gentleman called out.

Rowan dismounted and, crossing to the steps, shook the man's hand, taking his measure as he did so. He would have recognized Lord Rosewood as Primm's brother in an instant.

The earl's eyes were a hazel green whereas Augusta's were a stormy gray, but aside from that, their mannerisms and features were uncannily similar. Augusta wasn't as tall as her brother, but the earl's posture reminded Rowan of her.

Even as a young girl, she'd held herself rigid without appearing overly proud. She'd not been like the other debutantes who'd either hunched over giggling or stared down their noses at him.

Odd that the memories came so clearly. It had been a very long time ago.

Rowan cleared his throat. "Rosewood?" he confirmed.

"Guilty." The other released his hand.

Rowan introduced Rhys, and then a young man jogged toward them from a ramshackle building that Rowan guessed had once purposed itself as a stable.

"I can have young William care for your mounts. Looks like they could use some water and a good rubdown."

Rowan met Rhys's gaze and then, turning back to the earl, nodded, accepting for the both of them.

He then glanced up at the massive structure before him.

"I won't mince words, Rosewood," Rowan said. "This isn't just a project, it's more of a career."

Rhys laughed with a grunt, but the earl merely nodded thoughtfully.

"That's why I chose you specifically. I was tempted to build elsewhere, but my countess prefers that we live in the area, and she values the history."

"I didn't realize you were married." But of course. A woman would be at the bottom of such an outlandish project.

But the earl didn't appear bothered at all. In fact, he looked rather pleased with himself.

"I wasn't until a week ago," he said, but then allowed his gaze to drift over the castle. "I've some funds lying around, and as I've no intention of taking on the running of my father's estate, I'm more than happy to spend my money on anything she wants."

The three men took their time hiking around the perimeter of the stables, a dower house, a few other various listing structures, and the castle itself. They then hazarded a partial tour of the interior, and while Rowan and the earl discussed a tableau of issues, Rhys took careful notes.

Rowan knew Rhys would also be devising a rough estimate. Very rough at this point.

But when he eventually tossed out what Rowan knew would be a conservative number, a staggering amount actually, the earl merely nodded.

"It could go higher," Rowan added. "Depending on what we find. Rhys has included incidentals, and we're usually fairly accurate, but with a structure as rundown as this ancient lady, one rarely nails the final costs on the first go-round."

Rosewood faced the castle, and the trio of men fell silent until the earl turned back around.

"About what I suspected." Although he looked a tad disappointed, as though he'd hoped he'd been wrong. "Nonetheless, I want you to take on the project—from start to finish. My wife deserves the best."

Rowan stilled. Those investments the earl had made must have been lucrative, indeed.

And then he took a moment to stare up at the castle.

This would be the biggest project he'd undertaken to date. A buzzing vibrated down his spine.

The bones of Longbow Castle called to him.

But before he could accept, the earl spoke again.

"I have one condition."

Of course, there was always a catch…

"What's that?" Rowan asked warily.

The earl tapped his chin. "That you take a look at my sister's school. There's been damage to the foundation—possible vandalism. I'm no engineer, but it's in need of reinforcements."

Take a look at my sister's school.

Rowan ought to decline the project outright. The earl had no idea what he was asking.

And yet…

He was bound to run into her at some time or another—something he'd imagined with mixed feelings. Seventeen years was a very long time. He was a completely different man than he'd been while courting her. Likely, she was a completely different woman.

Furthermore, he could spend time with Fiona. He avoided his stepmother like the plague and in doing so missed out on visits with his half-sister.

Rowan reached out his right hand, and when Rosewood clasped it in his, gave it a firm shake.

"Let's rebuild your castle, then."

With that decided, a myriad of other details needed ironing out.

Fortunately, the previous occupant of the estate had kept the dower house in repair, and the earl and his new countess had made a temporary home there. Rowan and Rhys would bed down in the gamekeeper's lodge.

"I'm more than willing to put you up at the inn until something more comfortable can be made available," Rosewood offered.

"It'll be more convenient to stay on the property." Rowan

met Rhys's glance, the two men thinking the same thing. "Especially if there are vandals in the area."

It wouldn't be the first time one of Rowan's projects was targeted thusly. He and his team had learned that supplies, along with a dry space to sleep, were more than tempting for the occasional drifter.

"I'll send for my team, then. Once they've arrived, they'll set up a camp around the supplies and near the ongoing work. It's for the best that we have men here around the clock. They tend to get rowdy on occasion, but they're the best at what they do, and Rhys keeps them in check."

Rosewood frowned but agreed. "Very well then. I'm sure you'll think of other details while settling in, and I'll likely come up with at least a hundred more questions. I'm set to finalize the sale with Hardwood tomorrow morning, and if you're amenable, we can drive over to my sister's school afterward. You'll want to discuss necessary repairs with Auggie—or Miss Primm, as she's known in these whereabouts. You have my permission to include supplies required for the school in the orders you place for Longbow. Then let's hash out a contract later this week."

Rowan nodded thoughtfully. He'd be opening a can of worms that was seventeen years in the making—nearly two decades.

What the hell was he doing?

Asking for trouble. That's what.

HIM

*A*ugusta glanced down at her list. Miss Fellowes would deal with Allison Meadowbrook's intended, and then later, Augusta would meet with Piers's architect.

And hopefully the threats would subside.

And after she'd checked those two items off, she could finally get down to business, finalizing plans for the new term.

She'd dealt with worse than this. The school was going to be just fine.

She was going to be just fine.

Stiffening her spine, Augusta marched from her office, through the door that connected the corridor to her residence, and into her parlor, where she found a handful of her favorite teachers, along with her new sister-in-law, waiting for her.

That one student was capable of toppling Augusta's life-long efforts was more than irksome; it was deeply concerning. Allison Meadowbrook had held firm to her... demands. Either Miss Fellowes freed Allison from her betrothal to Lord Hard-wood, while *pretending to be* Allison, or the girl would tell everyone exactly what she'd seen the morning she and Miss Fellowes returned to the school on Christmas Eve morning.

More specifically, who she had seen—and what they'd been doing.

Idiot Piers! And in Augusta's own bed, no less. If he weren't truly her favorite brother, she'd never speak with him again.

But, although he'd lived something of a rakish life until now, he was the only member of her family to ever visit her at the school. He was the only one of her brothers who'd encouraged her when she'd needed it.

And he too saw their father for who he was.

But since they couldn't erase the past, they'd simply have to deal with the present.

With no other viable options, Augusta had given her approval, and Miss Fellowes had agreed to go ahead with the charade.

"We've no choice, really," the younger woman said.

More and more, it seemed, Augusta found herself in this position. Which was ironic, considering she'd opened the school so that women, in general, might have more choices.

Herself included.

Miss Fellowes would pose as Allison when Lord Hardwood arrived to finalize his proposal. The plan was so outrageous that if it failed, if the deception was discovered, he could ruin them all.

But if it succeeded, Allison would stand down and Augusta would regain control over the situation.

Having gone over all the details, Miss Priscilla Fellowes, Miss Chloe Fortune, and Miss Adelaide Royal excused themselves to put the plan in motion.

Which left Augusta sitting alone with Victoria, staring into her guilty eyes. "I'm so very sorry, Primm." It was at least the twentieth time she had uttered the apology.

It was done. All they could do was move forward. Augusta had forgiven her. It was time Victoria forgave herself.

And so Augusta changed the subject. "You said you had a

few ideas to improve the curriculum. I'm curious as to what you've come up with." Victoria had taught all things pertaining to social etiquette. The subject, although not one of Augusta's favorites, was indeed necessary.

"Yes! First, let me explain that I'm ashamed to admit that I've never felt more helpless than when you left me alone at the school. Tasks I have always taken for granted felt unsurmountable. And it made me realize that we need to teach the girls more practical skills having to do with the nitty-gritty of the running of a household—of how to survive without servants. Skills such as building a fire in the hearth, the best way to fetch water, and preparing simple recipes. These abilities seem mundane, and they may not be required on a regular basis, but at some point, our girls are bound to find themselves needing them."

Augusta nodded. "Most of our parents won't approve, of course, so if we incorporate your ideas, we'll have to do it under the guise of home management."

"My thoughts exactly... For instance, removing a stain from a favorite gown."

Apparently, diving into academic matters was precisely what both of them needed, and Primm took copious notes as they discussed lessons to enhance student self-sufficiency. Time flew by until the sound of a coach arriving outside interrupted them.

"That'll be Piers and his architect." Victoria rose with that love-struck gleam in her eye with which Augusta was becoming familiar. Oh, she hoped it remained there for a very long time.

As Jenny, Augusta's housekeeper and cook, was busy in the kitchen, Augusta strode to the entrance while Victoria followed.

"I do hope this architect is a sensible one," she muttered

with a glance over her shoulder. "I'm not looking to rebuild St. George's Cathedral, for heaven's sake."

"I don't think Piers would send over a man if he didn't think he'd be practical enough for you." A hint of laughter sounded in Victoria's voice, almost making Augusta smile.

Tugging her shawl around her shoulders, Augusta then opened the door and turned to greet the midday visitors.

Her brother had already exited the coach, followed by a second, vaguely familiar gentleman, but before she could wave, any semblance of a greeting died on her lips. Because the third man to emerge, the tallest amongst them, the one who held himself back…

Augusta blinked. *Him.*

No. No. *No!* She must be mistaken.

He was the same, but so very different. And yet even if he'd concealed himself completely, she would know his identity.

Rather, her heart would.

Awareness hummed in Augusta's chest as she stepped outside. And then her brother, who initiated the introductions, confirmed what she already knew. But she could barely follow the conversation what with the buzzing in her ears.

"Mr. Rowan Stewart… contracted to take on renovations at Longbow Castle."

Rowan Stewart. A name imprinted on her heart forever. If she wasn't the practical and independent lady that she was, she would have fainted.

But she was Primm, and this was her school. So she steeled her spine and stepped forward.

But dear lord, he was older now. His shoulders broader, his chest harder. And the set of his jaw lacked even a hint of weakness.

He looked magnificent.

ROWAN HAD KNOWN he would meet with her today and was determined to maintain a professional demeanor. Even so, upon his first glance, his composure nearly slipped.

Augusta Primm had changed in ways most people would consider to be dramatic. Not because a few lines creased the corners of her eyes, or because of a few barely-there strands of silver threading through her mahogany tresses. Her entire frame was thinner, harsher than he remembered, and she buzzed with tension.

He dragged his gaze away from her while Rosewood made introductions. Lord Hardwood had wished to visit the school as well, so their arrival was proving to be a convoluted procession.

"It's my pleasure to finally meet you." The Countess of Rosewood smiled as Lord Hardwood took her hand, and Rowan echoed the sentiment.

But with that introduction out of the way, Rosewood gestured toward Augusta. "My sister, Lady Augusta, but more importantly, the infamous Miss Primm." Her brother maintained his casual charm as he introduced her and then made a grand gesture toward the building adjacent to the residence. "Founder and headmistress of this grand institution." Rosewood chuckled. "Auggie, this is Mr. Rowan Stewart, the man who's going to restore Longbow Castle to its former glory—and keep your school from crumbling to the ground."

All the blood seemed to have drained from her face; even her lips looked more white than pink. And her gray eyes, which had once stared into his with openness and warmth, were cold and forbidding, reminding him of the North Sea in wintertime.

Rowan gritted his teeth. If she'd suffered, it was because of her own decisions.

The school that, in the end, was the culmination of all her dreams.

Augusta's pride and joy.

33

Neither he nor Augusta corrected her brother's assumption that they had never been introduced.

"My lady." Rowan shook himself and stepped forward. Augusta, who hadn't moved up until then, extended one hand. When he moved to bow over it, however, she turned her palm to clasp his and shook it firmly. After all these years, by God, she could still surprise him.

Her grip was firm, but Rowan hardly noticed.

Because, blast it all, although bitterness nearly clogged his throat, the rest of his person suffered the same response it had on their first meeting.

Awareness. Familiarity. And... that seemingly persistent attraction.

Betrayal apparently had failed to dispel this damned physical chemistry. As had time. But she was not the Augusta he'd known. She was Miss Primm—a professional woman—the owner of a grand institution.

The institution she'd chosen over him.

"The Earl of Hardwood, coincidentally, has also traveled to Warwick Village to meet with one of your students, Auggie."

Lady Rosewood exchanged a curious glance with Augusta, who'd dropped Rowan's hand and clasped both of hers behind her back.

She turned to face Lord Hardwood. "Indeed?" she asked.

"Is Miss Allison Meadowbrook in residence?" Hardwood asked. "I'd very much like to meet with her, if I may."

"She's unavailable currently. Perhaps you could return later in the day," Augusta said in a curt tone.

Lord Hardwood frowned. "But of course."

But Rowan had come here to do a job.

"I'd like to examine the foundation while I'm here." He held Augusta's cool gaze. If she expected him to return at a more convenient time, she'd be waiting another seventeen years.

It was Rosewood who replied. "If you'll show Mr. Stewart

the damages, Auggie, I'll accompany Hardwood back to the inn where we can have a drink to celebrate the close of the sale."

Augusta turned back to Rowan but couldn't hold his gaze and ended up staring just beyond his shoulder. Some of her color had returned, and he couldn't deny that she was as pretty now as she'd been before.

Not just pretty. In her own way, she was stunning.

Hauntingly beautiful.

But he only saw a mirage. Because he now knew she was a cold, driven woman. She only looked haunted because she lacked a heart.

"Very well." She nodded with a jerk. "Victoria, would you mind—"

"I'll find… Miss Meadowbrook and tell her Lord Hardwood will be returning shortly." Lady Rosewood nodded.

"Thank you."

And looking stiff, Augusta addressed him again. "This way, Mr. Stewart. The worst of the erosion is on the north end." She pivoted and marched toward the front of the school.

Even though his strides ate up more than each of hers, he had to move quickly to keep up with her. He didn't offer his arm, as he would to any other lady.

But staring at the thick coiffure pinned at the back of her head, he wondered if, unbound, it still fell to her waist. The mahogany colors gleamed in the sunlight, looking as thick and luxurious as he remembered.

And then he scowled, remembering the weeks he'd spent convalescing following the visit from her father's men.

He flicked the school a disparaging glance. All because she'd wanted this…

She marched with purpose, doing nothing to disprove any idea that she didn't deserve the reputation she'd gained—that of a rigid schoolmistress.

Following the spring they'd met, Rowan managed to live on

the fringes of society. It was Fiona who had brought Augusta's school into his realm of awareness. Once Addison mentioned that Fiona would be attending Miss Primm's, Rowan had been unable to pretend it didn't exist. The subject, surprisingly, came up more than one would expect. And not without controversy.

Her students often succeeded at landing the best husbands. But there were also whispers of criticism. It was said that a handful of those refined ladies showed more intelligence than was fashionable. And that they weren't at all biddable.

And that hadn't surprised Rowan in the least. She'd never been one to accept the status quo. It only made sense that she'd develop feminist tendencies.

Perhaps the criticism had merit. He scowled as he stared at the set of her shoulders.

She was angry, and that could only be because he'd shown up unexpectedly. He'd taken her unaware. Considering she'd been the one to break things off between them, her attitude was more than a little hypocritical.

"You've done well for yourself, Augusta." He spoke loudly enough so that she could not pretend she hadn't heard him.

She did not turn around, however, nor did she slow her pace as they rounded the corner of the school. "As have you." Her answer, of course, was succinct.

Damned woman.

Rowan nearly ran into the back of her when she suddenly stopped, and he got an unexpected whiff of her scent—lavender, soap, and chalk.

"There." She pointed at an amateurish fix made to repair the exposed foundation. The stone was chipped and scuffed in several places around the roughly fashioned patch.

This was why he'd come. Not to rehash the past. Definitely not to be distracted by her fragrance.

He crouched down and dragged his fingertips along the scar.

The building was three stories high, and although it was over a hundred years old, it seemed to have been maintained well.

Except for this.

He glanced along the lengths adjacent to the damage and then peered closer to the perimeter of where the repair had been made.

"My groundskeeper has been filling them in with mortar to keep larger animals from making their homes in the cellar." Her expression gave away her obvious dislike of the space. Because there would be nothing to keep smaller rodents from residing below the school. Augusta might be brave, but she hated rodents—nearly as much as she hated spiders.

Rowan nodded, pushed himself back to stand, and then stepped back.

Finally, she met and held his stare.

Spectacles rested on the bridge of her pert little nose, and behind them, worry lurked in her silver-gray eyes.

In all the time he'd known her, she'd only appeared defeated on one occasion. She'd come to his father's townhouse, and Rowan had chased the expression away. He'd thought she'd been as pleased with the resulting solution as he had been.

He shook his head, however, and returned his attention to the foundation. This type of damage was not caused by natural erosion.

Cold suspicion shot through his veins. His half-sister attended this school. Were she and the other students in danger?

"You said there were more. Show me to them."

THE PAST BELONGS IN THE PAST

"*Y*es. Yes, of course." Augusta nodded, amazed her legs supported her as she focused on the task at hand. She'd strangle Piers for bringing Rowan here except he'd not been in London that spring. Rowan had met Eli and Liam. And on a few occasions, they'd taken Noah and Theodore on outings with Addison.

But Piers had been out of the country, and with the breach in his relationship with their father, aside from the few details Augusta had provided him, he apparently had never learned who Rowan was to her. Or who he had been, that was.

Leading him around the building, she couldn't block out the full force of his presence.

Augusta cleared her throat. "It doesn't make sense to me," she said without turning around. "The overall condition, other than a few places, looks to be perfectly sound."

But was it?

She arrived at a second patch, this one larger than the first.

"This isn't erosion," he announced. "It's—"

"Vandals," Augusta finished for him. Although disappointed, she wasn't completely surprised. "I was afraid of as much. But if the damage was caused by vandals, then that means the foundation itself is sound. That's a good thing, isn't it?"

"Show me the rest." Rowan didn't agree or disagree. "The nature of the damage depends on the vandals themselves. On whether they're a gang of local troublemakers, passing vagrants, or something—"

"Worse." He wasn't glossing things over for her, as many gentlemen would attempt to do.

Augusta blinked and then proceeded to lead him around the perimeter of the school.

By the time they'd circled the building and arrived back at the front of her residence, he'd examined over a dozen patches.

He rubbed the back of his neck, a gesture that should not be, but somehow managed to be, achingly familiar to her.

"The best I can tell, the damage was caused by a pick axe or something similar. When did it begin?"

"Mr. Driver, my groundskeeper, found one shortly after the session began in autumn. Will our patches suffice? Or does the foundation require a more substantial repair?"

Is it safe for my girls? For my teachers?

Augusta met his gaze, forcing herself to focus on the importance of this meeting. It didn't matter that she had dozens of questions she wanted to ask him. Did he have a family now? A wife? Did he ever think of her?

Why didn't you come after me?

Only the school mattered—the safety of her students and staff.

She glanced down at her hands, clasped so tightly at her waist that her knuckles were white.

She hated being afraid. First this Allison Meadowbrook problem, then vandals, and now the sudden appearance of Rowan Stewart.

But she could handle these blows. She'd handled far worse.

He didn't answer immediately, and while he studied her,

Augusta refused to squirm. He'd told her she'd done well for herself, but she'd heard the sarcasm in his voice.

Best they leave it at that.

He did nothing to try to hide a pessimistic sigh, and then returned his attention to the building.

"I can't say for certain without making a more thorough inspection."

"You'll want to see the cellar."

"Yes."

She dipped her chin. "I... I have a meeting this afternoon that I absolutely can't miss, and Mr. Driver has gone to Exeter to visit his mother and won't be returning until Sunday. If you come back next week, he can take you down then."

Augusta had no wish to show him herself, even if she didn't need to handle this Hardwood business today. The one time she'd been down there had been one too many. The rickety stairway led to a space that was dark, damp, and the perfect home for all manner of spiders and other creepy crawly creatures.

Rowan studied her again, this time not bothering to veil his resentment for being here. His next words, therefore, surprised her. "My half-sister is one of your students."

"Miss Fiona Briarton." Did he think she would not realize? "She's one of our best students."

His jaw ticked, something she didn't remember from before.

"Can I tell Mr. Driver to expect you, then?" It would be so much simpler if he refused. She'd hire someone else—perhaps someone from the nearby village.

"Very well," he agreed.

Augusta had once known all his expressions, but this one was inscrutable. He was not the same man she'd known years ago. Nor was she the innocent girl who'd trusted him to protect her—to keep her safe.

Although, where her father was involved, anyone would have been hard-pressed at doing that.

The past must remain in the past. She must keep focused on the school.

She managed to bid him good day, but he only nodded before taking his leave of her.

And long after Rowan departed, Augusta stood in the foyer, clutching her list of today's tasks, organized primarily by priority and time sensitivity.

Her mind raced even as errant thoughts paralyzed her.

She couldn't escape her mind, which was determined to fixate on his face, a face that had once been more familiar to her than her own.

Rowan.

His onyx eyes were as piercing as they'd been before but held none of the warmth she'd grown accustomed to. And his voice had changed. It was deeper, gravelly.

Distant.

Rowan had towered over her when they'd first met, but since then, he not only seemed taller but more imposing for his powerful physique.

Where most gentlemen his age, well into his fourth decade, had either begun to shrivel or grow soft, Rowan had done the opposite. His shoulders were wider, and his torso tapered to a slim waist.

He'd been nine and ten when they met. He would have turned five and thirty just last May—the sixteenth. Despite herself, she'd acknowledged the date without fail.

Overwhelmed by all of it, she closed her eyes.

That hair, the glorious curls she'd once loved, was shorn so short as to be almost non-existent. How many times had she told him she loved his hair? Her fingers remembered the springy texture, silky and thick, and she found herself gripping her pencil.

He looked utterly different from the boy she'd left in London, and yet... the same. His rugged clothing today contrasted starkly with the fashionable ensembles he'd worn in Mayfair. One could almost mistake him for a common laborer.

But one would never make that mistake. Because, despite the circumstances of his birth, he was the son of a duke. He had always carried himself like one.

"Miss Primm?"

Augusta jumped. She'd been so lost in thought, she hadn't heard her housekeeper approaching. "Yes, Jenny?"

Jenny was not unlike Augusta herself—hard-working, confident, and not at all sentimental. But in that moment she stared at her employer with concern.

"Are you all right? Can I bring you some tea?"

Lord in heaven, Augusta needed to pull herself together. She unclenched her fists and forced a smile. "Yes, yes. I'll be in my office if you don't mind bringing it to me there."

"Of course, ma'am. Be sure to light the fire before you start working. You don't want to catch a chill just before the students return." The comment was as much a reminder as a reprimand.

"You know I never get ill," Augusta reminded the other woman.

"Let's keep it that way, shall we?" And then the housekeeper spun around and disappeared toward the kitchen.

Which spurred Augusta toward her office.

What with Miss Fellowes being forced to pose as Allison Meadowbrook, Augusta already had too much to fret over. She summoned all the resolve she could muster and did what was necessary.

She shoved Rowan Stewart out of her mind.

And for four whole days, it wasn't all that difficult. Because along with tending to her usual tasks, their little charade hadn't achieved the desired outcome.

Lord Hardwood hadn't accepted Miss Fellowes's rejection of his proposal on Allison's behalf. He'd demanded Priscilla, as Allison, attend a house party first. Only then would he release her from the betrothal.

Of course, having committed to the deception, Augusta had no choice but to allow Miss Fellowes, with Miss Fortune as chaperone, to travel to Hardwood Cliffhouse so that he would agree to end his betrothal to Allison.

The scenario was chock-full of possible complications.

Furthermore, with students returning after a long holiday break, she and the remaining staff were forced to rearrange their schedules to cover the absent teacher's classes.

To compound her troubles, Mr. Driver had located yet another damaged section of the foundation. He had returned from Exeter the day before and made the usual repair, but Augusta struggled to comprehend the possibility that the school was being targeted by vandals.

More than a possibility, if Rowan was correct.

Even thinking his name summoned a wave of turmoil. A wave of heaviness that consisted of heartbreak and disappointment, but also guilt.

Years ago, he'd attended the Willoughby Ball, for her, he'd said—and then every other festivity she'd told him she would be at. With or without an invitation, he'd never been denied entry. His father, the Duke of Bedwell, had wielded great power.

He'd explained this to her and they'd pretended not to notice those who didn't acknowledge him, but Augusta had also heard the whispers and seen the stares.

She'd dismissed them as unimportant to her. She didn't care that he was a bastard. The person inside, Rowan, was unlike anyone she'd ever met. She'd fallen hopelessly in love with him. And at the time, she'd been convinced anything was possible.

So she'd flirted with him. She'd danced with him.

She'd gone walking through moonlit gardens with him. She'd made promises...

Shaking off the unwanted memories, she pushed open her office door, and sheer force of habit carried her through the day.

When an intrusive thought cut through her concentration, she rejected it.

Is he married?

Augusta decided to inventory academic supplies.

What did he do after I left London?

She not only counted the items in the closets but in the classrooms as well.

How many women has he had in his life? He is a virile, handsome man. He would have had many. Wouldn't he?

A few of the student desks required maintenance. She began a list of minor repairs for Mr. Driver.

When Rowan had taken her hand and nearly bent over it, she'd experienced the same jolt she had before. How was that possible? She was twice the age she'd been back then!

Or had she simply imagined it?

She wiggled her shoulders and studied the windows, which were due a cleaning. Augusta would assign these to Miss Royal and Miss Wolcott, both of whom were keeping Allison Meadowbrook out of trouble for now. Augusta didn't mind assisting them. With nine classrooms in all, and twelve tall windows in each classroom, cleaning them would be a Herculean task.

Mrs. Driver would help without being asked.

By the time she arrived back at her office, the sun sat low in the sky, casting long shadows across the room. Augusta ignored the empty hearth in favor of her desk, but as she did so, one corner of her shawl caught the edge of the cup of tea Jenny had brought up, toppling it over. With nothing handy to wipe it up, Augusta watched, feeling quite powerless, as the cold brown liquid seeped into several of her lists.

For years, she'd functioned like a finely tuned clock. A problem arose, and she fixed it. A teacher required reprimand, and Augusta did so in an encouraging manner.

But lately... something inside her was coming loose. Some part of her needed to be repaired—and quickly.

Sadly, every time she closed her eyes, her traitorous mind wreaked more damage.

Rowan.

The events of 1815 were far behind her now. What was done was done.

When he didn't come after her, distance had proven to be a most effective barrier. She stopped looking for him on the streets, in the shops in the village, or even when an unexpected visitor rolled to a stop outside her aunt's ancient home.

The months turned into years then, and eventually, time went to work on her wounds. And because time and distance hadn't quite been enough, she'd learned to wall off sentimental emotions—focus on the details involved in running a school. And it had worked.

If not for this recent hiccup, she'd be perfectly fine.

Rowan was not the same person she'd fallen in love with, as she very well knew. Nor was she the young girl who existed only in his memories.

He'd grown more handsome whereas she had grown...

Into precisely what she'd intended—an independent spinster. Of course, she was capable and fit. She'd taken the money her aunt gave her and turned it into a thriving, respectable school. She'd defied her father's expectations and intended to keep right on doing so.

Everything was fine.

And except for the foundation and Allison Meadowbrook's threats... everything was perfectly normal.

The trouble was, nothing *felt* normal.

The students were already arriving from the winter holiday,

she was currently down by three teachers, and she'd made zero progress in discovering the identity of the person chipping away at the school's foundation.

By the time Monday rolled around, she had one eye on the lookout for anyone acting suspiciously, and the other watching the road for a lone rider…

In a professional capacity, of course.

But why, exactly, had he promised to examine her measly little foundation? Rowan's reason could be exactly what it appeared—as a favor to her brother for being awarded the contract to bring Longbow Castle back to its former glory—a project that no doubt would prove to be enormously challenging.

Not to mention lucrative.

She refused to imagine his being here had anything to do with her.

Monday passed, and Rowan did not return. And then Tuesday, Wednesday, and Thursday. By Friday morning, Augusta was torn between giving up on him and riding over to the castle to give him a piece of her mind.

He'd said he would return this week and the week was all but over. Why come at all if he had no intention of returning? He'd not been fickle when she'd known him before.

Perhaps his character had changed. Hers certainly had. Augusta stared down at her desk, disconcerted at the thought.

But now was not the time for such introspection.

Shoulders tight, an annoying buzzing in the back of her mind, Augusta dipped her pen in the nearly full jar of ink and focused on the task at hand—reconciling a balance sheet.

Her least favorite part of her job. She doubted it would be as distasteful if she were turning a profit.

She'd barely begun the tedious task when the sound of a horse approaching outside caused her to jump, knocking over the bottle of ink.

Drat and…

Damn!

Augusta smoothed her hair back, feeling to make sure her chignon was still intact, and then rose to greet whoever was outside.

She would not allow the composure she'd maintained for most of her adult life to abandon her now!

"One problem at a time," she muttered under her breath.

It could be anyone—a vendor, a prospective set of parents, or possibly one of her alumni. Many of her graduates often made return visits to inform her of their progress. A few returned in search of employment.

But a tingling at the base of her spine assured her that the man atop the lone horse who'd just ridden up was none of those. Ignoring it, Augusta slipped her arms into her coat and made her way outside.

And, of course, it was him.

THE CELLAR

*B*y the time Rowan dismounted and secured Whisky to a post outside the front of the school, Augusta— *Miss Primm*—had appeared at the entrance, arms folded in front of her, looking as prim and stern as she had last week.

"Good morning," he greeted her as he approached.

"I'd nearly given up on you." Her answer was cold.

Smudges of black ink framed the sides of her face, and he barely managed to bite back a grin. Rubbing a hand over his mouth, he covered his amusement.

A decent gentleman, under similar circumstances, would likely point the smudges out to her in gentle tones. Some might even simply make some excuse and take their leave.

But seeing as years had passed since Rowan had deigned to play the part of a decent gentleman, he ignored the black smudges and got straight to the point.

"You asked me to come this week," he said. "I believe Friday falls within those parameters."

"Yes, well. It's not very responsible to leave it to the last minute." She narrowed her eyes at him, making the streaks of ink look all the more comical.

This time, Rowan chuckled, earning himself a frown.

But then she turned her face away, focusing on nothing in particular. Tension strained the muscles in her shoulders and neck, subduing his humor.

Augusta might have achieved her dream, but she was not a happy woman.

She was Miss Primm, a woman with great responsibilities— responsibilities that included Fiona, currently threatened by some prankster or worse. He'd get back to business. It was foolish to think of her as Augusta.

"Has your groundskeeper returned?" he asked.

"Yes," she sighed. "But he's taken my cook into town." After a hard swallow, she met his stare. "But seeing as you've finally made time in your schedule to come, I suppose I could take you down myself."

"How gracious of you." Rowan nearly added a bow to his sarcasm.

Her distaste at going down to the cellar showed in her expression. Apparently, her fear of spiders was one thing that hadn't changed.

Or was that expression of distaste meant for him?

"That is why you came, isn't it?" she asked.

He answered in the affirmative. There were shadows etched beneath her eyes, clouded with worry.

A very long time ago, those eyes had glowed for him—with hunger, longing, passion.

He smoothed his hand over his head, feeling an illogical urge to growl.

What the hell was wrong with him?

"This way." She gestured toward the formal entrance.

Rowan followed her inside, down a long hall, and then into a maintenance room. Augusta struck a flint to light a candle, and then opened a door—one that he couldn't help but notice required leveling. Rowan's eyes took a moment to adjust as the flickering light illuminated a steep, narrow staircase.

If Augusta were the same woman he'd known before, he would have insisted on going first, in case one of the steps had been damaged or some creepy crawling thing might be hanging from a web.

But she was *Miss Primm* and likely wouldn't appreciate the courtesy. So instead, he allowed her to duck into the stairwell first, and then followed closely, prepared to grab her in case she lost her balance and went tumbling.

"I've only been down here once. Years ago. Even then, spiders had all but taken over. Before my aunt and I purchased the building." Her admission surprised him.

"When did you buy it?"

"April 12th, 1816." Pride laced her voice.

That would have been nearly one year after they'd met. Oh, but how quickly she'd moved on.

"You never married," he said. It wasn't a question. She had gone on to do precisely what she'd told him in her note. That she'd had an opportunity to be a woman of independent means—to run her own school. She couldn't do that while saddled with a husband—especially with a husband who was a bastard.

Not if she wished to be taken seriously, that was.

"I did not." She sounded uncertain but provided no further explanation. And then she twisted her neck around to momentarily hold his gaze. "Did you?"

They'd arrived at the landing. The floor was mostly dirt with a few brick platforms where additional supports were placed. The air settled around them, deep and thick.

"I did not marry." Rowan set his jaw and reached out for the candle. "I need to examine the joists. Do you mind?"

"Not at all." His hand grazed hers as she handed it off, and she immediately folded her arms in front of her.

She'd once told him that his touch brought her to life. Now, however, it seemed to chill her to the bone.

He shoved the ridiculous thought aside and held the light out so he could begin his inspection.

"What are you looking for?" she asked.

"Bowing joists. Intentional cuts." And as though speaking it to life, he caught sight of freshly cut wood. He stilled, and Augusta's momentum had her bumping into him from behind.

She gasped, and Rowan exhaled a curse. Her warmth along his back sent a streak of heated current shooting through his limbs, to his brain and, unfortunately, his family jewels. By God, such a stern, hard woman ought not to affect him physically—past or no past.

"I'm—I didn't mean to—How clumsy of me." She retreated, and his temperature instantly cooled. "What do you see?" she asked.

Rowan traced his fingers along the freshly cut wood. "Right here." And then he lifted the candle. All along the length of the building, similar cuts marred the smooth lines of the joists. This was not good.

This was not the work of a gadabout vandal. "Whoever did this has very bad intentions, Augusta. A good deal of work has gone into making all these cuts and eventually, the joists will fail. Every single one that's been cut needs replacing. But you need to think beyond that. If you don't catch whoever's doing this, they'll just keep damaging the new ones."

"Are we in danger?" she asked, surprising him with her calm. If the issue wasn't addressed, the entire structure could be on the verge of collapse. Any other woman would likely be in hysterics.

Rowan didn't answer right away but moved about the dark cellar, checking the depth of most of the cuts and ensuring he hadn't missed other issues. "Block off the two northernmost classrooms. Those are the weakest. Otherwise, for now anyhow, you ought to be safe. But not if this is allowed to continue."

"Can you fix it?" Her voice remained unruffled—emotionless almost. "Can you replace the joists?"

"Yes." But the repairs would require a good deal of lumber—thick, long stretches of sturdy wood.

"It's going to be expensive," she guessed.

"Your brother—"

"Piers is not going to pay for this. He has enough on his plate with that monstrosity of a castle." She was all business. "Can you provide me with an estimate, Mr. Stewart?"

In that moment Rowan wanted to throttle her. He'd called her *Augusta*, and she was making it quite apparent that she wasn't interested in acknowledging the past.

Rowan spit out a number. "Give or take a hundred pounds." The cost would be far greater than his estimate; Rhys would have conniptions when Rowan informed him of the quote.

But Fiona was involved; his sister would be living and learning in this building. And her safety would always be his business.

Which made Augusta's school his business.

"I have some savings," she answered tentatively.

Rowan hummed noncommittally and moved to where the vandal had destroyed a small section of the masonry. "The culprit did not enter from inside the school."

"I could tell no one's come down here in ages. I felt too many spiderwebs on the way down." An almost violent shiver ran through her.

"No live spiders, I hope?" Rowan wasn't above teasing her.

"I certainly hope not," she answered stoically.

Was this the woman she'd been meant to be all along? Was it time that had changed her—that had locked up her exuberance for life?

This Augusta Primm didn't match up with the woman he'd fancied himself in love with. Had their affair only been an illusion?

It would be impossible to know... seventeen years was a very long time.

Rowan marched across to one of the patches. "Your vandal created openings just wide enough to fit through, and then entered at various times to work on the joists. When did you say this began?"

"We discovered the first one last August. I'm surprised we never heard anything."

"Well, when one has no reason to be suspicious, one tends to ignore subtle sounds. Besides, I don't imagine the school suffers from an abundance of silence."

Augusta trailed her hand above her, her fingertips touching one of the intentional cuts.

"There are times when we've left the school unattended. Occasionally, we take the girls on outings—into Warwick Village or over to Cambridge. I suppose the vandal could have done his dirty work then."

Which meant that whoever had done this would have been watching the comings and goings of the teachers. And of the students. Young girls. Women. Children.

The thought must have struck Augusta at the same time. "He's watching us..."

"Yes." Rowan wouldn't pull any punches. Not with something like this, anyway. "Let's go upstairs. The sooner I order supplies, the sooner I can begin the repairs."

"And those will be enough? My girls will be safe?" She reached out and touched his arm.

Rowan stilled. Everything had changed except for this—her touch. The cool damp air between them immediately charged.

The candlelight flickered over her face, and staring at the

trail of ink, he couldn't help but remember tracing his fingertips over similar lines.

His gaze flicked to her eyes, and even in the dark, he noted shadows etched beneath them.

She'd obviously not been sleeping well.

"They'll be safe," he said. "As long as I have anything to do with it."

She studied him, looking for more reassurance.

"You have my word, Augusta," he added.

She'd once given her word and then broken it most spectacularly. That blow hung unspoken between them.

"I—" she began. "Thank you, Rowan."

He stepped back, forcing her hand to fall away from his arm. He didn't need her touching him. Because when she touched him, feelings threatened to rise to the surface—feelings he'd prefer remain dormant.

Hell, he'd been tempted to kiss her. Thank God sanity stepped in to remind him of who she was—of what she'd done.

"It's nothing more than I would do for any other client. I have a reputation to uphold, you know," he said.

For years, he'd wanted answers. Why had she told him she'd run away with him? Why string him along if she had no intention of going ahead with it? He'd been nothing more than an amusing diversion.

Seeing her all these years later, he realized he'd known those answers all along. She'd been perfectly clear in her letter.

She'd walked away from him for a bigger dream. He couldn't blame her. He was, after all, a bastard.

Rowan jerked around, forcing her to follow him up the stairs as they exited the dank cellar.

Neither spoke until they emerged into the long corridor, lit from above by the large windows.

"If you come to my office, I can write you a banknote. I'm sure you require a deposit."

But Rowan wasn't in any mood to take her money. He'd fix the foundation and that would be the end of it. "I'll send you an invoice. Until then, you need to be more diligent about who is allowed on school grounds. Hire a watchman—better yet, hire two."

"O-of course." And when Rowan would have turned and left, she called out, "Just the north rooms are compromised? Otherwise, the building is safe?"

If Rowan had any doubt whatsoever, he'd insist she shut down. "For now, yes. But I wouldn't want to see your life's work collapse into nothing." Was that cynicism in his voice? It shouldn't be. She'd accomplished a good deal for a woman. Hell, she'd accomplished more than most men were capable of doing. "Hire a few watchmen, Augusta," he advised again.

"I will." Even with the lines of ink streaking her face, she managed to look stern and professional.

Unwilling to endure another second of her company, Rowan exited alone. He climbed on his horse and rode as though demons chased him to the castle.

Much easier to feel apathetic from a distance. And that was all he really wanted.

~

AUGUSTA STARED out the window long after Rowan and his powerful mount disappeared.

He had never married.

She had just learned the school required major repairs and this was what she would dwell on.

She shook her head.

Of course, there would have been other women in his life. But he, like her, she guessed, was likely more dedicated to his career.

For different reasons, perhaps. But with equal dedication.

She'd felt the tremor roll through him when she'd placed her hand on his sleeve. Had it been revulsion or something else?

Or had it been her imagination?

From the first time she'd met him, his presence, his nearness, and especially his touch, had incited a thrill inside her unlike anything she'd known. An odd sort of understanding had existed between them. Had that connection been damaged permanently with the death of their love?

That tremor could just as easily have been hers. Standing in the dark, knowing spiders lurked all around her.

She steeled herself and turned her thoughts to what she'd learned—about the school, not the man.

Find a watchman.

She'd speak with her housekeeper, Jenny, first. Perhaps one of the woman's cousins would be interested in earning extra coin as a watchman. It was wintertime, and with less to be done on the local farms, families always welcomed additional income.

But there must be more she could do. She could set traps. She owned a pistol and knew how to use it. If necessary, she'd keep watch herself. Since Rowan's arrival, she'd begun having the dreams again—dreams she'd thought could no longer plague her. Once she woke from one of them, she rarely went back to sleep...

She marched to the end of the corridor to the door that connected the school to her personal residence. When she swung it open, she nearly walked right into the woman she was in search of.

"You're just who I was looking for," Augusta said, but Jenny narrowed her eyes, staring at her with a frown. "What is it?"

"Er." Jenny reached out. Augusta leaned back but the housekeeper pointed to Augusta's cheek. "You have something along your face. Black."

Perplexed, Augusta frowned, pivoted, and strode to the nearest looking glass.

"Ink." She vaguely remembered the accounts she'd been working on. The ink that had likely ruined a morning's work.

Rowan had said nothing. Oh, how he must have been laughing at her!

Augusta scurried to the bedchamber and leaned over the wash basin to study herself once again. If anything, in the light from her window, the streak appeared even worse. Not only was the ink on her cheek, but there was a little on her nose and in her hair. She glanced down, and sure enough, her fingertips were covered with it.

This was how Rowan had seen her. She'd thought she'd met him looking composed and professional, but in the end, she'd come off looking like a madwoman.

His opinion of her shouldn't matter.

Augusta poured water into the basin, soaking a cloth in the process. And as she squeezed the excess water out, her hands shook.

Now was the worst possible time for her to be distracted. Too many problems needed all her focus. The school faced too many threats.

And classes must continue as scheduled. If the school couldn't operate normally, the students couldn't return.

If the students couldn't return, she'd lose...

Something far more precious and dear.

Besides that, this institution was the only place she'd ever truly belonged. It was hers. And so many people depended on her.

Her staff, the students, not to mention the people in the village whose livings were bolstered by providing supplies that kept them operating.

Her heart skipped a beat. The school was so much more

than an educational institution. It was practically a living, breathing thing.

It was the place where her heart resided.

She needed to defend it at all costs.

SPRINGTIME AT MISS PRIMM'S

"*J*ust because you've finished repairing the foundation doesn't mean you don't have to come visit me anymore." Fiona frowned up at Rowan. Today's trip to the school had primarily been to make one final inspection and load up the last of his tools and spare lumber.

Since he'd spent mornings at the castle and only worked on the foundation later in the afternoons, the job had taken nearly three months, longer than he'd expected.

In that time, however, he'd come to see sides of his half-sister he never would have otherwise. At six and ten, Fiona was not only growing into a lovely young woman, but she was also bright, outgoing, and popular.

"It has been quite entertaining to learn the fundamentals of engineering," the young woman who was Fiona's bosom friend added.

"Now I know you are flattering me, Miss Annesley." He smiled at the girl, whose appearance contrasted starkly with Fiona's. When the skeleton team Rowan brought over had first gone to work, a handful of the girls had shown inordinate interest in their efforts. But when it became apparent they were more interested in the workers than the work, Augusta had ordered them to keep away from the construction.

Except for Fiona. Not because she was allowed special privileges as a duke's sister, but because of her relationship with Rowan.

And Fiona rarely went anywhere without her little dark-haired friend.

Rowan pinched Fiona's chin. "I can't come every day, imp, but I'll come to see you next weekend."

Fiona scowled but then just as quickly perked up. "Will you take us into the village?" She bounced on the balls of her feet.

Having avoided his stepmother for years, this was the most he'd ever felt like a brother to her. Denying her anything was nigh impossible.

"If you have Miss Primm's permission."

"Will you ask her?"

"You'll have to ask her yourself." Rowan wouldn't budge on this. While shoring up the footings and then replacing the joists, Rowan had found it necessary to confer with Augusta numerous times.

She was always professional and mostly pleasant. They were never actually alone together, however, which prevented either of them from mentioning the past. But although they'd kept their distance, Rowan's senses never failed to alert him when she was near.

Furthermore, one could not be on school grounds as often as he was and not learn more about the blasted woman who ran it.

Students spoke of her with respect rather than fear. And since she was occasionally short-staffed, she spent her days in various classrooms and worked in her office late into the evenings.

In between that, she bustled from classroom to classroom,

assisting students who needed attention and reprimanding those who demanded too much.

For all this, she'd happily sacrificed spending her life with him.

And yet, he couldn't help but respect her for it.

Fiona hopped onto the half wall that framed the steps up to the school, leaning back on her hands. "You really should consider attending Addison and Chloe's house party this summer." Before he could explain that he had a job to perform, Fiona added, "Mother isn't going to be there, and I'm quite sure Lady Rosewood won't mind if you take off a week or two."

When he didn't answer, Fiona pouted. "Please, Row? I'm sure Addison can find some sort of construction project for you to work on while you're there."

He pinned his gaze on his little sister and then flicked a glance at her friend. "She isn't playing fair now, is she, Miss Annesley?"

"Not at all, Mr. Stewart." Miss Annesley was a very literal young lady, and quieter than most. Fiona rarely went anywhere without her, and Rowan was happy his sister had such a constant friend.

He'd expected working around nearly a hundred young women to have been annoying, but instead, he'd found his time at the school almost enjoyable. These girls, although overly inclined to giggles and squealing for no reason at all, possessed an innocence inherent in youth that he'd forgotten.

Hope. That's what that was. Optimism for the future.

Primm and her teachers were doing good work here.

"I'll think about it," Rowan answered just as Rhys appeared carrying a mishmash of tools that inevitably had been left behind by some of his less-seasoned workers.

"I think that's everything." Rhys hefted them on the back of the old farmer's cart they used to transport supplies between the castle and the school, and then brushed his hands together.

"I'll drive this back now while you make the final inspection." Rhys was already climbing onto the driver's seat, chomping at the bit to put all their efforts back into the castle.

Rowan nodded. He had ridden over separately, giving Whisky a chance to stretch his legs, and had promised he'd deliver the invoice to Augusta when the work was completed.

Who, as luck would have it, was presently marching in their direction. Not that he saw her, but an awareness ghosted over his skin. He narrowed his eyes and inhaled a fortifying breath.

As per usual, she wore her hair in a tight knot at the back of her neck and an apron over a dull gray dress.

And those shadows under her eyes had only gotten darker.

"Miss Briarton, Miss Annesley. Would you two girls be so kind as to ring the dinner bell for me this evening?" Although her tone was pleasant enough, their headmistress's request was, in actuality, an order.

Fiona hopped off the wall and rushed over to give Rowan a quick hug. "I'll see you on Sunday."

"Noon," Rowan confirmed, and then both girls took off running toward the school's entrance.

"It isn't a race!" Augusta added. "Ladies walk." She frowned.

At this, Rowan raised a brow. He'd never known Augusta to be overly concerned with such things.

She shrugged. "I'm teaching etiquette these days. I really must find a replacement for Victoria." But then she turned her attention to the full farmer's cart. "You've finished?"

"Once I've made my final inspection. I don't want to keep you from dinner..." He'd avoided being alone with her, and that was for the best. But with the job completed, without the possibility of getting a glimpse of her every afternoon, his chest felt curiously empty.

An odd expression crumpled her face but only for a second. "Do you have the invoice?"

He reached into his jacket and handed it over.

"I'll have a banknote sent over next week." And then she reached out and touched his arm. "Thank you."

Rowan found himself focusing on her hand resting on his arm, all but burning him with memories and something else...

Regret. Longing. Emotions that held no power over him.

She met his gaze, and in that instant, Rowan struggled against a tug of affection.

"I realize you have gone out of your way to help me—"

He jerked his arm away. "Your brother requested it." And then he added, "I want Fiona to be safe. And the other students, of course."

He ignored the hurt in her eyes. She'd chosen this life. She didn't get to imagine he would go out of his way to help her specifically.

She stared down at her hand, hovering as though frozen, and then allowed it to drop to her side. "But you have my appreciation anyway." Damned if she didn't look pale and helpless.

"Yes, well. I don't want it." He was being outright petulant now.

"Oh." He'd shocked her into silence.

And then, without another word, he marched off to make his inspection.

THE PLAGUE OF DREAMS

*M*usic floated across the lawn. It curled around the trees and danced across the blossoms, creating that romantic quality couples sought when slipping out of a ballroom for a private interlude beyond the terrace.

"Is there anything more magical than a garden on a warm spring night?" A very young Augusta clung to Rowan's arm as the two of them picked their way along the narrow path.

Exactly one week had passed since they'd met. Tonight was an anniversary of sorts, and Augusta fully expected him to mark it by kissing her.

It would be their first kiss.

"Your laughter," he answered, glancing down at her, that half-smile tugging at his mouth. "Your eyes." But his gaze focused on her mouth.

He was never this relaxed around others, amongst the guests. Not even when the two of them danced.

And oh, but he was a wonderful dancer!

Although the son of a powerful duke, he avoided mingling with the crème de la crème of society. Occasionally, he conversed with some of the friendlier gentlemen, but although he kept one eye on the person he was listening to, he kept the other on his surroundings.

It was almost as though he expected to be ambushed.

Inhaling the heady scent of soil and greenery and flowers, Augusta stuffed down the thought. Because this moment belonged to the two of them.

At every ball they'd attended, Augusta's mother had gone out of her way to prevent her only daughter from being alone with Rowan. She'd either insist on introducing Augusta to some distant cousin or long-lost friend, or send her to the retiring room, saying her hair needed fixing. Once, she had insisted Augusta dance with her betrothed, who'd not even bothered attending.

The Duke of Malum's son seemed as keen to marry her as she was to marry him.

And tonight, Augusta outwitted every possible effort and slipped away when her mother's back was turned.

Over the course of three different balls, she and Rowan had been limited to two dances. But they'd been aware of one another, conveying entire conversations with their eyes.

Until tonight. Tonight they could be together.

Alone.

They strolled to the edge of the garden, where the fading sounds of the orchestra competed with the sounds of nature. The windows in the manor sparkled in the distance, and a cool breeze teased her senses. They arrived at a wooden bench, and Rowan lowered them onto it. He did not, however, relinquish her hand—not even when he turned to face her.

Augusta's nerves danced in anticipation, and her excitement nearly made her light-headed. Moonlight reflected off Rowan's shiny black hair, casting shadows that emphasized the delightful curls she couldn't get enough of.

He took both her hands in his. "This is impossible. You know that, don't you?"

But his hands massaged her fingers, and his eyes blazed with adoration.

"Nothing is impossible," Augusta reassured him, but he shook his head.

"You are betrothed." He spoke softly, with a hint of admonishment.

And yet he still held her hands and his gaze flicked to her mouth.

Augusta's heart pounded violently. "Only because my father agreed to it a thousand years ago. I'm going to break it. A lady can break off an engagement, you know. My fiancé doesn't even like me."

She leaned forward. Could he hear that? The sound of her heart racing so fast that it threatened to jump right out of her chest?

"Of course he likes you. You're the most beautiful debutante of the season." His voice was low, gravelly.

His compliment lit her up inside. Because it came from him.

"You think I'm beautiful?"

He dropped her hands and raised his to cradle her face.

And then, he leaned forward and claimed her mouth. Tentatively at first, but then deeper, tasting her. It was an introduction of sorts— to intimacy between the two of them.

This feeling, this sensation, promised everything she ever wished for. Being in his arms felt like returning home. She would give him everything. She would be everything for him.

This man was her dream. Rowan was her future.

And she knew.

She was never going to be the same.

AUGUSTA SHOT OFF HER PILLOW, the heartbeat thundering in her head reminiscent of that night. She could no longer keep track of how many times she'd dreamt about Rowan Stewart over the past four months. Twenty? Fifty? The few times she had met with Rowan, their discussions had been perfunctory—with him explaining the details involved in the steps he'd taken to mitigate damages and her negotiating payment arrangements.

But she was not foolish enough not to realize he had avoided her.

And when she'd touched his arm, his expression of dismay had conveyed just how much he resented her. He believed she'd betrayed him intentionally. It was too late to make explanations—not that they mattered now.

And although he'd made the occasional appearance to visit Fiona, with the work complete now, she no longer had any reason to seek him out.

Not that she wanted to. He obviously wanted nothing to do with her.

And it wasn't as though she *needed* him.

She'd hired two of the older men in the village to act as watchmen, and the danger to the school seemed to have passed.

Even Allison Meadowbrook's threats had been resolved. Not in the way they'd all expected. In fact, they'd nearly been caught up in an even more distasteful business, but that too had blown over with the announcement of Miss Fellowes's wedding.

Sitting in bed, the sheets twisted around her, Augusta pushed back the strands of hair, damp with perspiration, and waited for her heart to slow. Apparently, her conscious thoughts could be controlled; it was her subconscious thoughts that required a heavier hand.

She had not met him as they'd agreed, but neither had he gone out of his way to find her. One might argue that she could be equally angry with him. Although her father had done nothing but discourage his courtship.

Perhaps their love wasn't what she'd thought it had been. Or perhaps it simply hadn't been strong enough to survive her father.

But none of that mattered now.

And Rowan was working nearby. Anytime she heard

mention of his name, or the castle, or anything to do with her brother, she was reminded that he was... here.

Not because he wanted to see her, but simply because of fate's coincidence.

She shook her head. *This too shall pass.*

She'd drawn on the mantra for years now.

But a rebellious thought niggled in the back of her mind.

What if it doesn't?

THEY'RE BACK

Rowan pinched the nail from between his teeth and placed it against one of the new shingles, pinning it to the replacement wood where the roof was charred.

A temporary repair that would have to suffice for now.

He hadn't made a conscious decision to do so, but as spring turned to summer, he'd found himself keeping watch over Augusta's school, nonetheless. Someone had to, seeing as she'd given the two watchmen time off. Even if she hadn't, both of the elderly men she'd hired had spent more time sleeping than watching out for trespassers.

When the vandalism had ceased and the students departed to various destinations for the warmer months, Augusta had relaxed. She'd become negligent.

And for the past two weeks, the school had been left empty but for Mr. and Mrs. Driver. One of her teachers, Miss Fellowes, was marrying, and with classes paused, the remaining teachers had made the journey to Lord Hardwood's estate to witness the nuptials.

Augusta relied too much on her groundskeeper and his wife. Mr. and Mrs. Driver didn't even pretend to keep watch.

Then again, it was unfair of her to expect that two elderly servants could protect the school twenty-four hours a day.

And so, without consciously doing so, he'd taken on part of that responsibility.

Lucky for Augusta.

Rowan had witnessed the glow of the fire from the road. He'd immediately sent Mr. Driver for help. Left alone, Rowan had then done his best to keep it from spreading until half the village arrived to form a brigade. By the time Rosewood was informed the following morning, the fire had been extinguished.

The northeast corner of the roof and the wall beneath it had nearly burned through, but other than some water damage, the building was mostly intact.

If Rowan hadn't made it a habit to ride by the school late at night, the damage would have been far more extensive than this.

With a rope secured around him, Rowan used his feet to fortify his position as he hammered in the last nail while all but dangling off the edge of the roof.

Judging by the evidence inside, it was obvious the fire had not been accidental.

Seeing what seemed like a perfect opportunity, the vandals had taken advantage and mounted another attack. More damages. More expenses.

Augusta was not going to be happy upon her return.

Rattling sounded in the distance, and as though he'd summoned her with his thoughts, the school's familiar carriage appeared from down the road. Rowan recognized Coachman John easily. While repairing the school's foundation, he'd become familiar with most of Augusta's staff.

Yes, he remained angry with her, and yet...

She'd accomplished a great deal. Even more compelling, she

obviously loved her students. This school was as much of a passion to her as he had ever been.

And he wasn't jealous. No, those feelings were long gone. He only wished…

A bead of sweat burned his eyes, and he wiped it away.

Glancing back at the carriage, he could just make out the teachers' faces peering out the windows. A breeze cooled the back of his neck, and a current of awareness swept through him.

After being absent for nearly two weeks, Augusta had returned.

Rosewood and his countess had arrived the day before, and Augusta's brother awaited downstairs to deliver the bad news. Rowan's presence would be unnecessary.

But he imagined her seeing the damages, even from a distance. It was going to be quite a shock for all of them.

He released some rope, kicked out from the building, and then swung inside through the absent window so that he could go to greet the group.

Not bothering to wash up, he descended the staircase, skipping two and three steps at a time, and by the time he arrived at the school's entrance, the earl was assisting his sister out of the coach.

The women were full of questions, and Rosewood settled them down with his usual calm. He, the countess, and Rowan had discussed the serious nature of what had happened, but Lady Rosewood advised against stirring up a panic.

The school was, after all, meant to be a place of nurturing and safety. Rumors to the contrary would have parents pulling students left and right.

"Was the fire caused by lightning?" Augusta asked, her eyes jumping from Rosewood to himself.

Rowan grimaced.

"Vandals," Rosewood answered.

"It was intentional," Lady Rosewood added.

"Are you sure, though?" Augusta removed her hat, and the sun caught the lighter strands in her hair. Having been pinned up, hidden under a hat for hours while riding through the heat of the day, mahogany strands clung to her forehead and cheeks.

"Quite," Rowan answered. She wore a blue gown and spencer, both of which were wrinkled from her journey. The weather was unusually warm for England, and the heat had left her cheeks flushed and damp. Rowan stepped forward and discreetly handed her the flask of water he kept with him while working. She stared at him but then took a long drink.

Since it was a little cooler inside, he motioned for her to pass through the front doors. The gesture was nothing less than he'd do for any other lady; he wasn't so resentful that he enjoyed watching her suffer under the sun.

"You'll want to see for yourself," he added.

Augusta glanced at him. "Is it safe?"

"I wouldn't allow anyone to go up if it was not."

Seeing her looking so tentative shook him. She was not an emotionless spinster as he'd convinced himself upon his arrival. All of this would be easier if she was.

Augusta inhaled a trembling breath, stiffened her spine, and strode past him.

Behind her, the small group of women filed into the school with a hint of hesitancy—almost as though they expected the arsonist to jump out from around one of the corners.

"The smoke is mostly isolated to the third floor," Rosewood explained as they passed the second-floor landing.

"We can't sleep in the teachers' quarters. That stench is awful," Miss Royal said.

Rowan observed as the ladies discussed how best to go about cleaning up the mess, along with the best alternate accommodations.

He'd already examined the copper bin where the fire had

originated. The arsonist had used tar and, from what he'd been able to identify, books—school papers.

Augusta reached inside the charred pot and pulled out a mostly-burned leatherbound book. "My *Vindication of Rights!*" Her chin quivered for half a second but just as quickly jerked up. He nearly moved to reach for her and then caught himself, averting his gaze.

How had he become tangled in this? Against all his inclinations, he constantly found himself here witnessing her struggles and feeling the need to help.

Blast and damn.

While Rowan kept one eye on Augusta, Miss Fortune was mourning some of the other kindling—journals she'd been collecting.

"He left his tinderbox," Miss Royal pointed out.

"He might have heard me approaching." Rowan hadn't exactly ridden up quietly. Augusta glanced in his direction, and he shrugged. "While the school's been left empty, I've taken it upon myself to keep an eye on things." Rowan returned her stare, almost daring her to challenge him.

"We have Mr. Driver for that." The blasted woman was nothing if not contrary. And stubborn as hell.

He'd learned this well enough while discussing the costs involved in the work he'd done on the foundation.

"Mr. and Mrs. Driver had already retired for the night." Rowan clenched his jaw, speaking as though explaining something to a toddler. She truly needed reprimanding for this. "It's too large a property for one man to look after twenty-four hours a day."

Her brother intervened. "I daresay, Auggie, if Stewart here hadn't come by, the roof would have gone up entirely."

Rowan didn't want praise. He simply wanted to catch the villain who'd done this. Setting fire to a school was a heinous act. He'd happily watch the man hang.

For all the bitterness he felt toward Augusta, she and her teachers did not deserve to come under attack like this. It was a *school for girls*, for God's sake! His sister spent most of the year here!

Augusta brushed her hands together and then dabbed her fingertips at the corner of her eye.

"The entire school could have burned." She blinked and turned to Rowan. "My thanks, Ro—Mr. Stewart."

"It's nothing." Rowan collected his tools while Augusta instructed her teachers on what to do next, but, for some reason, she remained until the sounds of their footsteps had disappeared down the stairs, leaving the two of them alone.

In the ensuing silence, he could feel the rising tension coming off her, filling the room, like the charge in the air just before a thunderstorm.

And he waited.

Because *he knew her.*

"I shouldn't have gone to the wedding." Her voice echoed off the walls. She paced across the room and, fists clenched, her face turning red, finally cut loose with a barrage of self-recriminations.

"I never should have allowed Miss Fellowes to go to Hardwood Castle last February. Certainly not with Miss Fortune— of all people! And neither of them would have had to make the journey if I hadn't left Victoria alone at the school over the holidays. All of this is my fault. What the devil was I thinking? Just say it! I know you want to. I deserve all of this!" She went to rub her hands down her face but her fingers caught on her spectacles.

Even though he'd half expected this crack in her composure, he was more than a little startled by the violence of her outburst. And so Rowan remained silent and still.

He did, however, jump when she threw her spectacles across the room.

One of the lenses shattered but the other remained intact, lying innocently in the frame near the damaged wall.

Rowan's fingers twitched. For four months, Augusta had exhibited unnatural control in the face of adversity but now that she'd proven him wrong, his satisfaction upon seeing her outburst was… fleeting.

The urge to take her in his arms—to offer some reassurance —nearly got the best of him.

But she'd offered him reassurances once. Promises that had turned out to be lies.

And so he left her standing alone, looking forlorn.

Lost.

"That's idiotic." He spoke through clenched teeth.

Her eyes flashed, pinning on his. They burned with such intensity they appeared more silver than gray.

"You stare at me with contempt," she accused. Twin spots of pink glowed high on her cheeks, and her fists clenched at her sides.

Rowan cocked a brow. He wouldn't argue with this.

Because that hadn't always been the case, and he knew all too well that arguing wouldn't get him far.

He had seen her lose her temper before. When she'd come to him right after her father forbade her to see him again. In the beginning of their relationship, her father had forbidden her to break off her engagement to Malum.

In her frustration, she'd wanted to strike out at everyone. Only after she'd tired herself out ranting had she settled into his arms, exhausted.

He'd been alone in his father's Mayfair townhouse… The door to the parlor had been locked.

She'd tasted like honey and tea, and they'd been frantic to touch one another.

He'd believed she was the other half of his soul. The light to his dark, his shelter in a storm… Neither had been concerned with where they were, or that they might be caught, but only of their need to be together. The magnetic pull had grown too strong to resist.

Their lovemaking had come on like the summer storm raging outside. Unfathomable strikes of lightning had illuminated the room, booming thunder, and then a torrent of warm rain. And afterward, they'd simply held one another. In awe at what they'd discovered…

Connection. Exquisite pleasure. A rightness that must surely last an eternity. He'd realized then that they'd have to elope. Her father would never willingly allow her to marry him.

They had made plans.

Rowan couldn't dwell on the details that had made it the most satisfying lovemaking of his life.

Not now. Not with her glaring at him as though he'd set fire to the school himself.

He shifted, adjusting his trousers. There was no rain today. Only oppressive heat and regret and betrayal more noxious than the smell left over from the fire.

"When's the last time you threw something in a fit of temper, Augusta?" He wasn't being sarcastic. He didn't have to love her but he… *he knew her.*

And he wanted her to acknowledge that no person could contain all of their emotions all of the time. Good lord, she was more fiercely independent than even he was.

She dropped her gaze. "I wasn't throwing them at you." She inhaled, attempting to regain control. "No. I am sincerely grateful that you were here to prevent further damages."

"Are you? Are you really? You just told me you deserved this. Would you have preferred the school burn to the ground? No one was inside. No one would have been injured. You could have walked away and been free of it forever."

"You don't know what you're saying." Her eyes flashed up at

him again. "I've spent my entire life sacrificing and working late nights, strategizing to keep this school running. No one realizes how impressionable young women are or how important it is that they learn to think for themselves. Knowing how to plan a dinner party is nothing compared to knowing how to recognize the difference between right and wrong—seeing the inequities in the world and believing someday they might do something to right them. No one comprehends that for some of these girls, this is home. This place is a touchstone. We are..."

"A family." Rowan finished for her.

She spoke with passion, her words unbearably noble.

"If I fail..." She smoothed her hands down the front of her gown.

Rowan resisted the pull even as he again imagined himself taking her in his arms. The urge to do so was almost impossible to fight. This woman struggled with not only her conscience but the threats to her ambitions.

She swiped at her eyes and then met his gaze. And for a moment, she hid nothing. She was not *Miss Primm*, but she was *Augusta*.

And she craved comfort. He'd not allow her into his heart ever again, but he wasn't the sort of man to sit back and watch any woman suffer. She would resist comforting at first, but something inside him knew...

He lowered his box of tools to the floor and, after two cautious strides, oh, so slowly, gathered her in his arms.

She remained stiff, but he waited.

And after a few trembling breaths, she relaxed, tucking her face into his chest.

"You're not going to fail," he said, and then exhaled some of his resentment.

He rested his chin on top of her head, and her hair tickled his throat and chin.

And dash it all, holding her like this landed his heart and brain in an otherworldly place. A non-existent place somewhere between the past and the present. In the past, he'd soothed her with endearments and words of love, promising her he would protect her—that everything would turn out just as they planned.

But he'd never been given the chance to carry out that promise.

And she was right, he'd stared at her with contempt all spring. She'd betrayed him.

Holding her was familiar and yet new. And he took satisfaction that this bristly woman, this carefully controlled person he'd watched all spring, would lower her defenses with him.

And as he wrapped her up against his much larger form, as he acknowledged the way her breasts softened against his torso, the curve of her hips, and knowing the promise of pleasure between her legs, he reminded himself that this wouldn't last. This breach in the barriers between them was only temporary.

Otherwise, he'd be as confused as hell. He shifted and loosened his hold just enough so that some of his blood remained in his brain.

"I could still fail." She sniffed. "Some days, I feel like everything could just disappear in an instant."

Rowan cleared his throat. "And what do you do on those days?"

"I make a—"

"List," Rowan finished for her. Whenever she'd come around while he'd been working at the school, she'd always had a list with her. Consulting it every few minutes, checking things off, and adding to it.

She tilted her head back and met his gaze, perplexed. This resulted in her exposing what was still a creamy, delectable throat. He nearly groaned while she continued thinking aloud.

"It helps me organize problems. Then I tackle them one at a time."

Rowan dropped his arms and stepped away from her. Too much. Holding her was too much.

As he retrieved his tools, he was surprised his hands weren't shaking. He couldn't allow her to look at him like that—like she cared—or as though he did.

Seventeen years ago, she had promised to meet him—to marry him. Neither had cared what the *ton* thought, and he'd had plenty of funds at his disposal. They could have made a good life together.

But she'd wanted her school. Rowan didn't fully understand her decision, he doubted he'd ever forgive her for it, but in an odd way, he respected it. After all, he'd gone on to make a name for himself as well. He couldn't very well have traveled throughout England, working on projects from here to Edinburgh, if he'd married her.

There would have been children.

Or would they have drifted apart because of their different ambitions?

He rubbed his hand over his head.

Their affair had ended a very long time ago. They hardly knew one another now.

"I keep finding myself thanking you." She grimaced, looking adorably shy, clutching her hands at her waist.

"One task at a time," he said. "And the damages from this fire will become a distant memory." The vandals weren't his problem. Rosewood would insist she hire better watchmen.

Rowan needed distance. He needed fresh air and a good, hearty ride.

Oblivious to his agitation, Augusta nodded and then turned to stare out the window. "If only it were just the fire…"

"Regardless." He found himself crossing the room to retrieve her spectacles. The broken lens would need replacing, but he bent the frames so they might prove somewhat functional before handing them over.

In doing so, he was very careful not to touch her again.

"Thank you." Her voice caught. "I'm sorry," she added.

"Why would you be sorry?" he asked before he could stop himself.

"For throwing them. For…" She waved a hand around the room and then gestured toward herself. "For such an undignified display."

He waited.

What else are you sorry for, Augusta?

She shook her head. Apparently that was all she was capable of giving him. Rowan shifted his tools from one hand to the other and made for the door. Being alone with her like this was the last thing he needed.

"You'll find a way. You've managed well enough until now." He didn't look back when he spoke but strode out the door and then purposefully made his way down the winding staircase.

Would she find a way this time? He shot a glance toward the burned section of the building. Or was she out of her depths?

Blast and hellfire.

The wretched woman needed protection. Her brother showed some concern, but he was a nob, and members of the aristocracy had a tendency to underestimate their vulnerabilities.

Augusta was worried; that much was obvious. But she seemed almost paralyzed when it came to acknowledging the danger she and the school were in. And by not comprehending that danger, she—and the school—were unprotected.

Good Lord, was he going to have to provide it? What with the agreement he'd made with Rosewood, he could always appoint one of his workers. A chat with her brother was in order, as would be a chat with Rhys.

Nonetheless, while watching out for Augusta Primm, Rowan was only going to do so from a distance.

Because as dangerous as these vandals might be, Rowan might very well face an even greater threat. Because having held her in his arms, he'd learned that even after all these years...

She fit.

Damned Augusta Primm.

NEVER MEANT TO BE

"*I* *wasn't sure you'd get permission to come out today.*" Rowan covered Augusta's hand with his, glancing sideways at her as he drove them out of Mayfair.

"*My mother thinks I'm going to a recital.*" She didn't want to talk about her mother and father. They were doing all they could to keep her away from him. "*Where is Addison today? Is he settling in with his newest tutor?*"

"*He has to be.*" Rowan frowned. "*Father's giving him no choice.*"

Augusta nodded. She understood the dynamics of aristocratic fathers well enough, but even she found herself baffled by Rowan's position in his family.

Rowan had lived the first seven years of his life on his father's plantation in Barbados—until his mother's death. Upon hearing that his former mistress had died, the Duke of Bedwell brought his son to England where he'd taken him into his home.

Rowan's relationships with his stepmother, half-brother, and father were complicated.

"*Is he really such a tyrant?*" Augusta asked.

"*My father loved my mother, and he has treated me... well. Very well, in fact.*" Rowan exhaled. As they drove toward the outskirts of town, he explained that his father outwardly favored him over his legitimate offspring—over poor Addison—whom the duke considered feeble and weak. "My father's marriage to the duchess was an arranged one. They don't get on well. But Addison is his legal heir, and my father makes him suffer for it," he said.

"He... is unkind to him?"

Rowan pinched his lips together and nodded. "I try to protect him, but Addison claims that my interference only makes it worse."

"Ah..." Augusta winced. Poor, poor Addison! But as the heir, his life would never be his own.

Driving on less-trafficked roads now, Rowan could turn and stare at her without having to worry about other vehicles. "I don't speak of this with anyone." A frown marred his smooth face.

"You can trust me, Rowan," she said. "They are your family."

"It doesn't always feel like it."

After rolling along silently, her mind bursting with questions, Augusta finally asked, "Do you love your father?"

Rowan pondered her question for nearly half a minute before answering. "I don't know." And then he turned the question back to her. "Do you love yours?"

This was part of why she loved being with him. Because they could talk about anything. She never had to worry that she would say something wrong. He was safe.

"No," she said. "I don't think I ever have. My father's controlled my whole life, it seems, but has never taken a moment to consider anything I want—or who I am, for that matter." She exhaled. She didn't want to talk about her father. As of yet, he was an unresolved obstacle between Rowan and her. "Where are you taking me?"

"My father owns a cottage, a small estate on the river. But for a few servants, it's empty most of the time." He swallowed hard. "It's not entailed."

What was he saying?

"It belonged to my father's mother, and my father has promised that upon his death, it will come to me." More clearing of his throat.

"If I marry before his death, however, ownership passes sooner. It will be my home." He nervously squeezed her hand. "I wanted to wait until you'd broken things off with Malum before mentioning it..."

Was he saying what she thought he was saying?

And then they turned down a narrower road. The cottage, made up of red brick with flowered trellises climbing to the roof, was the most charming home Augusta had ever seen.

"This is yours?"

Rowan dipped his chin. "Lockstone Cottage."

"Cottage" was a conservative word to describe the house, really. It stood three stories high, and two massive wings flanked the tall, rounded door set in the center of the arched entrance. Despite its size, however, the home felt warm and inviting.

"It's in need of numerous repairs and new furnishings, of course. But I think it will be more than comfortable. Will you live in it with me?" he asked. But then he scowled. "Dash it all, this isn't the proper way to do this, is it?"

But Augusta nearly burst out laughing. "Are you asking me to marry you?"

He frowned again. "Didn't I say that?"

"You did not."

He drew the horses to a halt and then turned to take her hands in his. "I'm horrid at romance, and I'll never be good enough for you. But the minute I met you, I knew you were the other half of my soul. I love you, Augusta. Will you make me the happiest of men and be my wife?"

Augusta swiped at a tear. "You aren't horrible at romance. In fact, you're really quite good at it." And then she added, "Of course I'll marry you."

She would be Mrs. Rowan Stewart. She would live in this beautiful cottage with him. They would have children. They would grow old together.

But first, she needed her father to break his agreement with the Duke of Malum.

He had to! Because living without Rowan was not something she was willing to do.

SHE'D HAD the same dream three nights in a row, a memory from a time long past, one that lingered in the back of her head until well into the afternoon. These nighttime assaults of memories best forgotten were getting ridiculous.

Seeing that it was nearly dawn, she threw her feet over the side of the bed and, after washing and dressing, marched from her residence, through the door to the school, and directly toward her office.

The dreams were brought on by his presence and the growing fear for her school. They would diminish when matters settled down—or when he left.

But could she wait that long?

In the past, she'd never had difficulty pivoting when faced with some unexpected challenge. Why was she struggling now?

One task at a time. She contemplated Rowan's advice. It was sound; in fact, it was advice she'd give to any one of her students or even one of her teachers. It was why she relied so heavily on her lists.

But even before attending Miss Fellowes's wedding... she'd experienced a few occasions when she'd been so overwhelmed her heartbeat thundered in her ears. Panic hovered, making her gasp for air. Thankfully, these episodes hadn't lasted long. She could wait them out while locked in her office. And going over her lists never failed to bring calm.

But what did one do about problems she couldn't resolve with a list?

One resolved them anyway.

And not in the manner she'd attempted yesterday. Good heavens, she had *thrown a pair of spectacles across the room like a madwoman!*

After he'd left, she'd barely kept her tears in check. Instead, she'd done what she did best. She threw herself into work. In an attempt to shrug off his... rejection, she scrubbed soot off the walls, in the hallways, the classrooms, and even the closets. She scrubbed until she could no longer lift her arms over her head and then she'd gone downstairs to her chamber, unpacked her clothes from the wedding journey, and washed up for bed.

One would have thought she'd get a good night's rest, but Rowan had managed to invade her sleep as well.

Augusta squinted and straightened the pencils on her desk. Today was a new day.

But first things first. Opening her drawer with shaking hands, she removed the old pair of spectacles she kept on hand. It had been foolish of her to give in to such a fit of temper. Now she'd have to go into the mercantile in Warwick Village and order a replacement pair. What had she hoped to accomplish?

She froze, staring at the lenses in her hand.

He'd not contradicted that he'd felt contempt for her.

But then he'd taken her into his arms. She'd heard his heart beating—it had been racing.

And then it had slowed. She'd been alone for a very long time, but for those brief moments, she'd felt a little less so.

It didn't mean anything. She exhaled a shaky breath.

Slipping on the older spectacles, she read through her list of priorities and then her secondary lists that broke each priority into detailed tasks.

And then she read through them again.

Three times. Five times. When she still felt itchy, she opened a second journal. She would break each individual item into lists of their own.

And yet she was avoiding the most recent hurdle to come along. Augusta removed her spectacles and rubbed her eyes. While returning from Priscilla and Lord Hardwood's wedding,

Miss Fortune had finally admitted what Augusta had suspected.

Chloe had confessed that while at Hardwood Cliffhouse earlier that year, she'd had an affair with Captain Edgeworth. And that affair had resulted in... a rather delicate complication. Even as early as March, Augusta had noticed Miss Fortune's change in appetite, the texture of her hair, the woman's tendency to become queasy for no reason at all.

Augusta had recognized the signs all too easily, but she'd hoped she was wrong.

She had not been.

And now she'd have to replace Chloe as well, yet another of her students' favorites.

But far worse than that was the uncertainty of Chloe's future. If the captain didn't do the right thing, Chloe would need protection and... money.

With all of Augusta's personal funds going toward keeping the school standing, she had little extra to spare.

All the lists in the world weren't going to solve the sort of problems she faced—circumstances utterly out of her control.

And of course, events came up the following day, events that ought to be welcomed, but with the recent fire and Chloe's situation, Augusta wasn't prepared.

Lord Hardwood's mother and all his sisters arrived to tour the school unexpectedly, along with a handful of titled gentlemen...

Normally she would have had weeks' notice before hosting such affluent visitors. She'd have planned meals, outings, and had the school shined from top to bottom.

But Augusta was currently short-staffed. She had sent Chloe to London, in her own carriage with Coachman John for protection, to track down Captain Edgeworth and Miss Royal had gone along as chaperone.

Furthermore, the scent of smoke persisted to drift around

the school, and there was no hiding the other remnants of the fire or the charcoal stain on the corner of the roof.

And of course, who was one of those lofty gentlemen who'd arrived with her unexpected guests? Captain Edgeworth himself.

At least she'd been able to send him after Chloe, leading Augusta to believe he was willing to take care of his responsibilities.

Averting that particular crisis, thank heavens!

But that left herself and Miss Wolcott to act as hostesses to the other guests.

And Victoria, who was nearby and willing to help.

But for how long?

Any month now, Augusta had no doubt that Victoria would make an announcement of a very personal nature.

Augusta wasn't naïve enough to believe her brother would exercise restraint as far as marital intimacy was concerned. And Victoria, despite all her prim and proper ways, was likely just as bad.

Augusta winced. As of now, she was going to need to add a minimum of four capable women to her dwindling staff—three and a half teachers and a part-time assistant.

And seeing as Victoria would no longer be handling the school's fundraising efforts, Augusta was going to have to brush up on her social skills as well. As much as she abhorred the pretentious events, they were a necessity she couldn't ignore. Because such events didn't only garner funds, but attracted new students.

And new students meant more tuition payments.

More money—of which the school was in desperate need.

The pounding in her ears was so loud now that it was almost painful.

One problem at a time.

Blinking, she read the top item aloud: "Hire new teachers."

Breathe.

Normally—there was that word again!—she took her time hiring her staff, taking advantage of those serendipitous referrals or meetings that came along when she least expected them. She'd hired intelligent ladies who needed a place to belong or a purpose. But with four vacant positions, she couldn't rely on fortuitous circumstances this time.

She'd be forced to rely on total strangers to teach her girls—yet another decision she wasn't entirely comfortable with.

Before leaving to attend Miss Fellowes's wedding, Augusta had sent notice to an employment agency in London. The director there had said she would send four applicants to be interviewed. Augusta only hoped she'd be as lucky with the new candidates as she'd been with the ladies she was losing. Not once had she regretted hiring any of them.

Every single incident this year that had resulted in scandal, and each termination of employment that followed, had been Augusta's fault.

Likely, she was somehow at fault for the vandalism as well.

Or... *my little annoyance,* as she'd begun to think of these incidents. It sounded far less ominous.

Augusta set the staff list aside and stared down at list number two: *Protect the school.*

Beneath that, she'd written, *Convince Lord Sexton to investigate my little annoyance.*

Seeing as she'd had no choice but to entertain all of Lord Hardwood's womenfolk, along with their gentleman chaperone—who just happened to be a marquess but also a prominent detective—Augusta assumed he'd be happy to look into the matter. Someone with such lauded investigatory skills could surely solve their little mystery.

And he'd agreed to examine the crime scene this morning.

So when a knock sounded on the door, Augusta rushed across the room to unlock and then open it. Miss Beatrice

Wolcott, the last remaining teacher residing at the school over the summer months, stood tentatively on the other side.

Miss Wolcott was one of those hires Augusta had made on instinct alone. Augusta had barely sat down for their interview before a knowing stirred inside her. Miss Wolcott was hiding from something—or *someone*—and needed a safe place. Such a lady would never do anything to bring undue attention to the school, and in her appreciation for being hired without references, worked harder than anyone.

Augusta hadn't expected the latter, but in the light of recent events, she appreciated the woman's work ethic, which was almost as relentless as her own.

"Good morning, Miss Primm," the other woman greeted her.

"Is it?" Primm muttered, but then glanced up. "I suppose we'll know soon enough." Augusta caught herself and then added, "I trust you slept well."

Miss Wolcott lowered herself into the chair opposite Augusta.

"Very. I'm not used to the quiet of sleeping in my own chambers. I'll enjoy it while I have the opportunity." She brushed her skirts and quickly changed the subject. "I'm going to work on lesson plans today and clean out the storage closets in my classroom. That is, unless you needed me for anything else."

Discussing mundane summer tasks comforted Augusta. The school had been too quiet, too empty lately. Surely that was why she'd struggled to silence her mind.

"Always a good practice to keep ahead with lesson plans." But Augusta glanced down at her list. "And later this week, we'll need to pen the orientation letters to the parents of our new students."

"We won't mention our little—?"

"Definitely not." Augusta frowned. "But I suppose we'll need to mention something about Miss Ship—*Lady Rosewood's* departure from her position." Seeing as it had been Victoria who'd recruited most of them and then finalized their admissions.

Miss Wolcott offered a few vague suggestions for the welcoming picnic before she rose and backed toward the door, looking eager to get to work.

"Oh, and, Beatrice?" Augusta called, standing as well.

"Yes?" Her employees always looked surprised when Augusta called them by their given names. They were her employees, not her friends. But although she shouldn't, there were some days when she slipped—when she needed to feel a smidgeon of closeness to another human being.

"Unlock the dorms upstairs, will you? Lord Sexton has offered to take a look into the identity of our... *little annoyance* and I'll need you to fill him in. He is scheduled to inspect the premises in"—Augusta glanced at the clock—"ten minutes."

Miss Wolcott hesitated, her expression becoming a little pinched. "Don't you think you ought to meet with him personally?"

Augusta ought to. Not because she enjoyed the arrogant man's company, but because he could be the answer to one of her problems.

Unfortunately, yet another item on her list had reared its ugly head.

Donations.

Augusta returned to the seat at her desk. "Trust me, Miss Wolcott, I'd far prefer your task over mine. Allison Meadowbrook's father is due to arrive to discuss his conditions for this year's donation." The man was one of their most generous donors, but unfortunately, currently their most disgruntled one.

Showing unusual reluctance, Miss Wolcott dipped her chin in agreement. "I'll do my best," she said.

"As I'm sure you do all your duties." That pounding in her ears was returning.

And then an unfortunate possibility occurred to her.

"Beatrice?" Again, she stopped the woman before she could exit.

"Yes?"

"If you can, keep the marquess away from my office, will you? I cannot have Mr. Meadowbrook seeing an investigator lurking about. He'll have questions, and even without the threat posed by our *little annoyance*, it's going to take everything I can to maintain his sponsorship."

"I'll do my best."

Which was, in fact, all Augusta could hope for.

In what remained of the day, Augusta managed to smooth matters over with Mr. Meadowbrook, convince Lord Sexton to spend the night on school grounds in order to advance the investigation, and prepare for an orientation of sorts for Lady Hardwood and her daughters the following day. One of the daughters was interested in teaching, but she was too young to fill any of the current spots and may need to attend as a student first.

Students from prominent families were always welcome.

Furthermore, her visiting detective had admitted that their case was not unsolvable. He'd limited their pool of suspects to a person with dark hair, likely male, who had been in possession of tar. Upon examining the tinder box left behind by the arsonist, he'd declared that the vandal was either a thief or a member of the nobility.

Which, when one considered such descriptions, could be almost anyone... but it was something.

Very late that night, Augusta stared at her bed, feeling physically exhausted without feeling sleepy. The day had been a productive one, but her brain was already preparing for hurdles she'd have to face the following morning.

Her bones ached, her spirit ached, but her mind still raced from the happenings of the day.

If she slept, she'd dream of *him*, forcing her to remember bittersweet moments over and over again. The dreams only served to remind her of what she'd lost.

But she couldn't discuss them with anyone. Not Miss Wolcott and certainly not Rowan!

They would subside eventually—once he returned to London.

But then she pictured the condition of Longbow Castle...

Drat and damn! Her brother's project was going to take years to complete.

So rather than changing out of her practical gown and into a night rail, she wandered through the foyer, past the parlor, and stepped outside.

The night was dark except for a sliver of light from the quarter moon highlighting the swaying treetops in the distance. Although the temperature was no cooler than her bedroom, a gentle breeze stirred the air, and the fragrance of wildflowers and dirt and grass soothed her.

A lonely cloud drifted overhead, casting an eerie shadow. She flicked her gaze to the treetops. Who might be lurking beneath them? The person who'd set the fire?

Unbidden, her father's image came to mind. His face ought to bring her comfort—security. Instead, a wave of dread swept through her.

Last December, upon receiving a letter from Liam that their mother's health was failing, Augusta had made a hurried visit to Starbridge Abbey. She'd done her best to keep out of her father's way, spending time reacquainting herself with Noah and Theodore. She had been grateful that for the most part, she'd been invisible to the man who had sired her.

She only wished she'd been invisible before, the year she'd met Rowan.

An animal howled in the distance, and a shiver rolled through her. She clenched her jaw, however, refusing to be afraid on her own land. She'd known enough fear for a lifetime. She'd fight these vandals herself rather than hide.

And so, instead of being chased back inside, she purposefully strolled down the walk, across the grass, and wandered around along the three-story building. This school belonged to her—to her and her students. It was a beloved institution, known throughout all of England. How dare someone attack it?

The silhouette of a man striding across the lawn caused her to gasp and then freeze.

She didn't exhale until she realized... Broad shoulders. Tapered waist. Thick, powerful thighs powering his legs, making quick work of the ground between them.

He carried his shirt, draped over one shoulder.

Which left his top half to gleam in the moonlight.

"It's you," she said.

"What the devil are you doing out here all alone? Have you no sense?" Rowan ran his hand over the top of his head, stopping when it reached the back of his neck. In that motion, she caught sight of all kinds of rippling muscles.

"The better question is why are you here? And why aren't you wearing any clothes?" He wore breeches and boots, of course... The cloud shifted and shadows rippled over his skin.

She'd once known that skin intimately. He'd been more slender then, but she'd kissed that skin...

She'd tasted it.

"Too damned hot to sleep." He shuffled his feet. "And muggy. Thought I'd look around... in case your arsonist was in the area."

Piers had mentioned that Rowan had assigned a few workers to keep watch. If she'd known Rowan participated in the effort, if she'd thought he might be just outside every night when she climbed into bed... Would she have slept at all?

"I appreciate that." She didn't look at him. He'd admitted to feeling responsible for the school—the school his sister attended. She wouldn't fool herself into believing he'd come because he cared about her. "Lord Sexton is in residence this evening. He's promised to look into our little problem." No one would dare attack the school with the famous detective in residence—not with a hammer, tar, or anything else.

Rowan shifted but didn't meet her gaze. "Augusta... Sexton's going to return to London soon, and as good as he is, I doubt that even he'll be able to solve the mystery in a matter of a few days." He shook his head and then finally pinned his gaze on her. "For once in your life, would you admit that you need help?"

"I don't!" she instinctively contradicted him. She'd taken drastic measures to capture the person plaguing the school. She was going to rehire the watchmen, all the doors were ordered locked unless someone was present, and she had a pistol in her nightstand, which she operated with great proficiency. She would not be afraid!

And yet, Rowan tilted his head, challenging her in his stance.

It was he who had repaired her foundation and charged her next to nothing, and then he'd put out the fire, saving the building again. And without even asking, he was repairing the damages from the fire.

Who was she fooling?

She hugged her arms in front of her. "Well, perhaps a little."

His brows lifted. "A little?"

"Fine, a lot," Augusta half growled. "I need all the help I can get. Is that what you wanted to hear?"

He studied her and then chuckled. "Damn, I didn't expect that."

His laughing at her expense ought to feel insulting. So why didn't it? As two youths in love, they'd faced their fair share of challenges, and yet they'd always found something to laugh about.

"It's true that I can be a little... controlling. I realize this, and I'm not afraid to admit when I'm wrong. And contrary to..." She waved her hands between them, not sure what to call their current relationship. "I do appreciate all you've done." But perhaps she'd stumbled on him for a reason. An isolated incident for fate to step in?

Perhaps she ought to take it as a sign. It was time they talked... Time they put the past to rest. If that was even achievable.

But she needed a good night's rest!

So at the risk of making a fool of herself, she swallowed hard. "I'm actually glad I've come across you."

"Is there a problem with the roof?"

"No... No. Nothing like that. I'd like to... talk to you, about what happened." And then, before her courage fled, she added, "*Before.*"

His brows rose even higher now. She'd gone out of her way to avoid discussing anything personal in all the time he'd been here.

She'd thought that would be best.

But these dreams... Would airing their differences make them go away?

Augusta glanced over her shoulder. The two of them were alone, but she had to be sure.

She needed to sleep again. She needed to find peace. Any other problem, she would have addressed already. But this...

Was different.

And suddenly she didn't know where to begin.

Rowan initiated the conversation for her.

"You wish to apologize for failing to meet me as promised?

For choosing your independence over me?" His tone was sarcastic. Bitter.

For choosing her independence...? "But I—"

"No need to explain. I understand now. But, I'll admit, I never thought you'd turn to your father to end things for you."

Wait! *Go to my father?* Willingly?

"Ending it wasn't my choice. Surely you realize that." She frowned.

He shrugged, and Augusta couldn't keep her eyes from trailing over his chest. It wasn't fair that he'd aged into an even better-looking gentleman, and she'd simply... aged.

"Surely you didn't imagine you could send your message via one of your father's henchmen without him becoming involved? I knew you were frustrated when he refused his support, but hell, Augusta..." He stared into the distance. "You could have simply told me."

She narrowed her eyes. What was he talking about? "I didn't send any message." And if she had, she certainly wouldn't have asked one of her father's men to deliver it.

She'd not had a chance to send any sort of message at all.

Before she could sneak out of her bedchamber to go and meet him, she'd been grabbed from behind, bound and gagged, and thrown into a carriage that had transported her as far from London as possible without having to leave the country.

It had been one of the most terrifying experiences of her life and her own parents had been behind it all.

She had not told her father anything. He was the last person in the world she'd have turned to. She shook her head. "I didn't come that night because... I couldn't."

The brief glance backward, the glimpse of that memory, made her stomach churn.

Rowan's expression weighed heavy with skepticism.

Perhaps she shouldn't have dredged up this nightmare.

He was right. She had been terribly naïve. She'd been a fool to trust Martha with the very personal aspects of her relationship with Rowan. Her father paid Martha's salary.

Augusta had paid dearly for assuming her maid would be loyal to her.

But she'd thought Rowan would come after her—she'd been so very sure he would know something untoward had occurred.

So she pressed onward. "I thought you'd come looking for me. I didn't expect you would know, but I hoped…" She had experienced very lucid dreams of him forcing the carriage to stop, of him breaking through the doors, taking her into his arms, and… rescuing her.

Because he'd loved her.

But she'd been disappointed over and over again.

Memories of staring at miles of passing scenery flashed through her mind. The windows and door had been locked from the outside, making escape impossible. Her hands had chafed from being bound, and she'd had to relax in order to keep from choking on the cloth tied around her mouth.

Initially she'd been terrified, but once she'd realized her captors were familiar servants carrying out her father's orders, she'd been shocked. And then furious.

After traveling north for nearly a week, her aunt welcomed her with apologies and comforting words. But under what amounted to nothing less than house arrest, she could not go back to London. She could not send word to Rowan.

It hadn't taken long for Augusta to realize the hopelessness of her situation. The Marquess of Starbridge was too powerful. She'd even wondered if her father had paid Rowan off. It was possible that his feelings hadn't been as strong as hers.

Devastated, all she could do at the time was make the best of her circumstances.

"Come looking for you?" His harsh tone brought her back

to the present. "After being met by your father's men instead of the woman I expected to marry, I was laid up for two months."

"Laid up?"

He'd been a young and vigorous man. But of course... he'd been vulnerable.

The meaning behind his words had her swaying until she blinked.

His assertion answered questions she'd kept to herself for years. Her father had been willing to use force with his own daughter, why wouldn't he use violence on the man she'd fallen in love with?

Guilt ran down her spine like a venomous spider. She opened her mouth to speak but nothing came out.

In those days, her father had relied upon three particular men to carry out more delicate matters, all of them scarred and angry-looking.

Only one of them had accompanied her. Leaving the two others...

Bile burned in the back of her throat. Rowan had been hurt because of her. *Because of her!*

Why hadn't she realized this? Was it possible she'd suspected this all along? Was this why the dreams left her feeling so on edge?

She could have gone to him once she was free, but...

Back then, she'd made assumptions about his own freedom. If he had still cared about her, he could have come, or so she'd thought.

As the truth became clear, black edged Augusta's vision, and her limbs began turning numb.

THE DETAILS

*A*ugusta swayed from side to side, and even in the dark, Rowan could see the blood draining out of her face.

She hadn't known?

Flashes of memories raced through his head. Her promises echoed in his ears. And then the punch of pain and betrayal he'd experienced when he realized she wasn't coming.

Because two angry giants had shown up instead.

Of course she hadn't known!

Disgust swept through him. He'd been a blind fool. Apparently, that was what love did to a man.

"The message…" Rowan frowned. "It wasn't really from you."

His words weren't a question.

He'd thought he'd had all the answers. He'd read the message over and over again, written on her familiar stationery. She'd even spritzed it with her perfume, adding insult to injury.

He had believed the worst of her.

For years.

Nearly two decades.

Of course she had not gone to her father to end things for her. She'd had nothing to do with the beating he'd been given. Why in God's name had he been so quick to think the worst of her?

She'd never willingly hurt him. In the wake of self-disgust, consoling relief ripped through him.

And then sadness, a heavy, bittersweet sadness.

Somewhere deep down, he must have realized this. If he hadn't, he never would have accepted the job at Longbow Castle, let alone agreed to Rosewood's addendum.

He and Augusta had been so caught up in their feelings, they'd made plans for a future together without taking reality into consideration.

Melancholy showed in Augusta's eyes as she made a wan attempt at a smile.

"Does it matter?" Augusta hugged her arms in front of herself.

It mattered. The details always mattered.

But before he could press her, the door to the front of the school swung open in the distance. And oddly enough, Lord Sexton stepped outside.

He, too, looked to be suffering from a bout of insomnia as he marched across the lawn toward the trees.

Rowan kept silent, and so did Augusta. Neither of them was in any mood to make polite conversation.

Of mutual accord, they continued on around to the back of the school. But when Augusta turned as though she'd enter through the back of her residence, Rowan reached out and caught her arm.

"It matters." His voice came out husky-sounding. By God, this woman was going to drive him mad.

She stiffened, but he pulled her against him anyway. "Rowan—"

He didn't stop to think what he was doing, but cut her off before she could finish, crushing her mouth against his.

This kiss was nothing like any they had ever shared before. When he'd courted her, when they'd believed themselves in love. In those stolen moments, she'd parted soft lips, inviting him. Now, she pinched them together—not fighting him but not welcoming him either.

"It matters," he growled against her mouth. If ever a kiss could communicate regret, it was this one. But Rowan was also filled with anger, frustration, and a thousand questions.

And lust, *damn his eyes.* Lust drove him as much as anything else.

Because it was the one thing that hadn't changed.

She tried shaking her head to evade him, even as her body melted into his. She slid her hands up his chest, her fingertips tracing the cords of his neck. Even as her lips sighed open, tension rolled off her frame. But she wasn't resisting him.

She was resisting herself.

Nothing about this woman was the same as the one he'd fallen in love with. This woman bristled while systematically maintaining a fortress around herself.

"It's too late," she cried, her fingers clutching the back of his head.

With his cock stiffening, wedged between the two of them, he fought his own battles. She'd had years to find him—to explain that she'd not jilted him willingly.

Instead, she'd kept hidden away at her school.

Rowan tore his mouth away from hers and gripped her wrists.

"Is it?" he demanded.

"I'm so sorry, Rowan..." Moonlight reflected in her stormy eyes. "I know it doesn't really matter, but at least we know now... I was devastated to believe you hated me."

I only hated you because I believed a lie, damn it! He'd been a fool to fall for it so easily—a fool who'd been blinded by what he'd thought had been her selfish betrayal.

But a voice whispered in the back of his mind. *Had he been wrong about all of it?*

Because... The details mattered. What was he missing?

"What happened?" He squeezed her wrists.

Augusta paused before answering. "I was sent to live with my aunt."

Rowan nodded. "But you started the school a year later."

She struggled, and he loosened his hands.

And then, shaking her head, she exhaled. "I wanted to find you—" She stared straight ahead as though the button on his shirt suddenly fascinated her. "I made promises..."

So, he hadn't been completely wrong. She'd chosen the school over him.

"Your father provided funds for your school if you stayed away from the bastard." It was just as he thought. Perhaps she was right; the details weren't all that important.

Her eyes flew open wide, but then a woman's voice shattered the quiet of the night.

"Miss Primm? Are you out here?"

Rowan waited a second, then released Augusta's wrists and stepped back.

"Jenny," she explained. "My housekeeper. She'll be wanting to lock up for the night." Augusta frowned before calling over her shoulder, "I'll be right in!"

She touched her lips, lowered her lashes, and then held his gaze for what could have been a single second but also could have been a lifetime.

"I'm sorry, Rowan," she said, and for a brief second, he saw something of the old Augusta in her. She took two more steps backward, still holding his gaze.

"It mattered that much to you?" It was a ridiculous question, spurred by more than curiosity. She professed to be a spinster, but needs simmered beneath her stern demeanor. "Is there someone else?"

"No." Her answer was vehement. "Of course not."

"I never stopped thinking about you." The words were out before he could stop them.

Oh, lord. He was making a fool of himself.

She shook her head. "Don't say that. Haven't you realized yet, Rowan? You and me. The life we wanted. It was all just a dream. We were living in a fairytale!"

And then, almost like a ghost, she vanished inside.

Listening to the distinct sound of locks being set, Rowan fisted both hands at his sides and then flexed them.

Was she right?

One by one, the glow of candles in the windows of the old building disappeared. And with a thousand thoughts racing through his head, he studied his surroundings.

Her father had sent her away against her will. She'd given up on him the same as he'd given up on her.

And since he'd given up on her, he'd failed to protect her.

A fatal weakness on his part. It wasn't the first time he'd failed to protect those who'd needed him most—his mother long ago, his brother, and now, unwittingly, Augusta.

He would not make that mistake again.

Rowan prowled the grounds, his eyes watchful and his strides stealthy and silent. He didn't return to Longbow Castle until the eastern sky turned dusky purple.

Nothing more than a fairytale? Perhaps, but they were different people now. Could they exist together in some form of reality?

A LAPSE IN FORTITUDE

"I hope Jenny hasn't gone all out for dinner this evening. This heat has robbed me of my appetite." Beatrice's voice followed Augusta into the small dining room.

"I believe she made her famous chicken salad." Augusta smiled.

Augusta liked Beatrice, even if she suspected the woman had come to her with secrets. Beatrice Wolcott had shown exceptional intelligence and exhibited the no-nonsense sort of practicality required to effectively teach. But most importantly, Augusta had recognized caution in the other woman's eyes, and a need for safety, a need for peace.

The school had lost many brilliant teachers in the past year, but at least Beatrice would be staying on.

However, recently, and against Augusta's better judgment, she'd allowed the line between employer and employee to become blurred. Even if neither of them was willing to discuss their past, they'd found comfortable companionship with one another over the past few days. With it being just the two of them, it only made sense they take meals together.

"It's quiet now that our guests have departed." Beatrice

spread her napkin across her lap. "I'm looking forward to the students returning this autumn—more than usual." For the most part, Beatrice carried on what amounted to something of a single-sided conversation.

But she was right. The school did feel too quiet.

Lord Sexton hadn't remained as long as Augusta had hoped. After just two days, he, along with Lord Hardwood's women-folk, had made their goodbyes earlier that morning.

Rowan had been right about the marquess. He was probably right about most things.

Except for me. He didn't know everything about her. Her reasons for not finding him were more complicated than he could ever imagine. He didn't really want to know the truth. It was messy, sad, and another aspect of her life that she had no control over.

Augusta's hands shook as she unfolded her napkin.

He'd kissed her!

How many times had she relived the moment over the past few days? More than any spinster ought to, that was for certain.

For seventeen years, she'd decided she didn't miss it. She hadn't missed the feel of her heart racing when he leaned closer, nor the taste of his breath in her mouth.

Feeling his staff grow hard against her belly.

Sex. Intimacy.

Love.

And she'd been right to deny herself.

But oh, when he'd gathered her closer...

All it had taken was the reappearance of Rowan Stewart to undo those efforts.

Not because she was a weak person, or because she'd secretly been harboring elicit passions, but because when Rowan had crushed his mouth against hers, the needs she'd squashed long ago combusted into a savage hunger.

Jenny entered the room and served two plates of bread and salad, made colorful with the addition of deep red strawberries.

Which, since she was dwelling on the past, only served to remind her of very old memories. She would not allow herself to relive the picnic they'd shared at Lockstone Cottage, the place they would have made their home. *Plump, red, juicy strawberries.*

They'd been so very young then.

And stupid!

She'd been a foolish and curious girl, and he'd been a randy young man. The one time they'd succumbed to their desires, it had been clumsy and hurried.

But it had been the most exciting and wonderful thing she'd ever done.

Augusta grimaced at the food in front of her. That had been the last time she'd seen him.

Augusta thrust thoughts of him aside and spread some of the salad over the slice of bread even as a stinging pierced her heart.

It hadn't mattered that they'd been unexperienced. That one time had been...

Perfect.

She'd treasured their lovemaking because it had been the two of them. Because she'd been in love with him. Not because she'd been rebelling against her father or looking to be ruined.

"At least our little annoyance has left the school alone lately..." Beatrice recaptured her attention.

Augusta cleared her throat. "Lord Sexton said he would follow up on a few leads, but that we ought not to get our hopes up. Apparently, he's committed to taking over *The King's Society for the Advancement of Ingenuity of England*." It was a prestigious organization, purposed with utilizing advancements in science, of which he expected to be appointed permanent director. "I quite comprehend the headiness of ambition, truly. And I understand his decision." Augusta sighed. "But I'm not too proud to admit that I am exceedingly disappointed."

Exceedingly.

"Yes, it isn't quite the same without him underfoot… I mean, with Lady Hardwood and her daughters gone." A flush spread up the other woman's neck.

Augusta eyed Beatrice. Perhaps his leaving was for the best, after all.

Three times she had caught the man sending Augusta's English teacher inappropriate smoldering glances. Beatrice had returned a few of them.

And the sheltered young woman could only be hurt by such a man. Moreover, the school was in no position to lose yet another teacher.

Augusta was in no position to lose yet another teacher.

She went on to inform Beatrice that the applicants were expected to arrive sometime over the next week and that they ought to put together some sort of itinerary. Furthermore, both Augusta and Beatrice agreed to keep silent about the troubles with their *little annoyance* until the new teachers were hired and settled in.

Best not to frighten the women unless it was absolutely necessary.

Having emptied their plates, the two of them carried their dishes into the kitchen, thanked Jenny for her efforts, and then went about to carry out their separate tasks for the afternoon.

But their conversation set Augusta once again to worrying over the new hires. She'd not even met them and already, the process felt hurried and rushed.

How was she going to trust these women with that which was most dear to her on such short acquaintance?

These completely unknown women would be responsible

for shaping young lives, and Augusta knew next to nothing about them.

And was it fair that she keep them in the dark about the vandalism the school had suffered over the past year?

That guilt, that increasingly familiar sense that she was doing the wrong thing, summoned an unease she couldn't shake.

Wouldn't it be fair that her new employees be informed? That way they could weigh the potential danger before making a decision.

But it was possible that there wasn't any danger at all, and that telling them might scare them away from accepting a prestigious and fulfilling position, leaving the school short-staffed for however long it took Augusta to find more willing—and possibly less-qualified—candidates.

She rubbed a fist over her chest.

To maintain the school's reputation, Augusta needed to hire the very best teachers she could find.

And to attract the best teachers, the school needed a pristine reputation.

Besides, there had been no further signs of vandalism in nearly a fortnight. She couldn't know for sure if her little annoyance had moved on, or if the seeming calm that had come over the school was due to Rowan and his workers' diligent watch, but Augusta enjoyed the sense of normalcy regardless.

The end of summer was in sight, her teachers who'd fallen into times of trouble were all safely married, Miss Fortune's wedding announcement was expected any day now, and with new applicants en route to the school that week, Augusta no longer dreaded the new term.

In hindsight, she ought to have known better than to relax her defenses.

Because while breaking her fast with Beatrice later that

week, scanning the *Gazette* for Miss Fortune and Captain Edgeworth's wedding announcement, she nearly choked on her tea.

There was an announcement, but it was not at all what Augusta expected. No, the announcement was about the recent secret marriage between *Miss Adelaide Royal and Viscount Bloodstone.*

But...!

Miss Royal had only traveled to London to act as Miss Fortune's chaperone! Miss Fortune was the one who needed to marry!

Lord Bloodstone hadn't shown an ounce of interest in Miss Royal. The article had to be a mistake!

And yet, even if it was an erroneous report... the columnist had described that upon exiting one of the older churches just outside of Mayfair, the bride had tossed her bouquet and the groom had tossed a handful of coin. They had then driven off together. Alone.

"Oh, dear," Augusta said.

"They've exposed her past, the misdeeds of her father," Beatrice echoed Augusta's dismay. Because... yes. Her teachers were so very special, not in spite of, but *because* they had secrets.

Unfortunately, those secrets were coming back to haunt them—and the school.

And Miss Adelaide Royal's secrets, in the wake of their prior troubles, could, once again, make matters difficult for Augusta.

As she and Beatrice discussed the possibilities the why's and what if's—panic threatened Augusta's composure. The room felt as though it was closing in on her even as her stomach churned.

She pushed her chair back and shot to her feet.

New teachers are coming.

The school is safe now.

And this scandal wasn't really a scandal at all, was it? Not if Miss Royal was, in fact, married.

But was she? The facts in the *Gazette's* article didn't add up.

Augusta excused herself, wanting—needing—to be alone. The only place she could be assured of that was her office. As she stepped into the school corridor, her fingers itched to make some sort of list that would help her solve this new hiccup.

How many lists would that make now? Five? Ten? More lists than she could complete on her own. And some with items beyond her abilities.

And yet, she needed to read through them one by one. Make a plan. Schedule each task.

The sound of her shoes padding along the corridor raced along with her heart.

Black, then white crowded her vision. At the door to her office, her hands shook, and the lock eluded the key.

Stop this, Augusta! It isn't the end of the world.

With Miss Royal married, she was going to need to hire yet another new teacher. And Miss Royal was one of her students' favorites!

How many students would want to return when all their favorite teachers had been replaced?

Augusta leaned her forehead on the door, willing her thundering heart to slow. *Boom, boom, boom...* faster and faster! But the very instant her knees began to give out, a pair of warm hands encircled her waist.

"Hold on there, Augusta." Warm breath caressed the side of her face even as his voice sounded from far away.

Rowan. Try as she could, she couldn't open her eyes.

He gathered her shaking form into his. "What happened?" Worry and sympathy rumbled in his voice.

Augusta shook her head. She didn't want to need him, and yet he was the only thing keeping her standing.

"Can't..." She had to pause, gasping for air. "Breathe."

Rowan moved one hand up and over her sternum until he flattened his palm over her chest.

"Your heart's racing."

"I'll be... fine."

"Of course you will be." He lowered both of them onto the floor and went right about unfastening the laces at the front of her gown. When those were undone, she was vaguely aware of him doing the same to her short stays.

"Focus on my voice. You're safe here. The school is safe. I've got you."

She dipped her chin, trusting him implicitly. "Just breathe, sweetheart," he encouraged her.

"Trying..." She was breathing, so why did she feel like she didn't have any air?

Rowan's warm hand stroked the side of her face. "Remember the day that particularly obstinate swan stole our loaf of bread? And then I determined to recover it? Feathered little beast nearly pecked my eye out and you laughed so hard. I miss that—" Did his voice hitch? "—the sound of your laughter." He smoothed his hands over her shoulders and down her arms. "When I turned to reprimand you for such impertinence, my foot slipped. Do you remember what happened then?"

Rowan's matter-of-fact tones soothed her. She was almost breathing normally again.

"You fell in the water," she answered. Despite herself, she felt the corners of her mouth tip up.

"And you laughed even louder." He was sitting on the floor, and she was half in, half out of his lap. "We had fun together."

His voice was low, husky. They'd had great fun together. Perhaps too much so. Nothing that good stood a chance of lasting very long.

Augusta kept her eyes closed, remembering other times he'd

made her laugh. They had been utterly unworried back then—carefree when they ought to have been bracing for the worst.

With his arm around her, Augusta no longer felt as though an elephant was sitting on her chest, and the numbness was leaving her arms and legs.

But she didn't want to move. She wanted to pretend that sitting in his embrace like this was perfectly acceptable—normal.

She wanted to pretend that there was one person in this world with whom she could relax her defenses.

For the next few minutes, neither moved, both lost in their thoughts, until Rowan turned to study her.

"Has this happened before?"

"A few times. Not as severe. It's just nerves. And I didn't finish my breakfast."

But sitting with him was *not* perfectly acceptable. Mr. or Mrs. Driver could come along any moment, and how would she explain that she was curled up in Rowan Stewart's arms? Before working for her, they'd been employed by her father.

Her father was essentially incapacitated, however, and over the years, she'd surely earned their loyalty.

But she'd given her word.

Augusta reluctantly squirmed free of him.

"You should see a doctor," he said.

"I'm not sick. I'm just... anxious. I'll be fine." Besides, Dr. McBride and his wife were the worst gossips in the county—second only to Mrs. Pratt, the innkeeper's wife over at the Gray Swan.

Any doubts regarding her professionalism and sanity could hurt the school.

"What brought it on today?" His voice turned somber. "Has the school been damaged again?"

"No, no. I doubt anyone would dare with you and your men

keeping watch." Augusta shifted. "Thank you for that, by the way."

No longer almost in his lap, she still relied on his support. His arms warmed her sides, and his scent soothed her thoughts. And she wasn't so overwhelmed that she didn't remember the unique taste of his kiss.

Not the kisses he'd given her as a girl, but the one they'd shared recently. It had been desperate, forceful. It had been the sort of kiss a woman could lose herself in.

"You don't need to thank me." His voice rumbled beside her.

When was the last time she'd turned to another human for physical comfort? But, oh, how Rowan's touch flooded her soul. She couldn't allow herself to get used to this.

"Miss Royal is in some sort of trouble. I think," she said, in answer to his original question. "There was an announcement in the *Gazette*."

"Your brother mentioned something to that effect. It is a good thing, no? Bloodstone is a respectable fellow. I should think you'd be celebrating that she's landed such a good catch." But then he stiffened. "You've lost another teacher."

"Yes, no, oh, but it isn't just that. Something's... not quite right about it. Adelaide Royal is not the sort of woman who would flirt with a viscount. When she applied for a position at the school, she had no one. She wanted nothing to do with men. Her father... she needed a place to belong."

Rowan exhaled. "And you gave her that." He slowly stroked her arm.

"I tried. I try to do that for all my teachers, but in the past few months, I've failed in so many ways." She squeezed her eyes shut. "But something about that article is wrong. I ought to be protecting her, but instead, I sent her to London. And what of Miss Fortune? I expected her to be married off by now. If she isn't, then why was Miss Royal all alone? Oh! I never should have sent them. But—"

"You fear that a scandal would hurt the school."

"Yes." And she'd spent most of her life protecting this precious place. "And the school is a place of safety, a place where girls flourish into women. Parents expect them to be protected from threats, both physical but also sordid in nature."

Augusta brushed damp strands of hair away from her face, surprised at how clammy her skin felt.

"I can't sit here..." When she went to stand, Rowan rose first. If she was honest with herself, she doubted she'd have found her feet so easily without his assistance.

Flustered by her reaction to him, Augusta turned to her office door, her mind suddenly empty.

"It's in your hand." His gaze flicked to her fist where she clutched the key.

"I know that," she nearly snapped. She hated this—being out of control.

This time the key slid easily into the lock, and Augusta was rewarded with the familiar clicking sound.

And then she frowned. Surely, Rowan hadn't come to her office so he could help her deal with her temporary meltdown? So why had he shown up this morning?

"Will you come in?" she asked.

The warmth of his hand where he'd settled it on the small of her back spread up to her shoulders and even down her legs while he followed her into her private sanctuary.

His touch worked on her like a warm breeze.

She cleared her throat.

"Has our vandal been captured?" Such news was precisely what could lift her spirits today.

Instead of answering right away, however, he held her chair. Likely, he feared she'd keel over again. He then crossed the room and poured a glass of water from the pitcher she kept there.

"You could probably use something stronger but unless you

keep a liquor cabinet in here somewhere, this will have to do for now." He set the glass in front of her. "But I wish you'd see a doctor."

Augusta ignored the suggestion. Her breathing had returned to normal, and aside from feeling as though she'd just run to London and back, she felt perfectly normal.

But she wouldn't argue with him.

As much as she hated admitting it to herself, she was glad he was here. Over the past few months, she'd gradually taken solace in his steady presence—in knowing he was near.

Something she couldn't afford to rely on!

But he hadn't answered her question yet.

"Have you?" she prompted. "Learned something?"

"We don't need to have this conversation right now. In fact, you probably ought to return to your chamber and lie in for the rest of the day. The items on your ten thousand lists will keep until tomorrow. It is summer, is that not the time your school sits empty? Can you not allow yourself to take a day off?"

Augusta sipped the water, watching him over the glass, and then cocked a brow. "You should know me better than that. Now... tell me. Has someone been caught?"

Rowan scowled, somehow looking even more handsome than usual, and sighed. "No one's been caught. Sexton thinks your father has something to do with it." Seated across from her, his concern weighed heavily in the room. "You don't look surprised by this."

Augusta nodded slowly. In the back of her mind... in the *very back* of her mind, she'd considered the notion herself. And then she'd dismissed it. She had fulfilled all the requirements laid out by her father and her aunt—every last one of them.

Her father could be cruel and violent and unreasonable, but ironically enough, he'd always been a man of his word. And her aunt had passed three years before.

"It isn't him," she said and then pinched her mouth closed.

"How can you be certain of that?"

Augusta had kept the details of that year to herself for so long that the urge to tell him more surprised her.

He'd been at the heart of it, and yet, he had not.

She clasped her hands together and then rested them on her desk, taking a brief moment to organize her thoughts—what she could safely say and what she could not.

"The day I was supposed to meet you... that last day." The truth about her father's tyrannical activities wasn't something she shared with anyone. She'd not even shared this information with Lord Sexton when he'd interviewed her for the investigation.

It was...

Shameful. Humiliating.

Rowan crossed one booted foot over his knee, looking as though he had all the time in the world to hear her story. "I remember it well." Was that sarcasm in his voice?

It didn't matter. So she continued. "On the way to go to you, I was caught... and then forced into a carriage."

Rowan's eyes narrowed.

Augusta grimaced and nodded. She didn't want him imagining her darkest moment—or one of them, anyhow. Her hands and feet had been bound, a cloth tied around her mouth. She'd spent three days inside that carriage...

She had been... filthy. Disgusting. She'd purge the nightmare forever if she could.

"I was taken to live with my mother's sister on an isolated estate up north. I could see Scotland from my window."

Years before that, her aunt had lived with their family. Augusta had been a child and only remembered that Aunt Lucy had been one of her favorite people in the whole world. She'd been bold, smart, and... not afraid of Augusta's father.

And one day, she'd simply disappeared.

Her mother had explained that her sister wanted to live on her own. The truth was that her father had banished her. Apparently, Aunt Lucy had not been a good influence on his family.

"My aunt was good to me," Augusta insisted. As good as she'd dared.

Because circumstances had changed her. Years of isolation had beaten her down. "I quickly discovered my aunt didn't enjoy any of the freedoms she ought to have. The servants were in my father's employ. Her driver. The stablemaster. Even a few nearby neighbors were indebted to him. Aunt Lucy and I were practically prisoners."

Rowan kept silent but his eyes took on a cold, hard intensity.

Augusta could not share the most important events of that year. Events that tormented her but also, oddly enough, had provided her comfort over the years.

"I could only have my freedom if..." Augusta clasped her hands in her lap. "If I promised never to take up with you again." This requirement was only a part of the promise. "My aunt lived much of her life without freedom, and she wanted more for me. I didn't want to return to Starbridge Abbey, and she made it so I didn't have to. She convinced my father to release the funds for my dowry and then helped make arrangements for me to open the school."

"A dream for you," Rowan said.

A dream of sorts.

But Augusta had paid dearly for it.

Her father had not expected her to succeed, so he'd allowed it. By the time she'd truly claimed her freedom and established her independence, he'd lost interest in her.

He'd always preferred his sons. When she was no longer useful to him, he had turned his attention to Piers, the heir. But, ironically enough, as soon as he was able, Piers had denounced the marquessate to live his own life, far from their father's heavy hand.

Her father had then turned to Liam and Noah. He'd made no bones about his feelings for his youngest son—Theodore—whom he considered too weak to be of value to him.

But Augusta had kept every one of her promises. If she had not, she would not have been the only person to suffer the consequences.

"And yet." Rowan narrowed his eyes and stared hard, as though reading her mind. "I am here now. Anyone could imagine that you've taken up with me again."

"Yes, but the damage to the foundation occurred *before* you arrived. I went home over Christmas. My father is hardly aware of my existence, let alone the condition of my school."

"You are certain?"

"Trust me, I've considered the possibility. I have fulfilled my family's requirements. My father doesn't make sense as a suspect. I don't think he's left Starbridge grounds in over a decade. In fact, he hasn't been the same since Elijah's death. He's as mean as ever, but he has lost his power."

"Elijah was your father's original heir?"

"Piers's twin, yes. Elijah died almost four years ago." Augusta frowned. "Piers has no interest whatsoever in the title and has happily allowed our brother Liam to take over managing my father's affairs." And then she shook her head. "My father has committed more atrocities than I want to know about." Guilt flared in her again as she remembered that her father had ordered violence on him. *Because of me...*

She dropped her stare to her hands. "But he's not responsible for this."

"Very well." But Rowan didn't sound as certain as she felt.

His half-hearted acceptance of her explanation had her meeting his gaze again. He dropped a glance to her mouth, and in that instant, Augusta could almost taste his kiss.

It couldn't happen again.

Nor ought she to seek comfort in his arms, like she'd done today—though she felt so much better for having had it.

Was it even possible to return their relationship to a professional one? "Thank you for your assistance earlier." She straightened her back.

"Augusta." Onyx eyes saw right through her. Good lord, this man was... beautiful. He had never been formal and rigid like other English gentlemen. He'd been born with an abundance of natural grace. She drank him in, her heart in her throat.

"Yes?" She barely managed the word.

"Send for me. If you need anything."

He was smooth but also rough around the edges.

No wonder he'd disrupted her life so thoroughly. She didn't deserve his dedication to protect her. But...

She needed it. So she swallowed hard and nodded.

ROWAN RODE AWAY from the school, conflicted.

On one hand, Augusta had been vague, and he couldn't help but wonder what she'd omitted. Important details, or simply painful ones?

Or both.

They had fallen in love that spring, and yet she persisted in dismissing the particulars of the events that separated them.

No doubt she was conflicted as well.

He'd used the keys she'd provided to him, entered the school, and caught sight of her as soon as he turned toward her office.

She'd looked so damn helpless standing at the locked door. Her movements had been jerky, and then slow. He hadn't stopped to think but raced along the corridor. And he'd caught her just in time.

God help him, comforting her had come as naturally as breathing.

He couldn't be angry with her anymore.

This school was more than a vocation for her, it was a passion. And now the threats to it were making her half-mad with worry.

He'd left angry the night he'd kissed her. Why? Because he'd realized that Augusta's school would always come first. He'd intended to keep his distance. He'd only come today to discuss Sexton's suspicions.

The muscles in his stomach clenched.

She'd been on the verge of collapse. She'd looked pale, fragile... And once he had her in his arms, he could have held her all day.

Someone was threatening her life's work—her passion. Rowan understood passion.

He had plenty of his own for his work. Over the years, rebuilding, creating structures that would last long after he was gone from this earth, had taken up most of his energy. He often stayed up late working on plans for his current project, or ideas for future ones. Aside from visiting Addison and his new wife, he rarely took time for himself.

His work was all he had. It was everything.

Why would Augusta feel any differently?

And ironically enough, his passion had been threatened once as well. A grand project he'd taken on in Mayfair had been destroyed at one time, by vandals.

Rowan had been aware of the threat but failed to take it seriously. And because of his failure, both his brother and sister-in-law had nearly been killed.

It wasn't the first time he'd failed to protect Addison.

Rowan shifted in his saddle, haunted by memories of his father punishing his brother. The old duke had insisted it was for Addison's own good.

Rowan had known better.

And he'd done nothing.

Augusta was but one small woman, mighty in spirit, but nonetheless, essentially alone. The ache in his gut moved up to his heart.

Her own parents had stolen her away. Why hadn't he considered that possibility? He should never have allowed her to return to her parents' house that afternoon. He ought to have realized that her father would have had her followed—that she needed Rowan's protection.

Just as he'd failed Addison, he'd failed her—a woman he'd professed to love.

No wonder she'd told him their dreams had not been real—that their love had been nothing more than an illusion. *I failed her.*

And there was only one thing to do about it—protect this blasted school.

And the woman who ran it.

He shifted in his saddle for a different reason.

He'd nearly kissed her again. Despite all the time that had passed, he still wanted her.

No, that wasn't entirely accurate. He wanted her *more.*

He'd been involved with a few ladies since suffering from the loss of his first love. He'd slaked his lust, and learned a thing or two about himself and women.

While in London, he'd even been formally pursued by a few eligible ladies of the *ton.* But he'd never taken any of them seriously.

Not because they weren't desirable, or because their parents all thought similarly to Lord Starbridge. Hell, Miss Madeline Dudley was beautiful, charming, and possessed a hefty dowry. Her father, an American businessman, hadn't minded a bit that Rowan was a bastard. Son of a duke, even on the wrong side of the blanket, had been good enough for his daughter.

Had Augusta even come close to marrying? From what he'd gathered, the school was her one true love. Hell, she'd mentioned wanting to run one on the first day he met her.

And yet...

When he'd kissed her, he'd felt a rumbling of the passion she kept on a careful leash. She was no longer the naïve and innocent girl he'd fallen in love with back then.

She'd grown into a stunning, independent, and even powerful woman.

And she'd admitted to needing him.

Would she ever admit that she wanted him?

IT MUST COME FIRST

*S*itting at her desk less than a week later, yet another tricky situation had arisen. And yet, Augusta found that she wasn't quite as overwhelmed as she'd been before.

Just knowing Rowan was near—that he was willing to help her—she didn't feel quite as alone as she had.

Send for me. If you need anything.

She didn't send for him, of course. There were no fires or crumbling foundations. Her current troubles were hers to solve.

The day had started promising enough, with the applicants' early arrival, but had gone downhill from there. One of the young women seemed like a good fit, but the other three women, all of whom came with excellent references, expressed a little too much enthusiasm when it came to discipline.

Discipline had its place, but lacking warmth, it became more of a detriment to learning.

Augusta felt backed into a corner, however, because she had no other options.

Which meant she was quite out of sorts already when she

watched her coach appear on the road—the coach carrying Miss Royal and Lord Bloodstone from London.

Together.

Alone. What was the matter with everyone?

So when Coachman John drew the carriage to a halt, knowing the even less-pleasant task ahead, she all but snapped.

"Miss Royal." She leveled a disappointed glance at one of her last remaining teachers. "I've been wondering when you'd be so kind as to grace us with your presence again."

But Miss Royal lifted her chin rather than show any repentance. "We experienced inclement weather—"

"And yet you are here now." Augusta swallowed hard. Miss Royal had always been the humble one and a part of her was proud of the young woman's show of courage.

Dreading the meeting ahead, she asked Beatrice to take the applicants for an extensive tour of the school while Augusta led the newlywed couple into her office for a private meeting.

A meeting that left her heart in tatters—even if her decision had been a necessary one.

She'd had no choice but to sack Miss Royal. Not only sack her but ask her to leave the shire altogether. Because despite the Gazette's announcement, Adelaide wasn't married at all! And she'd just spent nearly a week with Lord Bloodstone—*unchaperoned*.

If the truth of their actual circumstances were to be made public, the resulting scandal could be the final blow.

Bloodstone was going to have to marry her.

Of course, Adelaide had seen her decision as a betrayal. It had certainly felt like one...

But the school came first.

Augusta only hoped Lord Bloodstone proved to be a man of honor and good character—moreover, a loving husband. In what Adelaide had witnessed over the past thirty minutes, she guessed that he'd be all those and more to Adelaide.

Augusta had seen the way he looked at Adelaide—the way he'd touched her hand, her back, offering comfort without being overbearing.

A happy marriage for those two was the only circumstance that might assuage some of this massive guilt.

And as the door closed behind them, Augusta exhaled a shaky breath.

She hated to lose Miss Royal. She hated losing any of them.

And when she reached for her increasingly growing stack of lists, she hated that her hand was shaking.

She was going to have to hire all four of the applicants. The agency had assured her they were all perfectly qualified, but were they right for this school? Augusta always considered a potential teacher's academic qualifications and intelligence, of course. But under normal circumstances, she had other, less obvious requirements. Upon interviewing someone to join their little family, Augusta listened to her heart, tallying attributes that indicated good character—attributes such as compassion, empathy, and... backbone.

Miss Fortune had first attended the school as a student, so Augusta had known precisely who she was getting when she'd taken her on. But when she'd met Victoria, Miss Fellowes, Miss Royal, and Beatrice, a sixth sense had supplied her with a unique knowing. She'd been one hundred percent certain they would not only be excellent teachers but strong role models for their students.

And they would have been if Augusta hadn't put them in impossible circumstances.

Thumbing through the letters of recommendation attached to each application, Augusta felt...

Nothing.

No connection, no visceral sensation urging her to award them positions.

She exhaled a shaky breath. Perhaps this was best. Perhaps she'd been too invested with the other women.

Now, she needed to decide which teachers would teach which courses. All but one of them seemed unusually stern—especially the older woman—Miss Agatha Black. Her students were going to hate her! But unless someone else came along before the new term began, Augusta was out of options.

She dipped her pen in the jar of ink but paused when a shiver ran down her spine.

Because nothing felt right anymore. Ever since she'd opened the school, listening to her gut instincts had mostly led to her best decisions. The trouble was, however, that over the past few months, her instincts had fallen silent.

She'd like to blame it on Rowan, but he wasn't really to blame. It had begun when she'd returned from the holiday visit home. Seeing her mother, her brothers, being in the home of her childhood but knowing she would never be one of them, had shaken her balance.

She climbed into her bed later that night feeling melancholy. And as usual, she couldn't fully dismiss the ever-present ache in her heart—the ache she'd carry there until her last breath.

And was once again assaulted by one of those dreams...

Augusta glanced up and down Adam's Row and, only after confirming that she hadn't been followed, stepped forward and lifted the knocker. She required all her willpower to keep from bursting into tears.

She and Rowan normally only met privately, in the park or at a shop on Bond Street, but since he'd said his family had left London two days ago, he ought to be alone.

And her news was too important to wait.

The door opened and a stern-looking butler stared down his nose at her. Why wouldn't he when, although she'd told her maid where she was going, she'd left Martha behind?

"Is Mr. Stewart in?" At least her voice wasn't shaking.

"And whom shall I say is calling?"

"Lady Augusta Primm."

Her title moved the man slightly, and he gestured for her to enter. "You may wait here. I'll see if he is in."

She stepped inside and was immediately overwhelmed with white marble, white statues, and gleaming crystal. The foyer felt cold and hard.

Or perhaps her circumstances had corrupted her perception.

"Augusta?"

She turned, and just the sight of Rowan, his affectionate gaze and half smile, brought relief. But she had bad news. Terrible, horrific, unthinkable news.

"I need to speak with you." Staring into his familiar eyes, her voice trembled.

A few swift steps and Rowan was at her side. "Of course." He placed a reassuring hand on her back and led her into a room on the left.

"Thank you, Fitz, that'll be all," he addressed the servant and then closed the door behind them. "Did you walk here alone? You should have sent for me! Good Lord, Augusta, you're shaking."

He took her into his arms and kissed the top of her head. And he held her until the shaking stopped.

But this wasn't why she'd come.

She drew back, forcing him to loosen his hold on her.

"My father refuses to break the agreement with Malum. He says he's going to set a date." She closed her eyes, but her tears managed to escape anyway. "I cannot marry him. Oh, Rowan."

"I'll meet with him," Rowan said.

"Malum?

"No. It's time I speak with your father."

Rowan was a confident and intelligent young man. He was also the son of a duke. But her parents had made their opinion of him crystal clear. And deep in her heart, Augusta knew that any appeal he might make would prove to be fruitless.

She shook her head. "You don't know him, Rowan. He won't change his mind." She didn't want to tell the love of her life that her father would most likely not even meet with him. She was already well aware of how uncomfortable Rowan felt while out and about in society. She didn't want to do anything that would make it worse.

"Then we'll marry without his approval. But I'm not letting you go." Rowan lifted her chin so she had no choice but to meet his gaze.

Elopement.

Was this really happening? Had matters really come to them having to take such drastic actions?

"Yes!" It was the only possible answer she could give. "Yes, of course!" All along, she'd known Rowan was the person she wanted to spend her life with. She'd give everything up for him! And yet fear shot through her.

She held his gaze. "My father will hate you. He'll hate me, but he'll hate you worse." And her father wasn't the sort of enemy she'd wish on anyone. She winced. "Are you sure—"

"I love you, Augusta. It's the only choice he's left us with."

"I love you, too." Augusta swallowed hard, feeling afraid, excited, terrified, and utterly relieved...

Rowan touched his lips to hers. "Trust me?"

"More than anything," she sighed.

"Then we'll leave for Gretna Green tonight." Rowan released her, pacing across the room and already working out the necessary plans. "I'll need to meet with my solicitor to access my funds. We'll need a carriage, money to travel. A driver, and at least one outrider. But I can have all that arranged before dark." Determination lit the back of his onyx eyes.

Augusta stilled, caught by the force of his gaze. The two of them had flirted, and then moved their relationship to a deeper level. They had shared secrets, fears, and dreams. But until now, a part of her had doubted they could actually be together. He was young, and he lacked standing. And her father was one of the most powerful men in all of London.

But he was not without means, and he was willing to risk her father's wrath in order to marry her.

Me! *Augusta Primm!*

As long as they were together, they could thwart her father. They could do anything!

They were going to do this!

He stopped his pacing long enough to take her into his arms again, and she remembered their first kiss. She'd been right to believe that knowing him would change the course of her life forever.

She slid her fingertips over his collarbone until they could wind around his neck. His kisses, although familiar by now, sent scorching sparks of excitement shooting through her. She parted her lips and not only surrendered but explored his mouth as well.

His tongue played with hers and then smoothed along her teeth. The kiss started out gentle and innocent. But as his hands moved down her back, around her waist, and hers tangled in his hair, raw hunger unleashed. The hard steel of his staff against her belly empowered Augusta, and she pressed onto her toes to be closer.

He dragged his mouth along her jaw, drawing a trail of fire along her neck, chasing away thoughts of anything but this.

These feelings.

Him.

Rowan walked them to the settee, and she fell back onto the cushions and in that moment, she relinquished her old life. She no longer belonged to her father.

She was Rowan's. She would be his forever. And he would be hers!

Furthermore, for the first time, the two of them were truly alone.

"Rowan," she groaned, her fingers threaded through his hair, clutching him. The time for waiting was past. She was going to be his wife. He was going to be her husband.

"Augusta." *His hands moved over her gown, palmed her breasts, and hers tore at his jacket. And then he covered her.*

Augusta embraced him with both her arms and her legs. These sensations meant everything. They would join, once and for all.

Nothing meant more than the two of them, as one. Forever.

She gasped into his mouth, breathing the same air. With Rowan, she feared nothing. With Rowan, anything was possible. The two of them together were invincible.

And surrendering to him was all she wanted.

When he settled between her legs, it felt right. When he moved his member along her seam, it was the most natural thing in the world. And when he nudged inside her body, she invited him deeper.

The pinch and stretching gave way to satisfying fullness.

There was no need to wait. They were going to marry. By the end of the week, he would be her husband.

He sank deeper, his hips moving with greater urgency.

And she welcomed it. She surrendered all to him.

And he gave her everything.

This was love. This was magic. They moved together, confident that love would always be enough. It would stand around them, an impenetrable fortress.

Unfortunately, many a fortress had fallen.

AUGUSTA SAT UP, her nightrail twisted around her legs. She didn't need to touch her cheeks to know they were streaked with tears.

The dreams hadn't stopped. In fact, she'd had one nearly every night.

Throwing back the covers, she crossed to the windows. Was he out there now? Walking the perimeter of the school? The temptation to don her robe and go see for herself was strong.

The need to see the person she'd loved in her dream nearly overwhelmed her.

But that feeling was utter nonsense!

She shook her head, closed the drapes, and then dipped a clean linen into her wash basin. Only after scrubbing her face several times did she feel herself again.

Until the distant sounds of breaking glass shattered the night.

From inside the school.

Where Beatrice was sleeping.

UPPING THE STAKES

*R*owan stood in the corner of Augusta's parlor, waiting for word on Miss Wolcott's condition as the sky turned from an inky black to a dusky purple.

Augusta's vandal had returned, this time to throw a rock through the second-story window. It had been a hurried attack and the blighter had escaped once again. It would be naïve to imagine the act hadn't been perpetrated by the same person who'd committed the others. Rowan pounded a fist on his thigh, cursing himself for leaving two of his less-seasoned workers to keep watch on this particular night.

Augusta had just begun to look herself again. The look of panic in her eyes had lessened.

I ought to have been here.

Instead, he and Rhys had been lounging in Rosewood's study, drinking, discussing the ongoing progress at the castle as well as other subjects of great import to males in general—such as the best brand of cigars, the characteristics of a good scotch, and the mechanics of the best vehicles for speed.

Stupid, meaningless conversation.

His feeling of inadequacy was eerily similar to the other times he'd failed.

He'd lowered his guard. What had he been thinking?

A glance around the room, however, reminded him that reinforcements had arrived.

Shortly after midnight, Sexton had arrived at Rosewood's residence following a long journey from Starbridge Manor—along with one of Primm's younger brothers, Lord Noah.

Pleased at the unexpected reunion, Rosewood had opened an old bottle of scotch and, as the night wore on, their discussion had turned to the investigation into Augusta's vandal. After his visit to Starbridge Abbey, Sexton had dismissed a number of suspects. Rowan had kept silent when he'd learned Augusta's father remained on the list. Just as they'd all decided it was time to retire for the night, a pounding on the door brought Mr. Driver and the news of yet another attack on the school.

This attack, however, hadn't been nearly as harmless as the others. As these sorts of crimes tended to evolve, someone had been hurt this time.

A hefty stone had crashed through the window over Miss Wolcott's bed, bringing shards of glass raining onto the unsuspecting and vulnerable teacher.

Sexton leading the charge, all four men had leapt onto their mounts and raced to the school to find the women all but paralyzed by the act. With broken glass everywhere, on the teacher and all around her bed, no one, it seemed, had known how to rescue Miss Wolcott.

Mrs. Driver stood at the far end of the room, stunned, and Augusta made tentative attempts at removing some of the glass. *"I didn't want to make her injuries worse..."* she'd apologized upon their arrival.

He'd never seen her so uncertain.

Lord Sexton had wasted no time and immediately swooped

in to carry Miss Wolcott down to Augusta's spare room. Ever since then, Lady Rosewood and Augusta had been tending to the young woman's cuts.

Rowan wavered between his desire to search the area around the school and his need to ensure Augusta wasn't going to suffer another of her attacks.

In the end, his need to reassure himself of Augusta's well-being won out.

He exhaled a breath he hadn't realized he'd been holding when she quietly appeared in the open door.

"She's sleeping," Augusta announced in a tired voice. Rowan jumped to his feet. Dark circles dragged at her eyes just above her sharp, pale cheekbones. The feeling of relief was a temporary one for all of them. If there had been any doubt before, tonight's attack only proved that the damages to the foundation, in addition to the fire, had not been random. There was a person or persons in the area who wanted to do the school serious harm.

Or was Augusta the actual target?

Either way, this attack proved that the villain wasn't concerned if innocent people were hurt as a result.

The apron Augusta wore over her night rail was covered with splotches of blood. She looked tired, shoulders slumped. Rowan held her eyes.

We'll find whoever did this, Rowan promised silently.

Augusta smoothed her skirt and dipped her chin.

"Physically, I think she'll be fine," she addressed everyone in the room. "But such a horrific attack can leave other scars— emotional ones."

Those, Rowan suspected, of which Augusta might be all too familiar. As a very young woman, she'd been forced into a carriage. She would have fought them. Had they hurt her? Bound her? Since learning what her father had done, these questions had haunted him.

This woman, no doubt, understood such wounds all too well.

Rowan forced the images out of his mind. If he dwelled on them he'd be of no use to anyone.

After answering Sexton's questions regarding Miss Wolcott's recovery, Augusta turned to Lord Noah. "What are you doing here?" she asked, looking as pleased as she possibly could following the traumatic events of the early morning.

"Isn't a younger brother allowed to visit his long-lost sister?" Lord Noah moved to embrace her, but she held him off, gesturing toward her soiled garments.

"I was there over the holidays," she reminded him, her voice wooden—exhausted.

Rosewood stepped forward. "Noah rode with Sexton on his way back from Starbridge Abbey." He sent his sister a hard stare. "A piece of Father's stationery was found in one of the chambers at the Gray Swan, Auggie, the morning after the fire."

"Interviewing your family members was a necessary aspect of the investigation," the marquess explained.

But Augusta didn't seem at all encouraged. "It wasn't my father." She reached into her pocket and withdrew a crumpled piece of paper—a message that had been attached to the rock. "The attacker's message was not written on Father's stationery."

Which, in Rowan's mind, didn't absolve the man. But he wouldn't argue the fact with her now.

The script on the paper was bold and clear. *This is only the beginning.*

Rowan lifted his gaze to Augusta's and knew exactly what she was thinking.

If this was only the beginning, and if this villain wasn't caught, she was going to have to delay the opening of the school, which could ultimately result in her having to close it.

A discussion broke out but when Lady Rosewood stifled a

yawn, the earl suggested they'd all have clearer heads after a little sleep. Rosewood, along with his countess and his younger brother, departed for the dower house at Longbow Castle, and Lord Sexton disappeared, presumably to gather evidence and question the guards who had been left to keep watch.

Rowan would join in the detective's efforts tomorrow—actually, later today.

But for now, that could wait. Because staring at Augusta, he saw right through her brittle composure.

She was near her breaking point.

This was too much even for the starchiest of schoolmistresses.

And so, rather than depart with the other guests, he silently watched the others take their leave, leaning against the wall, arms crossed as he considered the events of the evening. The sounds of the front door closing, locks being set, and the rumbling of horses riding away as the carriage drove off were exactly what he'd been waiting for.

Augusta reappeared silently, looking more than a little ghostlike.

"You stayed." She sounded more relieved than disappointed.

"You shouldn't be alone." Rowan's words were straightforward but might have suggested multiple meanings. Was he being intentionally ambiguous? He would sit here in the parlor, wait outside her window, or share her bed. But he was damned if he'd let anything happen to this woman.

Gripping the doorframe, she shifted her eyes to the hearth where fading red glowed from the coal Rosewood had used to start a fire hours before. The earl had not lit it because the room was cold, but because its warmth offered comfort in a time of uncertainty.

"You need to sleep." Rowan hadn't moved.

Augusta frowned and then glanced down at her apron. Her

limbs remained still, as though she was too drained to even answer, let alone get herself to her chamber.

For so long, she'd handled her troubles alone.

Without making a deliberate decision, Rowan pushed away from the wall and crossed toward her. She blinked and then widened her gray eyes.

"You're leaving?" she asked.

But when she went to step out of his way, Rowan bent down and scooped her into his arms, cradling her as if she was a child. "Which way to your chamber?"

This was the least he could do.

Miss Primm, school director, headmistress, and well-established spinster, would have fought him tooth and nail before allowing him to carry her like this. But tonight, she was Augusta—as vulnerable as any human would be following the events of the night.

"Last door on the left," she murmured.

The cool and distant woman she'd presented to the world for so long only inhabited part of her soul. Flesh and blood woman owned the rest.

The tired emptiness in her eyes was all too familiar. He'd occasionally seen it in his own. It reeked of that feeling of failure. Of having one's ambition and determination thwarted— the near death of a deep desire to prove one's worthiness to the world.

She'd been so busy being strong that she struggled to ask for help even when she needed it desperately. No wonder she was exhausted.

To top that off, she secretly nursed wounds inflicted by her father, the Marquess of Starbridge.

And wounds… Rowan swallowed hard.

Inflicted by me.

"I thought you'd come looking for me. I didn't expect you would know, but I hoped…"

Despite all evidence to the contrary, she'd kept a spark of hope alive that he could rescue her—that he would find her...

He'd been a fool.

"I thought she was safe inside, with the doors locked." Augusta dragged his attention back to the present.

"It was a natural assumption to make," he said. She had every right to consider the school safe for her teachers.

He ought to have been on alert, however. This was the last time he'd be caught unawares.

"I never wanted to put any of them in harm's way." She buried her face in his neck.

"But in order to protect the school, you had to take risks." Rowan pushed the door open, and as he did so, inhaled the scent that was uniquely Augusta. Soap, paper, leather, and just a trace of something floral—practical with a hint at her femininity—like the room's owner.

"But the ends cannot justify the means! Beatrice—"

"Is going to be fine." That woman had a backbone that was nearly as strong as Augusta's. And if she needed help, Rowan had no doubt, Lord Sexton would be there to provide it. "The marquess, I think, has romantic feelings for your Miss Wolcott."

The lofty detective had been unable to hide the panic he'd felt when they'd been informed of the attack.

Rowan lowered Augusta's feet to the floor, and when her knees didn't collapse, he set himself to untying her apron. She neither protested nor asked him to leave.

She stood, swaying slightly with her eyes closed. "The marquess has asked Beatrice to travel with him to London and pose as his fiancée to help him land that position he wants so dearly. She'd be chaperoned for the entirety of the visit, of course, and afterward, he's promised to catch whoever's trying to hurt the school."

Rowan raised his brows.

"But I'm not sure it's best for her," Augusta continued. "Her reputation could suffer once she calls it off—worse than that, *she* could suffer. Especially if her emotions are involved."

"He's a good man. He'll protect her." Rowan had recognized an intensity in the man's expression earlier. A gentleman only ever became so distraught when he'd formed an attachment. "And Miss Wolcott is a grown woman. She has the right to make her own decisions."

Augusta had opened her eyes and was staring at his mouth.

Rowan tilted his head. "They are all grown women, your teachers. And ultimately, they make their own decisions," he insisted.

"Because of me."

"Because they want to help you."

Augusta frowned at this. The trouble with being a controlling individual was that ultimately, you felt responsible for everything.

"I did nothing to stop them," she said. "In fact, I pushed them…"

"Yes." Rowan nodded. "But ultimately, they made their own decisions."

Rowan would have laughed at Augusta's perplexed expression if she hadn't just experienced such a traumatic night.

So instead, he tugged the apron off her arms and tossed it aside. She stood like a cloth doll, not frozen, but still, so Rowan reached up and fumbled with her gown's ties.

Her eyes widened, and she reached up to capture his hands.

YIELDING CONTROL

*R*owan was here, in her chamber, his eyes tired, his mouth set in a grim line, looking, for all intents and purposes, as though he intended to undress her. Her room was mostly in shadows, but even so, she couldn't let him see her.

Not because she was ashamed, but because her body told stories. Stories she wasn't prepared to explain.

It had been her aunt who first pointed out the delicate silver lines low on Augusta's belly. She'd emphasized that even if Augusta had wanted to, she could never marry a proper gentleman. The tell-tale lines were evidence of Augusta's deepest secret. Rowan might simply interpret them as a betrayal—more deception.

She couldn't have him seeing them, and yet she didn't want him to leave.

"Avert your eyes, Rowan." Her voice came out lower than usual as she loosened her grip on his wrists.

Most unexpectedly, over the past several months, he'd become a part of her life again. Old feelings encroached on the present. Or were these new feelings?

Not willing to examine the answer, Augusta drew a simple

day dress out of her wardrobe, whipped off her soiled gown, and covered herself as quickly as possible. It was morning, after all.

"You can look now," she said.

She stood in the center of her chamber, not knowing what she wanted as she watched him turn around.

She did know she didn't want to be alone.

And that she craved his touch, more tonight than ever before.

It was Rowan who broke the uncomfortable silence. He sent his gaze around her chamber, and then it landed on her unmade bed. "I always wanted to see Augusta Primm's bedroom."

The corner of his mouth twitched. Was he teasing?

Perhaps it was what the two of them needed. He usually knew what she needed, anyhow.

"Yes, well. Is it as glorious as you imagined it would be?"

"That depends, I suppose." He leaned his shoulder against the wall, crossing one ankle over the other.

At one time, everything between them had been glorious. Was he suggesting...? Surely not.

But Augusta held her breath. Was this why she'd allowed him in her chamber? Was this why he'd stayed behind?

She touched her fingertips to her hair. Even as exhausted as she was, his words sent longing coursing through her. Impossible. She shook her head.

"I can't..." She flicked her gaze to the bed. She suddenly felt as though she was seventeen again. "It's too risky."

The only worse scandal that could befall the school now would be for the headmistress to get caught having relations with her brother's architect.

Or worse, get herself with child. A lesson she'd learned the hard way.

Did he realize how important the school's reputation was to

her? Or did he think she was simply being prudish? It would be rather hypocritical of her, considering their past.

But she was more mature now—smarter—much wiser.

Rowan seemed to make some sort of decision for both of them and crossed to the bed. He fluffed a pillow and pulled the covers down. "In," he ordered.

"I'm dressed," she said.

"You're exhausted." He patted the mattress.

"I'll never sleep." But she found herself easing into the covers anyway. "Especially if you stand there watching me."

"I'm not leaving you alone." Had he always been this stubborn?

But Augusta held his gaze. Shadows underlined his eyes, and for the first time, she noticed the creases at the corners. Too many years had been lost, gone forever.

He was as tired as she was. And her heart ached at the thought of sending him away.

Her heart ached, *period.* And Rowan's presence was the only thing that could ever soothe that ache. He made her feel safe—strong.

"Then come," she found herself saying. "But just for a nap. You'll have to leave before Jenny returns."

"Just for a nap," he agreed. Augusta watched as he removed his boots and waistcoat before climbing into the place she'd made for him.

And it struck her that, years ago, she'd imagined this. Sharing a chamber with this man, a bed, perhaps with children across the hall.

They would have lived modestly as husband and wife, and they would have slept side by side for the rest of their lives.

Having him beside her was similar to those long-abandoned fantasies, and yet it was not at all the same.

In her fantasies, they'd worn nightclothes and sometimes nothing at all. In her fantasies, they'd been free to touch one another. She would have been as familiar with his body as her very own. He would have known every inch of hers.

A barely suppressed cry escaped her throat.

Rowan turned onto his side, facing her, resting his head on the pillow. When his gaze searched hers, he saw everything.

It wasn't fanciful to imagine that he saw right into her soul.

He reached out and stroked her arm. "My sweetheart," he said. "Don't be sad."

The ache in her heart moved to her throat—it was a hopeless and pathetic sob. Pathetic because they could not reclaim the past. They had separate lives—responsibilities.

And yet she leaned into his touch, her pulse racing even as he calmed all her fears.

"I see you," he said.

Augusta lay facing him, her eyes memorizing the shadows darkening his bronze skin, emphasizing the sharp angles of his perfect features. Dark stubble peppered his cheeks and neck. But he was smooth despite all his rough edges.

"I miss your curls." She allowed herself a half-smile. Unable to stop herself, she reached out a hand and smoothed it over the very short hairs on his head.

"They're not very practical when one is cutting lumber or handling hammers and nails."

"I like it this way too," she admitted.

Rowan had always seemed stronger, more powerful and dependable than any man she'd ever met. He was no-nonsense, never swayed by the winds of gossip that surrounded them.

She slid her hand down to cradle his cheek, and he pressed a kiss to her palm.

He'd been residing on the grounds at Longbow Castle for nearly half a year now. And he had not stayed away from the school. Even when he'd finished the repairs, he'd come to visit his half-sister. He'd been so close, and yet so very far from her.

"I checked the *Gazette* every day. I was sure you would marry." Her words floated between them.

"I've only ever proposed to one woman."

Augusta inhaled. *To me...*

"It wasn't meant to be," she said.

"It wasn't our time."

"No," she agreed. But it certainly had felt like it was. He dragged his fingertips along her arm, drawing invisible circles that sent molten shivers swirling in her chest, her abdomen, and between her thighs.

Once, they'd given into their voracious hunger for one another. It had been clumsy but wild and passionate.

How was it possible this pull still existed between them?

This attraction was the same but different. Tension coiled in her belly when the hand stroking her arm moved lower.

"When I learned that you had opened the school," he admitted in a husky tone, "I wanted to come to you. I waited for you to come to me instead."

But she could not.

"You had the school—your dream," he added. "Time passed."

So much time.

"I feel like everything is slipping away," she admitted.

"You can't control everything, Augusta."

Tears burned the backs of her eyes.

She had sacrificed him. It had been the only way she could take control of her life.

He rounded his palm over the curve of her hip and she shivered. Despite feeling hot all over, her desires warred with long-practiced restraint.

She was the stern and practical Miss Primm. Headmistress, dedicated and disciplined.

"I'm practically forty!" Even in her own head, the protest sounded weak.

Rowan chuckled. "Four and thirty," he corrected her. "You certainly aren't a debutante anymore."

What did he see when he looked at her? A tired spinster? And if he saw her naked, would he be able to read all those stories?

He grasped Augusta's hip, nudging her onto her back.

"We're different people now," she said. But like clay beneath a sculptor's hands, she offered little resistance. With each mesmerizing stroke, her body softened.

"In some ways, but your eyes have haunted me for seventeen years. You were so damn beautiful."

"I wasn't." Even in the blush of youth.

Rowan shook his head. "Now..." He studied her face. "You are stunning."

His words stilled her. Rowan had never been a flatterer. He was not the same man she'd known before. Aside from his outward appearance, his soul was quieter. More confident. Less moody.

"I've changed," she said.

"I hope so. Not doing so makes one a fool." He leaned forward, his mouth a tantalizing inch from hers. "I've changed too..."

"I know." She exhaled a trembling breath.

He licked his lips.

"I've been wondering something." His voice was little more than a whisper. "Do you taste the same?"

"But you kissed me already—"

"I was too starved to pay attention. I practically inhaled you. This time I'm going to savor you."

She inhaled. "I don't know." His nearness stole her ability to think, and she grasped for reason. "What did I taste like before?"

"Strawberries. Honey." His mouth grazed the corner of hers. "Wine."

"I didn't realize…"

"Augusta." His breath tickled her jaw.

"Yes?"

"Let go."

He rolled her onto her back at the same time he claimed her mouth with a slow, searching kiss.

Let go. He cradled her cheek before sliding his fingers into her hair.

Let go? Augusta's lips parted and the kiss grew heavier. More than the almost violent embrace they'd shared last week.

This felt like a second first kiss. But it was grown-up and filled with promise.

The warmth of his hand smoothed her skin from waist to thigh and tingling desire seeped to her core, her chest, and her limbs. She allowed herself to sink into the mattress, exhaling a soft moan.

She missed being touched. She missed… *this.*

His tongue delved inside and then tangled with hers.

"Even sweeter." His words vibrated between them. "*God, Augusta.*"

Augusta explored him as well, running her tongue along the surface of his teeth. His air filled her lungs. Unlike when he'd kissed her outside, this kiss was slow, deliberate…

Knowing.

Their lips parted with a sigh, and after staring at her mouth, he locked his gaze with hers.

"This hasn't changed," he said.

"No." She'd determined to leave this part of herself behind forever. But how had she lived so long without the taste of a kiss?

Without *his* kiss?

"You're beautiful," he said, and then he oh, so slowly, gathered her gown in his fist. "More than beautiful."

She should not.

She should send him away.

She eased her knees open as calloused hands stroked the delicate skin of her inner thighs.

"I cannot. We cannot…" But she didn't stop him. Instead, she treasured his touch.

"Augusta," he breathed. His motions remained gentle, even, and persistent. When his fingertips slid along her seam, he inhaled. He'd touched her intimately before when they'd made love. But neither had disrobed. Their lovemaking had existed in a frantic, chaotic storm. They'd been fearful of being caught but also blinded by their need to join.

And now, she wanted this. She wanted him. But she, more than anyone, knew how dangerous it could be.

Rowan's gaze flicked from her face to his hand, tracing her with deliberate patience. His touch was maddening, fueling the fire inside of her. Drawing out her anticipation.

No one would interrupt them here. There was no hurry. This was her bedchamber, and they had all the time in the world.

Her heartbeat matched the throbbing in her core. She wanted…

"No seed," she said. It was too risky.

He stilled. Something flickered in his eyes and then he nodded slowly. "No seed."

Hiding her belly, palm splayed, she closed her eyes and focused on him touching her intimately.

"Just this?" Augusta knew things, she merely lacked experience. But if there was no seed, there would be no consequences.

But, saints preserve her, how long had she craved this?

He pressed his palm to her apex, twisting his hand, pushing into her, creating friction that caught her unawares. It was so good. So very, very good.

"I've learned a few things." His voice came out gravelly-sounding even as he stroked her, stretching his fingers along her opening and circling his thumb around her nub. Rubbing and sliding...

"Yes."

Augusta surrendered. Just this once.

"You're so warm." Rowan whispered encouraging words. "Succulent velvet. Soaking wet."

He spoke with a passion she'd only ever felt from him, and she opened her eyes. His expression excited her as much as his touch.

His nostrils flared, his eyes blazed, and his jaw clenched. All his life force focused on her.

"Rowan." Was that her voice?

He curled two fingers into her channel, pressing and kneading his palm over her apex. It was too much but it wasn't enough.

Augusta thrust her hips up, and he buried his face in her shoulder.

"Sweetheart," he groaned, dragging his mouth down her neck. All the while, his hand pumped, working her. He used his free hand to pin both of hers above her head, trapping them against the mattress.

And when he lowered his body onto hers, grinding his hips, the sensations inside turned painfully exquisite.

"Rowan!"

Vibrations shot down her back to the end of her spine followed by white-hot fire shooting through her limbs to her fingertips and toes. The sound of raspy breaths echoing in the chamber came from her.

But he wasn't finished.

Rowan knew the perfect rhythm, the pace, and the pressure, and he didn't stop coaxing until her completion left her utterly spent.

She should feel embarrassed, ashamed. At the very least,

apologize for taking and not giving. And yet all her nerves rejoiced in the aftermath of *la petite mort.*

Just with him.

Just this once.

Because her mind swirled with chaos. She'd lost control.

He was the only man who'd ever owned her heart and the dream of him was too impossible to resist.

Just as her mind began racing, she felt a gentle kiss on her brow.

Her eyes flew open. "Are you leaving?"

"I'll be right outside."

She nodded and frowned. "We can't. I shouldn't have... You need to go." Of course, he couldn't spend the night in her chamber.

Rowan chuckled. "Stop thinking, Augusta, and go to sleep."

IT'S BETTER THIS WAY

"*One more push, Augusta. Oh, darling, you're doing so well. It's almost over. One more push,*" Aunt Lucy urged from beside her.

Augusta had known delivering her child was going to be hard, but women went through childbirth every day! How hadn't she realized it would be so painful?

But Augusta was young, strong, and healthy. The windows were closed and a great snowstorm raged outside, but the birthing chamber was warm—too warm, perhaps. Augusta gave one more push and felt sharp stretching below—so much pain! After an expectant silence, a baby's cries echoed off the brick walls of the stuffy chamber.

"You did it, sweetheart. It's all over now," Augusta's aunt crooned beside her.

Two minutes before, Augusta had felt like she must surely be dying, but with the baby delivered safely, new life surged through her. Pushing onto her elbows, she wanted to see her child!

"A boy?" she asked.

The midwife didn't answer until Aunt Lucy nodded.

"A girl." The woman continued working between Augusta's pale and shaky thighs.

Augusta held out her hands. That was her baby—her and Rowan's baby.

"Millicent is tending to her," Aunt Lucy said. "Lie back."

Augusta went to protest, getting only a glimpse of her almost maroon-colored child when she ached to hold her in her arms.

A girl. Her baby was a girl.

"Drink this." Her aunt put a cup to Augusta's mouth. Something sweet. With all of her attention on her child, Augusta drank.

"I want to hold her," Augusta demanded.

"It's better this way. Remember? We discussed it. The child will have a better life, and so will you. I promise, the family taking her in will treat her better than you or I ever could. But it's best you never know. Let go, Augusta. And once you've recovered, you'll be able to rejoin the world. You can have your dream of running a school for girls. You won't be trapped up here with me."

Augusta knew all this. But in that moment, nothing in the world mattered as much as holding her daughter. Her heart screamed to have her baby in her arms.

"But I want to hold her. I need to hold her." Augusta's gaze followed the midwife's every move as she snipped the birthing cord and then wrapped her in a clean linen. Only the top of her baby's head showed out of the swaddling blanket, showing curly black tufts of hair. Augusta's fingers ached to slide through them. Would they be soft and silky?

"I need to see her!"

Were her daughter's eyes dark like Rowan's or gray like hers? The baby was completely cloaked now.

"Take the child away, Millicent," Aunt Lucy ordered.

"No!" Augusta shouted. "No!" Her second cry was more of a howl. It sounded of unspeakable emptiness and loss. She barely sounded human. "I need to hold her."

Her aunt poured more of the sweet liquid into her mouth, and by the time Augusta swallowed, her limbs felt heavy. The sickly taste was laudanum.

"I need to hold her. Just let me see her." But her eyelids weighed heavy, and she struggled to form the words. *"I need to..."*

"...HOLD HER!" Augusta sat up, her own voice waking her.

She'd not had the dream in a very long time. Just when she thought it was gone forever, it snuck up on her. And every time it haunted one of her nights, the years disappeared. It was like losing Ivy over and over again.

Augusta hugged her arms across her middle, feeling empty. Shaking.

As her heart slowed, she glanced toward the window. Already, the sun was high in the sky. She'd slept half the day away. It wasn't like her to lay in bed so late.

And then the events of the night came back to her. She stroked her hand along the sheet where Rowan had lain beside her. Aside from a dent in the pillow, there was no outward evidence that he'd even been there.

Confusion threatened to erase her pleasure, but she dismissed it. She never should have invited him into her bed, but she would not be so hypocritical as to regret it.

She would not be intimate with him again. She *could* not be intimate with him again. If such recklessness on her part was ever discovered, the school would never recover.

She dismissed what might be a greater reason—that he would eventually leave the area, and she couldn't go through losing him again. She'd be a fool to invite that kind of pain.

Knocking sounded at her door, and Augusta jumped guiltily.

"Yes?"

"I've tea for you, Miss Primm." Jenny. Of course it was Jenny.

And then the other, very real, troublesome events of the night slammed into her.

The rock breaking the window. Beatrice covered in blood.

Beatrice admitting she was considering going to London with Lord Sexton.

Augusta ran a hand down her face. Where the devil were her spectacles?

Rowan had carried her to her chamber and then called her beautiful.

It had been easier when he'd been angry with her. When he'd kept his distance.

Because when he treated her like he had last night, he threatened to break down the barriers protecting all of them.

She couldn't let him in any further.

Even if she wanted to.

"I SHOULD HAVE EXPECTED the attacks would escalate," Sexton grumbled from where he paced to the far end of the long room that made up the teachers' quarters on the second floor of the school.

"You're not the only one who made that mistake," Rowan said as he studied his handiwork. He'd secured a large piece of wood over the empty space where the broken window had been removed.

The famous investigator merely grunted in response. "If I could stay on, I would."

"But you cannot. No one is questioning your decision."

Another grunt from Sexton. "Miss Primm would argue with that statement."

Rowan chuckled. Because when it came to the school, Augusta could be more than a little argumentative. Rather than agree with the man, however, Rowan decided to ease the investigator's conscience.

"I've assigned more of my men to keep watch." Rowan

brushed his hands together. "Rosewood agrees. Until this is over, Miss Primm's safety—" He cleared his throat. "Er... The safety of the school takes precedence over castle renovations."

But Rowan himself would make damn sure Augusta was safe.

The marquess had inspected the area outside and below the window that had been broken. There had been two sets of footprints, one of which had been smaller than the other. Neither matched the impressions left by any of the night watchmen's boots.

Sexton was going to dig deeper into the case, but first, he had to finish up his business in London.

Meanwhile, Augusta's newly hired teachers had been lucky enough to be at the Gray Swan the night before, planning on moving into the school later today. No doubt, the innkeeper's wife, who managed to hear all the latest news, had spread word of the attack over breakfast.

And the summer break was nearly over. Augusta's students were expected to return in a little over a fortnight.

Shadows darkened the door as the younger Primm brother stepped inside. Glass, dirt, and dried drops of blood evidenced the violence of the night before.

"I was just telling Piers that I'm happy to keep an eye out," Lord Noah announced. "I came along to help, after all." The young lord slouched a shoulder against the doorframe and, now that there was no impending emergency to occupy his attention, Rowan flicked a curious gaze over the man who had arrived so unexpectedly.

Lord Noah Primm had thick brown hair and the same blue eyes as his brother, and what he lacked in solemnity, he made up for in brawn.

Was he similar in character to his father, or had he developed a moral code that actually resembled honor? Only time would tell.

"Commendable." Rosewood sent his brother a smirk. "Although you've waited long enough."

"You'd know how tricky it is to get away if you bothered taking over your duties. Between Liam's heavy-handed orders and Mother's woeful entreaties, be grateful I'm here at all."

"Hmm." Rosewood's response was to look doubtful. "You have choices. But leaving requires establishing your own finances, and you haven't done much about that, have you?""

From what Augusta had told Rowan, their father's mental capacities had significantly declined over the past few years. Rosewood refused to move home and had handed over the running of the estate to the next younger brother, Liam.

Judging by this unexpected flash of tension, delegating may not be the perfect solution Rosewood imagined it to be.

Rowan pounded in one last nail as he pondered the dynamics of Lord Starbridge's grown children. Aside from Rosewood and Augusta, Rowan wasn't inclined to trust any of them.

"I've enough men for now." He would be vague in his assessment.

Augusta was the eldest and the only daughter. The twins, Elijah and Piers, had been born barely a year after Augusta, followed by Liam, then Noah, then the youngest, Theodore, with an average of eighteen months between them.

According to Sexton, Lord Liam was the most like Augusta's father; Theodore, the most loyal to their mother; and Noah was the most well-liked all around.

Rowan would have liked to trust the man across from him. He certainly trusted Rosewood.

But whereas Piers Primm had left home shortly after graduating from Oxford, Noah, although quick to complain about Lord Liam's harsh rules and the persistent cold inside the castle, had been content living in his father's house.

And Sexton mentioned that Lord Noah had been quick to

suggest plenty of alternative suspects—none with specific motives or opportunities.

Had he done this to protect his father or because he truly wanted to help with the investigation?

Lord Noah scowled in Rowan's direction but quickly erased it when Lord Rosewood spoke up.

"Why don't you ask Auggie what you can do to help?" the earl suggested.

"I'll offer to teach one of her classes." The younger man flashed a sudden grin. "Which one do you think, Piers? Knitting? Crocheting? Or husband hunting?" He waggled his eyebrows.

"I'm sure Auggie will come up with some way for you to help." And then Rosewood pointed toward the door. "I believe she's in her office now."

Rowan stilled. If he'd realized she was up and about, he'd have sought her out himself. Although he'd done his best to keep busy this morning, to keep himself from reliving the intimacy of the night before, he craved the sight of her.

His fingertips craved the feel of her skin. His mouth craved the taste of her lips.

And other parts of him... craved more, *damnit.*

Before drifting off, she'd as good as ordered him out of her bedchamber. She'd said that what happened between the two of them couldn't happen again.

He'd believed he'd been the one maintaining the distance between them. Had it been her all along? And if that was the case, what did he want to do about it?

As Augusta placed the last pin in her chignon, she reflected on the changes of the past week.

Beatrice had, in fact, departed for London with Lord

Sexton, taking one of the new hires, Miss Pepperspring, along as chaperone. And following the repair to the window, the other three newly hired teachers had already settled into the lodgings provided on the second floor of the school.

Noah, her little brother, was staying in the guest room at Piers and Victoria's dower house and was only complaining a little at having been put to work assisting Mr. Driver with some of the annual summer chores.

But each day that passed without solving the mystery of her little annoyance brought her closer to the launch of the new term.

She had not, as of yet, decided to delay it. If there was one more incident, she promised herself. Or one more attack...

But there had not been, so she did what came naturally and dedicated herself to familiarizing the new teachers with the school's procedures, rules, and schedules.

Miss Pope, although a quiet and serious lady, showed slightly more warmth than the other two women. She would step in and teach history and domestic studies, replacing Priscilla.

Augusta had directed Miss Webb to teach philosophy and dance in Miss Fortune's place, and Miss Black to fill Miss Royal's shoes, teaching science and math.

Augusta could only hope the students would not be too disappointed and eventually come to appreciate the new teachers as much as they had loved the old.

If not, she'd have to find replacements for her replacements. Already, Augusta was going to have to teach the less orthodox classes, such as Victoria's modern etiquette series and Chloe's ladies' defense. She would hand these off to Miss Pepperspring when she and Beatrice returned.

Furthermore...

She had a particularly interesting young lady in mind to bring on—Lady Eloise, the eldest of Lord Hardwood's sisters.

True, the girl held resentment toward the school, but while they'd been visiting, she'd asked astute questions that showed more than casual curiosity. Lady Eloise, although stubborn and a bit outspoken, was intelligent, independent thinking, and had a bossiness about her that would lend itself well to teaching.

Having slept on the matter and made her decision, Augusta marched toward her office, intent upon sending the young woman an offer.

But then she glanced up.

Her organized thoughts scattered when she spotted Rowan's black eyes watching her from a distance. He waited at her office door, looking fine in an elegant jacket and waistcoat, looking for all the world as though she'd arranged to meet him there.

Furthermore, he wore a cravat.

His knowing gaze held hers, making her knees weaken and her heart skip a beat.

She'd managed to avoid him for an entire week, which was rather impressive considering he'd unofficially taken over responsibility for the school's security.

Suddenly the man of her dreams from yesterday merged with this man—the man he was today.

"Good morning, Rowan." She would be friendly but also professional.

But she remembered how she'd allowed him to touch her and how she'd responded, and heat suffused her neck and face.

"Augusta." He grinned. "Have you been avoiding me?"

For his own good. For her own good. For the school. "Yes," she answered honestly.

He would know. Because *he knew her.*

"I thought so," he said.

Augusta couldn't keep her eyes from appreciating everything about him. His proper attire only emphasized the power beneath it.

Just as she had when she'd been a girl, she drank in his sturdy shoulders and the way a series of muscles stretched when he crossed his arms over his chest. Only, back then, his shoulders hadn't been as broad, and the muscles hadn't been quite as impressive.

These were not the sort of things she ought to be noticing.

She sighed and then moved to unlock the door. "Well, since you've found me, you might as well come in." She didn't want to seem ungrateful but... it wasn't as though they could take up where they'd left off seventeen years ago.

Too much had changed.

Even after all this time, too much was at stake. The lock clicked, and as she shouldered the door open, he raised his hand and pushed, assisting her. His scent nearly sent her spiraling all over again.

She'd been wise to keep her distance from him.

Pretending to be distracted by work when she was really distracted by Rowan, Augusta shuffled papers around on her desk before taking a seat.

He had already sat down, and when their eyes met, he leaned forward, resting his forearms on his knees.

"Have you decided what you're going to do?" he asked.

"About?" *Us? The past?*

But then he clarified his question. "Are you going to go ahead with the term? I'd thought you would have canceled it by now." She hated that she heard disappointment in his tone.

"Sexton has promised to return—"

"His vote won't be finalized until three days before students begin arriving." He grimaced. "I know this school means everything to you, but there would be no coming back if anything happened to a student."

Augusta nodded. He was right. Of course he was right!

But... "If I don't reopen, that means that whoever has been doing this gets exactly what they want." And then it dawned on her—the real reason she'd been dragging her feet making this decision.

It wasn't the money. It wasn't even about the school's reputation. It was that she'd sacrificed so much to come this far. She'd been bullied for most of her life. Bullied into giving up Rowan and her child. And now someone was trying to make her close the school.

"Augusta..." Rowan trailed off, a pinched look on his face.

"No, you're right. I know." She removed her spectacles and rubbed her eyes. "I'm just... weary of letting the bad guys win." It wasn't practical. Nor was it fair to her students and staff. But at what point could she stand up for herself and all that was hers?

She lifted her gaze and met his.

And, watching him study her, it struck her that... he *understood.*

"I imagine your *little annoyance* is going to be quiet for now. I've too many watchmen here for him to think for a moment he can get away with anything else."

"But every day that you have your workers here rather than working on the castle costs money." Money she didn't have.

"Mostly your brother's." He half-smiled.

Augusta winced. "Is there any chance it's over?"

She expected him to dismiss the idea outright. To tell her to be practical, but instead, he shrugged. "It could be. Whoever did this may not have intended to injure anyone. But..."

"The note."

This is only the beginning.

"I should delay the term," she admitted.

"Not yet. We'll catch him. And until we do, we'll double up on security. I'll see to it myself that every student and every teacher is safe."

"You can't promise that."

Rowan's jaw ticked. "Because you don't trust me?"

Of course she trusted him! But this was costing him a fortune! "I'll never be able to repay you."

"I don't expect you to. But I would ask one thing."

Augusta bit her lip. What could he possibly want from her? Because he was going to be tremendously inconvenienced to ensure she could open the school.

"What?"

"Come on a picnic with me," he said. The words were so simple. They should have reminded her of the past.

But they were no longer two innocents. And Rowan had grown into a fierce and proud man.

Even so, a hint of vulnerability lurked in his mesmerizing eyes. *This man.* He'd done so much already, expecting nothing in return.

"Today?"

"It's as good a time as any." He was impossible to resist.

"Yes," she said. And then again. "Yes."

SO MUCH TIME WASTED

Of course, Augusta couldn't just up and leave that instant. But following a harried quarter of an hour spent rearranging tasks and notifying Jenny that she was leaving, she stepped outside her residence to find Rowan sitting on the driver's seat of an old farmer's cart. Patiently waiting.

The rustic conveyance and single horse could not be more different from the high-flyer pulled by a matching pair that he'd driven when they were in Mayfair.

And that was good.

It was good that this was different.

And for no reason at all, she laughed.

"Are you making fun of my vehicle?" He hopped down, his dark eyes dancing, and reached out to assist her.

She stared at his hand—dark, sturdy, capable. When he wrapped it around hers, she felt the callouses brought on by years of hard work.

"Not at all, Mr. Stewart." Was she flirting with him?

She ought to be working with Miss Black today. She ought to make sure Noah was making himself useful.

Instead, she was climbing onto a farmer's cart, of all things, to take a picnic with the most attractive man she'd ever known.

"Ready?" He glanced over when she'd situated herself, and the look in his eyes tugged at her heart. The day he'd proposed, he'd asked the same question before driving her to Lockstone Cottage, his estate on the river. The familiarity of it all was nearly enough to make her hop off and rush back to her office where she could give in to a long bout of tears.

But that was ridiculous. Wasn't it?

"Do you reside at Lockstone Cottage while in London?" Aside from the very basics, she knew so little about his life. The years between the day she'd been stolen away from London and the afternoon Piers brought him to the school were a vague and empty vacuum.

"I sold it," he said. Augusta should not be disappointed. Why would a professional architect, a single one for that matter, need a sprawling estate on the outskirts of London? "After you... left, living there no longer appealed to me." He made the admission freely.

"It was better suited for a family," she agreed. After she'd accepted his proposal, he'd given her a thorough tour. They'd walked through every room and made their plans, fully convinced that they would one day make their life together in that place, discussing such things as what sorts of updates they'd make to the master suite and where they'd set up the nursery. "I'm sorry," she added.

"It wasn't your fault."

"I know. I'm just sorry for the way it turned out."

"Are you?" he quipped. "Perhaps we shouldn't look at it that way. You were presented with an opportunity to set up your school, and I've been able to travel throughout all of England, France, and Italy working on projects that will stand long after I'm gone." He sounded proud. "As will the impact you've made on every student who's ever attended Miss Primm's." It sounded rather exciting, really.

"I suppose." Each and every student mattered and would make an impact on the lives of others.

That was why she loved the school.

And she did love it.

I do.

It had served a great purpose for her, as well as the students and staff. So why did she feel... dissatisfied?

Rowan turned them onto a less-traveled country road, through a copse of trees that opened up to a vast meadow. Neither seemed compelled to speak, lost in their own thoughts. The absence of conversation, however, was oddly comfortable.

"Your dream changed," she finally said. "It was initially to be a husband, a father. Then to become a renowned architect. What is your dream now, Rowan?"

"I suppose I'm living it," he answered. "I pretty much do as I please—but I also have a purpose. You have your school now. What keeps your passion from ebbing?"

She focused her gaze on the horizon. Just six months before, she would have gone on about renovating the classrooms. She would have told him she wanted to build better lodgings for her students and hire more teachers.

"My aunt insisted that the school was my dream, and that I should never let go of it." She shifted in the seat and sighed. "Funds from my father and my aunt's encouragement made opening the school possible. And I was happy to take it on, but I had so much to learn. The first year, we had twelve students. Three teachers for twelve students. Can you imagine?"

With no one on the road, he was able to turn and meet her gaze. "My first project was a gamekeeper's cabin." He grimaced.

"There is some very lucky gamekeeper out there, then, living quite comfortably no doubt, in a Rowan Stewart original."

"Indeed," he chuckled and then turned the subject back to her. "When we were courting, you mentioned wanting to run a school."

"Yes." She'd considered the idea in an abstract manner. But had it been her dream? As controlling as her father had been, ultimately, he'd handed her all the tools she needed to either succeed or fail on her own merit. She'd been determined not to be a failure. "I liked the idea of it back then. Of course, I didn't know at the time how much work it would be, how long it would take to make that image a reality.

"But I realized, as I became acquainted with my teachers and these girls, how very unique each of them is. I also began to realize that traditional curriculums seemed designed to squash those very things that made these young ladies so very special."

"And so, you found your calling," he said.

She wanted so very badly to tell him another reason she'd been so dedicated to the school's success. One of the best reasons that kept her moving forward. But instead, she asked, "How did you know that designing—that building your creations—was your calling?"

He sat silent for a full minute. Augusta knew his answer had something to do with her—with the betrayal he'd experienced for having known her.

She consoled herself that, at the very least, he knew the truth now—or most of it anyhow. "Tell me," she urged.

"My father's wife never took to me," he said.

Augusta nodded, remembering comments he'd made in the past. "You told me once that your father made it worse," she inserted. "By favoring you over your brother."

"Yes. After your father's men… delivered the message, I had no choice but to convalesce at my father's house. Which had me living in my father's home for a good three months."

"And the duchess was there?"

"Yes."

Augusta turned on the bench to face him. But… three months? Dear God! "What exactly *were* your injuries?"

"Augusta…"

She didn't want to know, not really, and yet… "Please, Rowan."

But he shook his head. "Just the typical sort of injuries one suffers in a brawl. To get to my point, being confined to my bed for so long drove me mad. Lying there, day after day, I realized that I needed to keep both my mind and my person active. I needed to do something solid—of significance. In truth, I never truly belonged with the people I call my family. I wasn't made to live the sort of life they lived. And yet, I didn't know anything different. During the first few months after I recovered, rather than do anything about it, I spent long days sulking in one of the shadier London pubs." He shot her a rueful glance. "I was also heartbroken at the time."

Augusta winced. She knew that heartbreak all too well…

"Nonetheless," he continued, "As luck would have it, I became acquainted with Henry Toliver, a seasoned builder who took me on and taught me everything he knew. When he retired, I completely renovated Lockstone Cottage and then sold it for twice its original worth. The rest, as they say, is history…"

Augusta absorbed his story. He'd taken what he had and built a life that he could be proud of.

"I think that's marvelous," she declared. Some part of her had imagined him living a lonely and unsatisfying life. How very vain of her!

Or was it because, in the very depths of her heart, she had been the one who had never shaken the loneliness that followed after losing him?

And then Ivy...

He turned the horse off the road and onto a clearing, and the sounds of a brook bubbled musically in the distance.

Rowan drove the cart near the trees growing on the bank and drew the horse to a halt. But he didn't move to climb off right away. Instead, he turned to face her wholly.

"Your school, what you've built, is marvelous as well. Well known throughout all of England." Rowan frowned. "It is what you've always wanted, is it not?"

Augusta had kept her doubts to herself for so long, she wasn't sure how to voice them.

"It was, it is. Of course it is." But her words lacked conviction.

"It's a lot of responsibility for one woman—for one person."

"But it is my responsibility. I've managed well enough," she insisted. "I just..."

He waited, and when she didn't continue, climbed off the cart, secured the horse, and then came around and stared up at her.

"Let me help you." He reached up a hand. Was he referring to assisting her off the driver's seat or to something else?

He had already helped her more than he should have. More than she deserved! But why?

Augusta placed a hand on his shoulder. Rowan's hands encircled her waist, and he swung her easily onto the ground. Again, the simple interaction was bittersweet.

But his touch, this time, also carried a hint of promise.

Rowan kept his hands on her waist while she found her balance. And then a few seconds longer.

Getting her away from the school had been a brilliant idea. She left the *Miss Primm* persona behind and settled into being simply *Augusta*. When was the last time she'd spoken so openly with anyone? He doubted she'd ever shared her doubts with any of her brothers, nor did she seem overly friendly with the ladies she employed.

She was the face of the school, thus she needed to show strength and endurance.

"The school is your dream," he said. "But it's also a burden."

Her hand still on his shoulder, she leaned back and met his eyes. "Yes." But then she frowned. "I'm not complaining. This life, this… vocation. It's more than so many have. And the school has provided me with not only a comfortable living but with purpose…"

"And hope." Rowan comprehended this phenomenon all too well.

"And hope," she agreed, and then her gaze flicked to his mouth.

This attraction was like the tide; regardless of how much time passed, it seemed like it would endure forever. How many times had they been discussing matters important to both of them, intimate hopes and fears, all the while acutely aware of one another in a physical sense?

So Rowan did what came naturally. He brushed her mouth with his.

She stiffened at first, but then relaxed, parting her lips so he could deepen the kiss. His senses narrowed to nothing but the two of them. Perfect satisfaction rippled through him, stirring primitive urges. Images from time spent in her bedchamber flashed through his mind, rousing his cock, hardening it.

One kiss. One kiss from this woman and all reason fled.

He pulled her closer, gathering her fully in his arms. Had she always fit him so perfectly? She whimpered, and a tremble skittered through her.

Hell.

This wasn't the time for this. She'd made herself vulnerable to him while they'd been driving—admitting to her doubts—confessing to her fears. He didn't want to take advantage of her trust.

Drawing on all his self-control, he opened his eyes and reluctantly broke the kiss. She took a few additional seconds to come back to herself, and when she finally blinked up at him, confusion swam in her expression.

But she quickly gathered her composure. "It is difficult not to go back, is it not?" She made an attempt at cheerfulness, but her voice sounded tight.

"I don't want to go back," Rowan admitted. He wanted to go forward. Where? He wasn't quite sure, but going forward was their only option. Rather than bring up possibilities for the future, possibilities she might reject outright, Rowan stepped toward the back of the cart and lifted the basket Lady Rosewood's cook had prepared for him. He'd not rush his fences.

"Are you hungry?"

"I am." Augusta hugged her arms in front of her, unintentionally pushing up her breasts. As usual, she was all buttoned up, and yet Rowan could make out the hint of plump mounds beneath the thin material of her gown. She'd never been overly endowed but she'd been perfect in his eyes.

He flexed his hands. Another thing that hadn't changed.

Moving the basket to one hand, he extended the other toward her. "Shall we set up near the water?"

They'd gone on half a dozen picnics in Mayfair, picnics shared secretly, away from her father's prying eyes.

Not far enough, however.

This picnic, although private, felt... carefree. An odd word to use with Augusta involved.

"This is nice." She smiled up at him as she shook out the checkered blanket.

There was no pressure on either of them. No sense that time was running out.

"I hope these are still some of your favorites." While he emptied the basket, she assured him that she would always enjoy cheese and good bread and of course, ripe strawberries. And...

"Wine?" She quirked a brow.

"What self-respecting picnic doesn't include wine?" But in searching for two glasses, he realized they were going to have to drink it straight from the bottle. He lifted it to his mouth, swallowed, and then offered the bottle to her.

"Not very proper of us, Rowan," she teased but accepted, and then raised the bottle to her mouth, taking a delicate sip.

"Have I ever pretended to be proper?" Rowan stretched his legs in front of him, resting his weight on his hands.

Augusta Primm was teasing him—flirting. He was flirting right back. But what did he expect to come of it?

He didn't know the answer. He wouldn't think about that today. They'd arrived at a truce. Her school was still in trouble, and he had an enormous job to complete over at Longbow Castle.

Time was currently on their side.

"You managed well enough at the Willoughby Ball." She smiled.

She then went on to recount every single festivity he'd attended in order to see her. He'd courted her, and she'd enjoyed every minute of it. As had he.

Her ability to remember such moments in detail reinforced his opinion that their former relationship had not been insignificant to her.

Rowan mostly listened. He'd fallen in love with her, but even then had done so with mixed feelings. She had been the daughter of a marquess—he, a duke's bastard.

"But I have a confession." The smile she sent his way nearly knocked him over. It lit up her entire face. God, how he'd missed that smile.

"I'm all ears." Rowan bit into a piece of bread and tore it off, intentionally being more than a little uncivilized.

"I liked it better when you were improper."

He raised both brows, but she did not expand on her declaration.

"My dear Miss Primm." He couldn't take his eyes off her. "You cannot say something like that and then leave me hanging." Would she speak of the day she'd come to his father's townhouse?

The last hours they'd spent together that spring had been spent most improperly...

But despite it ending as one of the worst days of his life, it had been the day he'd made love to her. It had also been one of the best.

But that apparently wasn't what she was referring to.

"Around others, you exhibited extraordinary propriety. Mostly aloof, every inch the son of a duke. But... you were not my Rowan," she said, blushing slightly.

Rowan nodded. He'd emulated the demeanor his father maintained—but for entirely different reasons.

"I didn't belong with those people. Most wanted nothing to do with me. And I hated every second of it."

"Because you are a bastard?"

"That, and Barbadian. Because of my skin." This wasn't something he spoke of with anyone. Not even Addison. And suddenly he wanted to tell her the other half of it. They'd missed out on too much of each other's lives.

"Five years ago, I traveled to the islands—after my father died—at his solicitor's request. Addison was too young, and the plantation had lacked any real oversight for over a decade."

Augusta simply nodded. He'd discussed some of his origins with her all those years ago.

He'd been twelve when his father brought him to England—just after burying Rowan's mother. Rowan had described a few of those memories of his childhood—some poignant, but many disturbing.

Augusta would understand the significance of his going back.

"Was it as you expected?" she asked.

"I didn't know what to expect. But when I got there..." He ran a hand over his head and swallowed hard. "In Addison's place, I was the *master of the plantation.* Which meant *I was the master of my mother's family.* My mother's brother was the only one who acknowledged me as kin." The man's image still haunted Rowan. "My uncle was so worn out that he looked twice his age. I sacked the manager and hired a less demanding man. I ordered new workers' quarters built, new *slave* quarters. Increased their rations. Lessened their workload. But the one thing I couldn't do was set them free."

Why was he telling her this? Because she was Augusta?

"Because you were not Bedwell," she concluded.

"I could have, though." He could have gone against his father's people—the local regiment.

"Could you, though?" Augusta tilted her head, challenging him.

How many times had he chastised himself for not doing more—for not doing something that would have been truly significant for his mother's family? For her people? For his people? The thought never failed to churn acid in his gut.

For years, he'd wondered what it would be like to return to his homeland—the place he'd lived as a child.

He hadn't belonged there any more than he belonged in England.

"They hated me," he spoke the words that haunted him. "But unlike my stepmother, they had good reason to."

"Because of who your father was. Because you lived in the big house."

"Yes." He stared at her. "Not only was I hated by my mother's people, but the members of the West Indian Regiments nearly arrested me twice. If Addison had gone, as Bedwell, he'd have been appointed Lieutenant General of the militia." He made a wan smile at Augusta's obvious dismay. That had been the end of that dream.

"I no more belonged there than I did in England," he said.

"So you returned."

"Yes."

"You returned feeling guilty." She squeezed his arm. He hadn't realized she was even touching him.

He met her gaze. This woman, after all this time, understood him better than anyone else ever had. Being with her, he'd never failed to feel as though he... belonged.

Augusta drew her hand back and then exhaled. "The woman who is now Addison's duchess worked for me for a few weeks. Even though I sacked her, I see her occasionally. Whenever possible, she and the duke attend school events to support Miss Briarton. She told me once that your brother transferred ownership of his father's plantation to your mother's people. Such a radical transaction was quite extraordinary. I cannot think such a grand gesture didn't have something to do with you."

She was not wrong.

"He was not popular for it. Here, but also, ironically, on the island."

"But it was something."

"Yes." He held her gaze.

Since arriving at Longbow Castle, Rowan had done *something* to protect the school. Growing up, he'd done *something* to protect Addison from their father. Those somethings had never been enough.

"You are still close with him?"

"My brother? Yes."

"You were more of a father to him than the duke ever was."

"For what it was worth." Because he'd failed Addison when it had really mattered.

He tossed what remained of his bread onto the blanket. "I didn't bring you here intending to wallow in my past."

Augusta shook her head. "But your past, your feelings, your life—all of it is important. You are... very important to me."

INTIMACY

*Y*ou are... *very important to me.*

Augusta hugged her knees to her chest. She should have realized that a picnic with Rowan Stewart would not be a formal sort of outing.

So far, the two of them had discussed matters close to each of their hearts. They conversed about genuine matters, revealing their authentic selves.

It wasn't exactly like before. They had each grown because of their experiences—their trials.

And ironically, talking to him now was better. It felt more genuine somehow.

And of course, unspoken words danced between the spoken ones, sending her nerves sparking with anticipation. When he'd first arrived at the school, she'd found him attractive; how could she not? But coming to truly *know him* again, that attraction had increased a thousandfold. It was like a storm brewing around the two of them, circling, roaring. It would eventually collapse, and the two of them would have no choice but to become one.

Their gazes locked, his blazing and hers... utterly lost.

"As are you," he said. "Very important."

"But you said you didn't want to go back." The words, although practical, had stung.

"And I don't." They had been sitting beside one another. Rowan had removed his jacket and rolled up his sleeves.

He leaned closer and propped his hand on the ground behind her. His face was so near she could see the individual whiskers and the creases around his eyes. She could almost count his thick black lashes.

She dragged in a breath of air. "But—"

"I want to go forward." His words were heavy with conviction, his shoulders touching hers now.

Augusta felt herself frowning. Because how...? "What does that mean?"

And suddenly she was lying back on the ground, pinned by the weight of his hips between her legs, his large frame hovering over her.

"It means there is more for us," he growled, still holding her gaze as though waiting.

Was there more for the two of them? The heat racing through her entire body screamed that there was. But what would that look like?

An affair?

"There might be," she admitted, her voice barely more than a rush of air. They should discuss the details before going any further. They ought to lay out some rules.

And yet, absorbing the sensation of him nestled between her thighs, she really didn't want to talk about anything. She didn't want to control these feelings.

"There is definitely more for us." He kissed the corner of her mouth and then dragged his teeth along her jaw before claiming her mouth. This kiss wasn't soft. It wasn't tender. His desire possessed an edge of hunger that she felt too. Desperation from years of denial.

But...

"No seed," she gasped.

It was the one rule she couldn't risk breaking again.

He paused, drawing back to stare down at her. "No seed." He spoke the words like a vow.

"Yes, then." She exhaled, and her control broke free of her self-imposed shackles. "Yes." Augusta wound her arms around his neck.

After the horrid night when Beatrice had been injured, Rowan had stayed behind after everyone else left.

He had pleasured her. Because she had been broken. She'd been low, exposed, raw. She'd taken the comfort he'd offered but given nothing in return.

But outside, beneath this blue sky, in the grass, having enjoyed his comfort and honesty for a few hours, she wanted to do the same for him. Augusta licked her lips, a long-suppressed excitement dying to escape.

Even believing she'd betrayed him, he had been so very patient with her—for months now.

He'd come to her office this morning to ask her on a picnic.

She tilted her head back, giving him access to her neck. And when his hands began unfastening the front of her bodice, she wriggled to assist him.

The spot he'd chosen for their picnic was remote. Private. She felt safe and precious.

She trusted him.

With her gown loose, he sat back and drew it and her chemise down her shoulders. Sunlight warmed her bared breasts. And then the warmth of his hands took over.

Augusta wound her legs around his hips, grinding against the hard evidence of his desire. Letting go of her inhibitions felt decadent, wicked. But it also felt like she'd finally discovered her destiny.

He watched her with eyes that seemed heavy, and his

tongue peeked out to lick his lips. He looked as dazed as she felt.

Sensing rightly that she wanted more, Rowan went to work on her short stays, one lace at a time, relieving not only the bond around her ribcage but... her spirit—the woman inside.

"I missed these freckles." He pressed a kiss to her chest. "They've been hidden too long." How had she forgotten all the times he'd told her he loved them?

He spoke against her skin even as he tugged on her gown, drawing it down to her hips.

"Are you being improper again, Rowan?" Augusta lifted her hips to help him.

Since opening the school, she only ever wore gowns and blouses that buttoned all the way up to her neck. Her décolletage rarely, if ever, saw the light of day.

"You said you liked me improper," he reminded her.

"I do." She rubbed her hand over his head. He'd not shaved it recently, and the hairs grew like whiskers.

He rubbed a thumb over her nipple, rolling it between his fingers, pinching and provoking liquid desire rushing to her core. When he took the other in his mouth, she arched her back and cried out using words she couldn't distinguish.

"Sweetheart." His voice vibrated against her skin.

"Oh!" She wanted more and was ready to beg for it.

He lifted his head, and the savage hunger on his face made her heart skip a beat.

And yet, he hesitated.

"I want to take this slowly. I want to enjoy every inch of you. But when you make sounds like that, you make it very difficult for me to do either."

"What if I don't want to go slowly?" She felt needy and playful and demanding. God in heaven, she'd waited forever for this man.

"Then I'd miss out on tasting you." He licked his lips. "And that would be a travesty."

"But you are already tasting me."

He shook his head. "I'm going to taste all of you."

He lowered his chin and dragged it down her sternum. The weight of his chest dragged her gown past her hips so they tangled around her thighs.

With her breast dampened from his mouth, the gentle breeze tightening the tips into even tighter buds, Augusta pushed herself onto her elbows so she could watch his face.

His magnificent, beautiful, precious face.

His expression hinted at wicked and carnal ideas, and she willed him to try every one of them.

He managed to dispense with her gown, chemise, and stays in one efficient motion. His corded forearms rippled as he held himself up.

Beneath Augusta, the grass felt warm and soft, if not a little damp.

But she didn't care.

If losing him seventeen years ago had been a punishment, then this afternoon, this moment in time, was a reward.

A reward she refused to deny either of them.

Before she could analyze his intent a second longer, he slid his hands under her bum, lifted, and then buried his face between her legs.

"Mgrmph!" she gulped. Never had she imagined.

Never had she known such pleasure.

The sensation of his mouth, tongue, and teeth... The scraping of his whiskers and the squeezing of his hands was nothing if not a decadent banquet.

She struggled to keep her eyes open, loving the sight of him while collapsing into a heap of... feeling. Ultimately, her body gave out on her.

Falling back, she closed her eyes against the sun, her mind

focused on her core, on her sex. She parted her thighs wider for him and wiggled her hips.

Rowan knew exactly what she wanted. He rubbed his palm around her entrance, making delicious friction. He stretched her and pinched her with his fingers and thumb. All the while, he encouraged her, tasting her inside and out.

"So beautiful, sweetheart." He applied suction and gently grazed his teeth along sensitive flesh. "Sweet honey. So perfect." The vibrations from his voice nearly had her bucking.

Augusta fisted the grass beside her, pulling clumps out as lust coiled her insides. Primitive need pulsed in her belly, in her chest, from the arches of her feet to the top of her head.

Relief—satisfaction—was just out of reach.

"Let go, love." How was he doing that? How was he finding these places she didn't even know existed? A sharp slap landed on her backside and... Her body jolted as though struck by lightning.

This was the end of her.

The very end.

She would never open her eyes again. Never talk, or walk, or think clearly ever again.

Several seconds—minutes, hours?—passed before she returned to the present. Gradually, the nearby stream bubbled again, the birds sang, and the leaves rustled in the trees.

And Rowan watched her, his chin resting low on her belly.

"Well." Augusta met his gaze. "That was new."

"I'm not finished yet." He pushed himself onto all fours, his hands moving to unfasten his trousers.

And miraculously, his raw expression of want brought her to life again. He would put himself inside of her but only in the beginning. In order to prevent pregnancy, he would withdraw before spending.

He'd promised there would be no seed.

She flicked her gaze to her belly where tiny silver lines crisscrossed almost invisibly.

He hadn't noticed them. Something that was almost disappointment intruded on her bliss. But only for a fraction of a second.

Because he'd freed his member. And grown woman that she was, aside from certain Greek statues and less-than-detailed drawings, she'd never actually seen a man's engorged staff before.

She'd known it was large from when they'd made love. But over the years, even such a poignant memory had faded.

Studying it now, she couldn't help but think it must be larger than she remembered. Rowan fisted one hand at the base, staring at her.

Watching her watch him.

It was a moment that ought to embarrass any proper lady. It was a moment that ought to send a spinster like herself into a dead faint.

Augusta reached out and, the moment she dragged her fingertips along his length, a deep growl rumbled in his throat, and then escaped with a tremor.

AUGUSTA'S IDEAS

*R*owan's gaze shot to her bow-shaped mouth. How could he not with her touching him like this? He then leisurely skimmed his gaze over her body. Beneath rounded shoulders, her arms were toned and contoured. Her legs stretched long and inviting. Her firm breasts would have been creamy white if not for the tight and upturned buds, and other pink marks left by his mouth and whiskers.

Augusta's figure had been honed by years of hard work, of discipline. Beautiful in ways he never could have imagined.

Rowan wrapped his hand around her nape, sliding his fingers into silky hair. He removed two hairpins and then watched in satisfaction as those deep chestnut tresses fell nearly to her flared hips.

"If I were an artist, I'd paint you like this." The moment the words left his mouth, he felt foolish—like that nineteen-year-old youth from the past.

The flare in her eyes, however, proved she liked the compliment.

Augusta licked her lips. "You have always been beautiful to me." Her voice was low, husky, little more than a whisper. And then she rolled her lips together. "I want to see all of you as well. I want to taste you as you've tasted me." She moved her hand up to his waist and together they tugged the tails of his shirt free from his trousers.

He would give this woman whatever she wanted.

For months, he'd stewed around that damn school, worrying about the building, about threats, pretending he wanted nothing to do with her. And all along he'd wanted this.

He'd wanted her.

And more.

He tugged his shirt over his head, and her gaze devoured him. But that wasn't all. Her hands explored his shoulders, his arms, and his chest. She left a trail of fire behind.

Until she stopped at his side. "What is this?"

He didn't need to look down to know what she saw: the scar was a part of him now. He'd used it as a reminder to steer clear of the aristocracy.

"Caught myself on a knife." He didn't want to make her feel any more guilt for the past. It was more his fault than hers. He should have realized the danger they'd brought upon themselves.

Augusta lifted her eyes to hold his. A moment ago, they'd been a sleepy gray color. Now, storms swirled in those depths. "Whose knife, Rowan?"

He wouldn't lie to her so he shrugged.

"I'm so sorry—"

Rowan touched her lips with his fingertips. She seemed to understand but then surprised him by leaning forward.

Grasping his waist, she pressed the lightest of kisses to one end of the scar. Rowan gripped both sides of her head, stroking and threading his fingertips in her hair. His throat thickened as she dragged her mouth along the white ridge along his side.

When she reached the other end of the line, he expected her to draw away.

But she did not.

Her hands, tentative at first, wrapped around his staff—one at the base, the other sliding up and down the length. "It's like silk." She tilted her head back and stared into his soul.

The sight of Augusta Primm, seated between his knees clutching his manhood, was not one he ever expected to see in this world.

It was, in fact, unworldly.

And better than his most erotic dreams.

She applied a gentle squeeze, keeping her gaze locked on his face.

"Augusta." Rowen half-spoke, half-groaned her name. Without being conscious he was doing it, he'd wrapped her hair around his fist.

He would stop her, but he was wise enough to know that this woman had a mind of her own. If she wanted to explore, then damned if he'd get in her way.

And watching her explore him sent his heart sprinting. Without her spectacles, she peered at him closely. "I didn't see... before," she half-explained, drawing one delicate finger around the tip. "I didn't realize..."

"We rather rushed matters that day," he said through clenched teeth, trying to keep his breathing normal at the same time.

She stilled and, almost as though she was speaking to herself, said, "You, Rowan Stewart, are a stunning man in every way I could possibly imagine."

The soft warmth of her mouth massaged extremely sensitive skin. His nerves lit up like lightning and every ounce of blood, by now, flooded to his cock. Rowan required great restraint not to apply pressure to the back of her head.

"What are you doing, Augusta?" His voice sounded like crunching gravel.

"Kissing you," she answered, and then glanced up at him.

Her mouth glistened, and he marveled that her eyes could look so innocent and mysterious at the same time. "That's all right, isn't it?"

"It's…" He swallowed hard. "Spectacular, but you needn't…"

"I know I needn't." She went back to work. Velvety wet heat engulfed the tip, and then she claimed more of him.

Rowan locked his knees, bracing himself for anything she might do. In this matter, he'd give her complete control.

"You're tense," she said in between strokes. "Does it hurt?"

"No," he barely managed. But also yes. But it was the kind of pain any red-blooded man welcomed.

A coil of steel was shooting up and down his spine, and he required all his concentration not to thrust his cock deeper, so deep he'd feel the back of her throat.

Because his entire being wanted nothing more than to fuck Augusta Primm's beautiful, often impertinent, mouth.

"You, er, haven't done this before?" he asked, just to be certain.

She paused and lifted her lashes to meet his gaze. "Is it that obvious?"

"Not at all. But I wanted to make sure you realized what would happen if you…" She took him in her mouth again.

Deeper. So deep that this time, he did indeed hit the back of her throat. When she withdrew, he felt just a hint of scraping from her teeth. Just enough to make white spots appear in his vision, not enough to make him wince.

This wasn't the first time for him, but by God, it was already the most memorable.

"Stop if you need to. Push me away. Do whatever it takes because—" Rowan clutched her to him, giving a testing thrust.

The slight nod she made was enough to know she heard him. "I'll not spend in your mouth," he uttered, staring down.

Sunlight slanted across her naked shoulders, filling in shadows, bleaching out the different tones of their skin.

With each stroke, she grew braver; licking, sucking, cradling him from beneath. Rowan pushed back her hair more than once.

He loved the silky feeling but wanted to see the curve of her jaw, her thick lashes fanned out over her the tops of her cheeks.

He initially accommodated her pace, but then she whispered, "Let go, Rowan." And he knew. They were the same words he'd said to her.

He allowed his need to take over, moving faster. Thrusting deeper.

Feeling.

God, feeling everything. Claiming. Filling her. Harder. Faster. When that bolt of lightning finally shot down his spine, he jerked to pull out of her mouth.

But her fingertips gripped his buttocks, and she didn't let go.

The world careened around him as his seed shot hard and fast. "Augusta—sweetheart—God—" His knees threatened to collapse but her arms were wound tightly around his thighs. He bent forward, his fingers threaded in her hair, practically falling as he buried his face in those tresses.

Just when he thought he understood her...

"Good?" she asked softly.

He waited for his breaths to slow and then answered, "Very good." He inhaled, loving her scent, relishing the silken strands he'd claimed.

Before he could lower both of them back to the ground, just to hold her—just to absorb this intimacy—she shifted, squirming.

Augusta began working on her undergarments and putting herself to rights with as much efficiency as her shaking hands allowed. Was she going to take a step back as she had before, insisting this couldn't happen again?

She avoided his eyes, keeping her gaze downcast while she

found a napkin and began drying her face and hands. Was she going to pretend this didn't mean anything?

Rowan was torn between taking her into his arms to calm her down and allowing her the space she seemed to need. Not wanting to pressure her, he settled on the latter.

Rowan located his shirt and drew it over his head. He'd had every intention of making love to her. He'd never expected...

He would not have released inside of her. Not only because she'd requested he not, but because it was the safe thing to do. Not for all the king's gold would he allow a child of his to grow up as he had—as a bastard.

He didn't speak until she finished fastening her gown, located her spectacles, and turned to gather the remnants of the picnic.

"Are you all right?" he asked.

When she didn't answer, he handed her the bottle of wine— not quite empty. "Drink," he said.

She lifted her gaze to the bottle, which she accepted and lifted for a swallow. A rosy hue tinted her cheeks, and her hair, which he'd set free, swung heavily around her shoulders. When she lowered the bottle, she finally met his stare.

"It's just that I—I don't know. I don't know how this works. What people do..."

"You don't know the rules." Being out of control did not set well with this woman.

"Precisely. But I do know that nothing has changed." Conflicted eyes blinked behind her spectacles. "Nothing *can* change."

And yet... "Everything has changed," Rowan said.

She shook her head. "But the school. Your projects... Eventually we're going to go back to living separate lives. Mine keeps me here and yours takes you gallivanting around England." Was that panic in her eyes?

"Not presently." Now wasn't the time to make plans. Definitely not the time to make decisions.

Rowan reached out and clasped one of her wrists. A part of him was always a little surprised that the courageous woman she'd grown into could feel so dainty. He gave a gentle tug, and she allowed him to settle her onto his lap.

How could he explain what she needed to hear?

"Whenever I build something, large or small," he began. "I'm inundated with deadlines. The entire process must be planned out in an efficient manner—from ordering supplies to hiring the appropriate craftsmen. And before it's finished, I must look ahead to the next one—and begin planning the details it will involve.

"But once I finish, I always make a point to take at least one day to appreciate the end result. I walk through it. I touch the wood, the brick, the stone. I walk around it, up close and then from a distance. I do that because it deserves to be appreciated. Anything that required my lifeblood deserves to be appreciated.

"And this." He gestured between the two of them. "Has been a long time coming. Let's be grateful for a while before analyzing it."

She squirmed and turned to meet his stare. And then she nodded.

Her unique scent enveloped him—clean with a trace of something floral, but always the essence of the school. And now, he also recognized the aroma of sex.

No perfume would ever rival the combination.

Birds twittered in the distance and the soft sound of leaves rustled in the wind as he wrapped his arms around her. She nestled her face in his chest. He had never felt so at peace.

"When you hold me like this, I want to forget the world." Her words echoed his own heart.

The admission shook him nearly as much as when she'd taken him into her mouth—in some ways, more so.

"Sometimes it is not a bad thing to forget the world," he finally said. And that was why he'd brought her out today. "If only for a few hours."

"But—"

"Hush." He touched her lips. "If a human lives well into adulthood, he or she spends over half a million hours here on earth. You spend a third of those hours sleeping, and most of your waking hours working. A few hours with me doesn't mean you're being irresponsible—or weak. You cannot be everywhere all the time."

Damn, he'd been telling himself just the opposite since the attack on Miss Wolcott.

And yet...

"Trouble's going to find its way to us whether we're there to stop it or not," he added.

Was this admonishment for her or was it for him? How many times had he berated himself for failing to be diligent where the school's safety was concerned?

Or failing his mother? Or Addison? But he understood her need to stay alert.

"I have five of my workers keeping watch at the school as we speak," he continued. "Should I be there as well?"

She twisted around and studied him. "Five? Full-time?"

"Do you want me to appropriate more?"

"No. No!" She shook her head. "This has to be costing you and Piers a fortune." But she frowned and then bit her lip.

"What?" he asked.

"No person in their right mind will try anything with the type of security you've put in place. They'd be asking to be caught."

"Exactly."

"But if they don't make another move, there won't be any

more clues to follow up on. Without any clues, we'll never catch them. And the threat..." She exhaled. "The threat will never go away."

"They might give up." Rowan frowned, more than a little concerned at where she seemed to be going with this.

"But for how long? Your workers can't surround the school indefinitely, and eventually, we'll go back to normal."

Rowan simply nodded.

"And then they could come back. However..."

"No, Augusta."

"You don't even know what I was going to say."

"You're suggesting I pull the watchmen."

"Yes, but not really. We post them in less conspicuous places. And then we mention to Mrs. Pratt at the inn that we believe the vandals have given up—that we're no longer taking measures to secure the school..."

"Within a day the entire village will know."

"Precisely."

"And then we wait for them to attack again."

"Yes!"

"Absolutely not," he said. She was suggesting using herself as bait. "I refuse to put you in danger like that."

"But I won't be. Not if you're there." Augusta had moved off his lap now and was kneeling before him, her eyes alight with excitement. "It's our best chance at catching them before school is set to start up again."

"But what if—"

"I trust you, Rowan. I'll be safe with you." She was using his own arguments against him. He exhaled. It was a good idea, even though he hated it.

She hadn't looked this hopeful since he'd laid eyes on her last spring. But then she turned serious. "And Rowan. If we don't catch them, I can't allow the students to return. So we need to move quickly."

If he were to be perfectly honest, the plan had been in the back of his mind for weeks now. But he'd envisioned leaving the school empty, of setting Augusta up with her brother.

"You could stay with Rosewood."

"But then they might not come." And unfortunately, she might be right.

Was he going to allow her to do this? He'd barely found her again. If something were to happen, he'd never forgive himself.

And yet, this was Augusta's school. She was not going to let go of this. And the plan had merit…

It was her school that would be at risk.

And her person. And that scared the hell out of him.

"It's imperative only a select few know," said Rowan after a short pause.

"That might be difficult."

"But it has to be that way. We don't know who's behind these attacks, sweetheart. It could be someone associated with the school."

Rowan could practically see the thoughts racing through her head.

"Yes, I see what you mean," she agreed.

"You don't tell anyone. Not the new teachers, not the Drivers, not your cook."

She winced but nodded.

"Or Lord Noah."

"But he's—"

"Been living with your father his entire life. Rosewood will have to know, and the countess. Only my most trusted men will be involved."

"They will attack again," she said.

"But we'll be waiting for them this time." Rowan held her gaze as he took her hands in his and squeezed.

Augusta let out a shuddering breath. "Let's just hope they do it quickly."

THE DETAILS

$\mathcal{A}$fter agreeing to alter their strategy, they'd taken a stroll along the banks of the creek.

They'd discussed the finer points of their plan—where the school was most vulnerable, where would be the best place for watchmen to be placed, and how quickly they could have safeguards in place. They had not discussed the intimacy they'd shared earlier.

Truth be told, Augusta didn't know what to say.

The sun was low in the sky by the time Rowan drove her home. When he drew the farmer's cart back in front of the school, she moved his hand off of her knee.

Augusta wasn't prepared for anyone to know what he meant to her.

Because she had no idea what she meant to him. What their relationship was, or how long it would last.

Because she didn't know what she wanted—or what she could allow herself to have.

After assisting her off the cart, he showed all due propriety by keeping his hands on her waist for only a second and then putting the proper distance between them.

It wasn't because he didn't want to touch her, though. She knew by the look in his eyes.

It was because he was respecting her situation—their situation.

"Thank you." Augusta suddenly felt like she was seven and ten again. "I had a lovely afternoon." Only, no girl of that age would ever do what she'd done. Even now, she could hardly believe it herself. And drat if she didn't feel heat flood her neck and cheeks.

Women of her age ought not to blush!

"As did I." His eyes twinkled back at her.

"But Rowan, we can't—"

"We won't make any decisions now, agreed? Our plans haven't panned out very well in the past. Let's take this one day at a time."

"This?"

"Us."

A ripple of relief, but also fear, rolled through her. "I'm not like that, though. I need to know what's ahead. I need—"

Rowan locked his gaze with hers. "Let's just be. You and I. No one needs to know. We'll take what fate gives us."

Augusta nodded. "But no one must know."

"Agreed."

Augusta stood before him. Not feeling awkward, but wishing for a few more minutes in his arms. And the question of telling him about Ivy confused her again. Would it hurt him? Would it make any difference?

Would telling him be selfish on her part?

Not knowing the answers, she exhaled and forced her mind back to more urgent matters. "You'll speak with Piers, then?"

"I'll return tomorrow afternoon. The changes shouldn't be too difficult. And then you can tell Mrs. Driver."

Augusta nodded. "I'll send her into the village with an

errand. She's good friends with Mrs. Pratt, so I've no doubt word will spread before nightfall."

His gaze flicked to her mouth. "I'd kiss you if I could," he declared in a low voice. "In case you're imagining I've forgotten what it feels like to taste you. In case you're imagining I don't have plans to do it again."

A handful of words and her pulse raced again. She shooshed him, almost frantically, glancing about briefly to make sure nobody was close enough to hear, but she didn't contradict him. "Good night, Mr. Stewart."

Her use of his surname had him shaking his head. "Until tomorrow, Miss Primm."

She contemplated saying more but was too flustered to manage anything intelligent. Because what would she say? That she'd never forget his taste either? Or how he'd felt like silken steel in her mouth? How pleasuring him had been one of the most fulfilling things she'd done in her entire life?

Afraid to open her mouth again, and in case Jenny watched from the window, Augusta pivoted away from him and marched into her home.

She felt him watching her until she closed the door behind her. Leaning against it, she waited a full minute until she heard him drive away.

Somehow, that bond she'd thought was broken forever had slipped around the two of them again.

It was a bond that held up more than just friendship. It included intimacy and trust, and excitement and pleasure she'd long since given up on.

She'd told him that these slips of intimacy didn't change anything, and he'd told her the opposite.

And yet, she'd never before felt so utterly... whole!

The overwhelming feeling of euphoria and unspeakable contentment energized her and terrified her at the same time. And, although he insisted they live in the moment, she couldn't ignore the fact that he would be in the area for a year, perhaps longer, but would eventually move on.

She would not be giddy. She had a school to run—a school to save.

And yet, still, when she went to bed, his face was the one foremost in her mind.

$$\approx$$

THE NEXT MORNING, sitting at her desk, Augusta felt slightly more in control than she had for months now.

Having a practical plan in place was exactly what she'd needed—a plan that didn't involve sending any of her teachers off on some questionable journey or putting her students at risk.

And she had no choice but to admit that if this did not work, she would delay the autumn term—cancel it if necessary. Even if it meant not seeing Ivy through her final year, she would not put others at risk to suit her own needs.

Doing so would have been reckless and beyond selfish.

She'd confessed as much to Rowan, although she'd not told him everything. As much as she'd felt the pull to do so, she had not told him that he had a daughter—nor that he'd met her.

Knowing would cause him pain. But was it not his right?

She shoved the unease away, went to work on some letters that needed writing, and did not look up until a knock sounded on her door.

Victoria stood at the threshold, her eyes knowing, but not stepping inside.

"Are you busy?" she asked.

"You know?" Augusta hastily gestured for her sister-in-law to enter, relieved that she'd finally come to some decisions.

And since Victoria was her sister-in-law, not an employee

or a parent or one of her vendors, she could trust the other woman.

The thought settled on her like a warm blanket.

"Piers told me." Victoria glanced down the corridor in both directions.

"Come in, come in! Close the door behind you." Augusta pushed her letter aside and sat up straight.

"It isn't a terrible idea, is it?" she asked once Victoria had sat down.

Before getting caught in the scandal with Piers, Victoria had always proven to be level-headed. "I don't think we have much choice. But you're putting yourself in danger, and Jenny, not to mention the new teachers."

Augusta and Rowan had discussed this.

"I'm giving Jenny the week off. She'll be happy to spend time with her family. And we've decided to put the new teachers up at the inn. I'll tell them I'm going to have some last-minute renovations completed. It's not an outright lie. Rowan still needs to replace the window."

"Rowan?" Victoria narrowed her eyes at Augusta. "You've grown rather fond of our architect, haven't you?"

Augusta stared down at her hands. It was difficult to maintain close friends when one had so many secrets to protect. Nonetheless... "He has gone above and beyond to help protect the school." And then she added, "Fiona Briarton is his half-sister."

"Yes." Victoria stared silently for a moment but then returned to the topic at hand. "You'll be here alone. Won't you be afraid?"

"I won't really be alone. The Drivers will remain in their cottage, and remember..." Augusta lowered her voice. "There will be watchmen. They'll just be out of sight."

"You aren't afraid the vandal will try something?"

"I'm afraid that they won't." Augusta winced. "We can't open the school unless they are caught."

"I know. That's what Piers said. Why don't I come stay with you—?

Augusta held up her hand. "I'll be perfectly fine. Besides, I doubt Piers would allow it. And remember, I won't really be alone."

"Of course." Victoria reached out and took her hand. "This is going to work. I know it will."

"I hope so," Augusta agreed. "I certainly hope so."

LAUNCHING THE PLAN

Augusta hugged her arms in front of her, absorbing the unusual silence. After reminding Augusta of the meals that could be easily put together, Jenny had left less than an hour ago. The hardworking housekeeper and cook had been pleased to have a few days to visit her family and hoped to make it to the next village over before the sun set.

Miss Pope, Miss Webb, and Miss Black, not without grudging complaints for the inconvenience of being temporarily displaced, were safely ensconced at the inn.

Augusta crossed the kitchen, pushed open the service door, and stepped outside. With the sun low on the horizon, the grass, trees, and waning garden were cast in a golden glow.

Not a single watchman was in sight.

For the next week, she would be the only teacher in residence. "Go ahead, you despicable cad," she whispered. "Do your best."

She ought to be afraid. Any normal woman would be afraid.

But Augusta was not unfamiliar with adversity. She would face this.

Besides, she was not alone.

Rowan had assured her there would be no less than seven men watching from hidden vantage points. Even now, she imagined one of them hunkered down in the distant trees. At least one would be watching from each floor of the school. One would be in the stables, and a few others in places where even Augusta didn't know.

Rowan would be one of them. The thought sent her nerves dancing. He'd told her he'd move between her residence and the school.

He'd keep watch in her home overnight.

Augusta fanned her hand in front of her face. Because the thought not only set her nerves dancing, it set them on fire.

As though summoned by her thoughts, the door to the kitchen opened behind her. Her heart jumped. She didn't need to turn to see that it was him—her skin lit up.

Her body would always know when he was near.

"Do you think he's out there now?" she asked, still facing the spectacular sunset.

"I think he'll wait at least a day. Word's still spreading tonight." Rowan's voice all but wrapped around her. She ought to be scared. She ought to be going over all the last possible details they might have missed.

Instead, she chuckled. "Mrs. Pratt's chatter spreads faster than if it were put in the *Gazette*."

But then she turned around. He hadn't stepped outside to join her.

And yet, with only his silhouette visible, she saw *him*. She *knew* him.

One powerful shoulder slouched against the frame of the door, the oval of his head, the straight lines of his jaw. There was nothing superfluous about this man.

She'd touched him intimately. She'd tasted him.

And she did not regret it.

She was not unaware of the possibilities presented to them

over the next week. She was alone in her home for the first time in… She could not remember.

She'd left Victoria alone here over the holidays last year, and then Piers had arrived in the middle of the snowstorm.

No wonder they had…

Augusta shook herself. "Have you had any supper this evening?"

"I was hoping to share a meal with you." Was that promise in his voice? Because the last time they'd broken bread together…

"Of course." Augusta straightened her shoulders out of habit. "Jenny left some stew on the stove. There's more than enough for two." She strode toward the door and chuckled. "In fact, I do believe she made enough to last me the entire week."

When she reached the door, she expected Rowan to step back.

He did not.

Instead, he barely moved out of her way so that she had no choice but to place her hands on his arms on order to pass.

In a flash, spinning effortlessly, he closed the door behind her and pinned her up against the wall.

Then he crushed his mouth against hers.

She should resist him, but in that moment, she could not recall why. Instead, she parted her lips and slid her arms up his chest.

She was four and thirty, for God's sake. Rowan wouldn't be here forever.

They would capture her vandals, he'd go back to working on Piers's castle, and he'd inevitably move on to another project.

But for tonight, for this moment in time, they were utterly alone.

"I can't stop thinking about you," he growled, lifting her thigh so it wrapped around his waist.

She felt the same. Yes, she'd gone over and over their plan but not a minute went by when he didn't invade her thoughts.

Imagining his taste on her tongue again. Touching him everywhere.

If possible, this was worse than when she'd fallen in love with him the first time. Or was it better?

She tilted her head back, allowing him to drag hot, wet kisses down her throat.

Definitely better.

But was this love? Or was this the manifestation of a deep friendship, enhanced by mutual satisfaction of shared intimacy?

Was that, in fact, what love really was?

Both of Rowan's hands grasped her thighs now, and she tightened her arms around him as he lifted her up. Only... he didn't walk her to her bedchamber or to the parlor. No, he set her on the large working table in the center of the kitchen.

The day before, he'd been going to make love to her—to put himself inside of her—but she'd not allowed him the opportunity. Because she'd been so bold as to acquaint herself with his sex.

Which had been a revelation—opening her mind to all manner of depraved ideas. She'd learned his taste, his texture, and she'd been fascinated as blood surged there, turning him hard, increasing his length and girth.

Stroking his length, becoming familiar as she rubbed, explored... licked, had been incredibly satisfying.

But it had also left her wanting more.

She'd wanted him inside.

Him.

A tremor ran through her. "I want you, Rowan," she admitted. She'd wanted him since the day he'd arrived.

Only she'd believed it impossible. Foolish.

Dangerous.

So what had changed?

He shoved her skirts up while she unfastened his falls. She needed him. She needed him now. Her body was primed for this moment. Had been for a lifetime.

Clothing was shoved aside, mouths clashed and hands explored.

"Augusta," he groaned, running the head of his member along her seam.

"Yes," she answered. Madness. This was madness.

But she would be mad. Tonight. This week. Because the future held no guarantees.

"Perfect." He entered her fully, stretching her, becoming a part of her. It was a poignant pleasure, so acute as to be painful. Rowan's hands clutched her from behind, his face buried in her neck.

Lust drove both of them but this was more than that. It was as though two halves of a whole had been lost and then found one another again.

This was Rowan, the man she'd surrendered her heart to years ago. She cradled the sensation of holding him inside.

Needing to be closer, to feel his skin, she clumsily tried tearing his shirt over his head. He impatiently released her so she could get it off his arms. And then he tore at her bodice, sending buttons flying across the kitchen. He wanted it too. He wanted skin-to-skin. Nothing between them.

And then he was moving inside her again. Deep and purposeful, knowing where she wanted him to touch her, knowing what she needed.

His calloused hands branded her, stroking, gripping.

She smoothed her palms over him—over every muscle and sinew and tendon.

"Augusta—" The tenderness progressed into something more violent, and he shoved himself deeper.

"More." She clutched at him. Years of pent-up passion, of

being kept apart, of feeling betrayed fed their joining. It was love, but also anger, hatred, and the frustration of regret.

She jumped off a cliff and was flying. Thunder roared in her ears amidst the wet sounds of their bodies moving together and the table shaking.

She inhaled his breath. She received his length. And when completion came, a sob rumbled up her chest and tears burned her eyes.

Or was that sweat? His? Hers? Waves of pleasure rolled through her.

Only after her orgasm ebbed did Rowan stiffen, push in once, again, and then…

Withdraw.

No seed.

He fisted himself at the base, sending creamy liquid onto her belly. She knew the taste. It would be salty and warm. It sputtered once, again, and then less so a few more times. Once it was over, Rowan lifted his head and met her gaze.

Looking into his eyes like this felt more intimate than what they'd just done. And Augusta had the same sensation she'd had the night he'd first kissed her.

For better or for worse, nothing would ever be the same.

ROWAN STARED AT AUGUSTA, her small breasts bared, caressed by the golden sunset, her belly covered with his seed.

"I've never seen a more beautiful sight than this moment." He was not exaggerating. How long had he imagined her like this? Vulnerable but not embarrassed? Disheveled from making love but not regretful?

How often had he imagined her as… his?

"You remembered." Augusta's lips glistened from his kisses

as she stared up at him with eyes not yet recovered from passion.

"No seed." He nodded, drawing her into him. He embraced her in the aftermath of that storm. It had been messy, chaotic, and... by God, something he'd needed desperately. "I'll never do to a child what my father did to me."

He didn't really need to explain, because Augusta would understand the challenges he'd faced. It had been like that from the beginning.

Being a bastard didn't bother him now nearly as much as when he'd been younger, but the condition inherently brought disadvantages.

She squirmed but didn't say anything.

"I put you in danger once, Augusta. I'll never do that again."

She reached up and cradled his cheek with one hand, and then tugged at the back of his neck, kissing him with more heart than he thought possible.

But after the kiss, she slid off the table, located a white linen, and, turning away from him, wiped at her belly.

Rowan glanced around the room. He'd nearly shoved the table to the opposite side of the kitchen. Various utensils that had been neatly lined up were scattered on the floor.

But Augusta was being unusually quiet and this time, he refused to give her a chance to ignore the step they'd taken.

Without any particular plan, he wound his arms around her from behind. "I didn't hurt you, did I?" He'd wondered when he'd had a few seconds of rational thought. But she'd met him thrust for thrust. Her arms had been like a vice around his shoulders, and she'd only loosened her legs to invite him deeper.

"No," she reassured him. "That was..."

"Indeed," he chuckled, inhaling her clean scent. Only now, it mingled with the scent of their sex. Tonight he would taste her again. Her sweet bottom nestled him.

Tonight he'd take her from behind.

They had nearly two decades to make up for.

She shivered, and he turned her around to face him. He tilted her chin so she had no choice but to meet his gaze. "What's going on in that brilliant brain of yours?"

She bit her lip. "Too much." She laughed at herself. "And yet nothing at all."

He'd overwhelmed her. Of course. "You need food," he declared. But he didn't let go of her. Instead, he deftly did the best he could to restore her chemise and gown. When he stared down at the bodice curiously, he realized there were no buttons.

"I'll never locate all of them." Augusta laughed.

The sound loosened his chest, and familiarity engulfed them again when she went to work on his trousers.

"I'll buy you a new one," he said, shaking his head at himself.

"Nothing a needle and thread can't repair." She smoothed his shirt over his stomach, touching him.

Rowan ran his hands down her arms.

Touching her.

Long ago, they'd imagined a future together, but they'd been torn apart. He touched her because he realized how tenuous this really was.

As much as he wanted it to be, nothing between them was a certainty.

So he would touch her when he could.

HIS FATHER'S MISTAKES

"*I'll never do to a child what my father did to me.*"

Rowan's words echoed over and over again in her thoughts.

She'd barely recovered from the most exquisite experience of her life and he'd tossed out those words.

"*I put you in danger once, Augusta. I'll never do that again.*"

"There's bread in the larder." Her voice only shook a little when she found it again. "Jenny's had the stew on the stove all afternoon, so it's ready to eat now."

Tell him! Her conscience screamed at her.

No! It'll only hurt him!

Furthermore, she'd promised to keep their daughter's existence a secret. And Ivy lived a safe and comfortable life. Her parents were good to her.

Augusta had been allowed a single glimpse of her newborn daughter before losing consciousness. Each time she woke up, she'd begged to see her baby. Each time she had begged, she'd been sedated again.

By the time she emerged from the bog of laudanum and

whatever else her aunt had dosed her with, her emotions had become so dulled that fighting ceased to matter.

Her infant daughter was long gone—taken away by a well-off family who had sworn to love her like their very own, her aunt had promised.

Augusta had only become interested in life again when her aunt had brought her to Warwick Village and shown her the school. *"It can be yours,"* she'd suggested. *"You can live the life of an independent woman."* With money from her father, secured with the contract promising never to seek out either Mr. Stewart or the child, Augusta had clawed her way out of the unrelenting darkness.

But now Rowan was here.

Tell him!

"Shall we eat in the dining room?" Augusta ignored the voices warring inside her. She wanted to enjoy this time along with him. It was an unexpected and wonderful gift.

Rowan carried the bread, plates, and utensils while Augusta transferred two bowls of steaming stew into the small dining room.

"Wine?" Rowan asked, a grin dancing on his mouth.

"It's in the cabinet behind you." Part of her felt like celebrating despite the secret burning in her heart. For now, anyhow, she had found the other half of her person.

Once seated, Rowan poured two glasses and then lifted his. "To us. To tonight," he said.

Augusta swallowed hard. "To now," she answered.

She was going to have to tell him. But not tonight. With everything they'd gone through, keeping this secret from him felt wrong.

But there was nothing he could do to change anything. Nothing she could do. And so she'd save tonight for just the two of them.

The vandal might very well return tomorrow. They would

catch whoever had caused her so much trouble and then Rowan could go back to work on the castle once again.

"What would you be doing right now if you were not here with me? If you hadn't come to work on Longbow Castle?" she asked. She knew him, and yet he'd lived a life that was wholly unfamiliar to her.

"I might have purchased a long piece of property in the center of Bath. In the past it was used by the town's blacksmith but the location is spectacular and I considered building a row of houses there."

"Are you disappointed to have abandoned that idea?"

The look that blazed in his eyes was answer enough, but then he said, "I'm more than happy with my decision."

As was she. She stared at her plate as desire swept through her again. They were eating a meal, for heaven's sake! She could make proper conversation.

"Is Longbow really salvageable?"

"Just barely." He told her about the challenges posed by the castle but also about his skilled workers. She'd met Mr. Rhys, his foreman, but she hadn't realized how much Rowan relied upon the man.

Much as she'd relied upon Victoria up until Piers showed up and swept her off her feet.

When they'd both finished their meals, Rowan pushed his plate aside and held her gaze. "It feels like we've been doing this forever."

"Doesn't it?" Oddly enough, Augusta didn't know whether to feel happy or sad about it. "Does it bother you to talk about the past? About what could have been?"

"It doesn't bother me to discuss anything with you," he answered without having to mull over her question. "As long as we eventually discuss the future. Does it bother you?"

"I don't like thinking about what my father's men did... I hate imagining what you thought of me when I failed to show up. But…" She allowed a soft smile. "There were far better memories than those between the two of us."

"And far more of those."

Rowan poured what remained of the wine into her glass, and the two of them reminisced over a handful of those finer times.

She was startled to realize how much of that spring she'd forgotten—other debutantes who'd come out with her, all the candles at the Willoughby Ball, and suffering through some of the most atrocious musicals she'd ever attended.

Clearing the table and then washing the dishes, they waxed nostalgic, like an old married couple. Only they weren't married, and nothing about her feelings felt old.

His shoulder brushed hers as he returned the bread to the larder, and her heart skipped a beat. Covering the stew, he reached around her, his forearm skimming her waist, and heat pooled in her core.

By the time the kitchen had been put to rights, the time for conversation had run its course.

And yet the tension was so thick, it practically sizzled between them.

"I suppose…" Augusta backed up against the table again. The very same table…

"I'm going to check the doors and windows." He crowded her, dipping his face so his jaw brushed hers. "And then I expect to find you waiting for me in your chamber."

All she could do was nod.

Because she wanted him more than anything. And if she didn't have him tonight, she thought she might scream.

Very un-Primm-like. Un-Primm-like indeed.

IN ANTICIPATION of Rowan's promise, Augusta lit the candles she'd strategically placed around her chamber and then stared into her wardrobe and sighed. How was she expected to seduce Rowan when all she owned were two decade-old night rails that both covered her from neck to toe? From the hallway, she heard locks clicking and doors closing. He was checking the house thoroughly. And then he would come to her.

This night might very well be their only opportunity. She didn't want to waste it.

After tossing the least tattered of her gowns onto the bed, she returned the other and crossed the room to her vanity.

Not having to even think about her movements, she removed the seven pins she used every day to secure her chignon. Seated in front of the looking glass, she peered close. The dim light of the candles warmed her chestnut strands. They also enhanced the emerging gray ones.

Rowan had wound the length of her hair around his hand. What did he see when he looked at her? She was who she was, a thirty-four-year-old spinster—a woman of middle age.

And yet Rowan Stewart found her desirable.

"I love it down." His simple words, deep and heavy with emotion, brought the room to life.

Augusta stilled, meeting his gaze in the reflection.

"The younger ladies are wearing it short these days." Was she nervous? She glanced toward the drapes, which she'd drawn closed. "We are safe?"

"For now. For tonight."

Most importantly, they were alone.

Not allowing his stare to waver from hers, Rowan stepped into the room and closed the door behind him. It wasn't the first time he'd reminded her of a great lion, stalking his prey.

Only, once he reached the vanity, rather than pounce on her, he took up the brush, knelt behind her, and smoothed it down her back, halting only when it caught on a tangle.

"Look at you." He dragged the brush the entire length. "You're magnificent."

The compliment drew a short burst of laughter from her, and he frowned.

"I'm not sure we're looking at the same person." Augusta winced, reaching up to touch her face.

"I know who I'm looking at." Genuine, unfettered intensity burned in his eyes, but he didn't expand on his words. Instead, he focused on the task at hand, working the brush through her hair lovingly until it slid through the long strands effortlessly.

The even movements comforted her at first. But as his motions grew languid, anticipation burned hotter and hotter. And by the time he placed the brush on the surface of her vanity, tingles of excitement had worked a sensual magic on her body. Her breasts ached heavily and liquid heat swirled to her core. She squeezed her thighs together.

Rowan rose, and after assisting her to her feet, he directed her to stare at her reflection. "Look at you," he ordered again.

He pushed her small bench to the side, grasped the hem of her gown, and with no buttons to unfasten, it slid off easily.

"You, Augusta Primm, have conquered me."

If arousal was an actual sound, it embodied his voice. The bronze of his hands contrasted against her pale arms, reflecting hard work as much as his mother's heritage. He gathered her chemise and lifted it over her head as well.

Cool air skimmed her exposed skin and she shivered.

Of course, she'd seen herself naked before—thousands of times. And although she was not ashamed of her body, it had been for her eyes only.

She wasn't afraid of physical labor and worked in her office as well as out of it. She walked the school grounds every day and had been active for most of her life.

But she was not a nubile debutante, nor was she well-endowed with generous curves. And her body showed subtle clues to her deepest secret.

She trailed her gaze down her neck, following the slim

cords of muscles over her shoulders and along her arms. The tips of her breasts, which had returned to their normal size in the weeks after giving birth, pointed up. Her stare shot straight to the slim silvery lines but Rowan didn't notice them.

She could just make out the shadows of her ribcage, a subtle ladder that sloped to her abdomen. Rarely, if ever, exposed to the light of the sun, her skin glowed an almost creamy alabaster but for a smattering of those barely noticeable striations.

Her train of thought vanished when Rowan's hands moved from her hips to cradle her breasts. "More perfection."

Augusta smiled at his use of such a word to describe her.

"Flatterer." Only she knew he was not.

He moved one hand to cup her sex. This pose brought to mind a Greek statue and she had the sudden urge to arch her back.

"I've been wanting to do this all night." Rowan's movements took on greater urgency. "Look at you." But he did the looking. "How have I gone so long...?"

He pushed her forward, took her hands, and placed them palms down on the table.

The position ought to cause her to feel vulnerable, but instead, she felt owned.

She was his.

Tonight, she belonged to him. Had she always? Even when they were apart?

She watched in the looking glass as he unfastened his falls, stripped his shirt off over his head, and lowered his breeches.

His lips landed on her shoulder and she arched her back.

"*Look at you,*" he growled this time. "*Look at us.*"

In the glow of the flickering candles, the sight in the mirror did, in fact, resemble a priceless painting. Her hair cascading around both of them, his skin bronzed and golden, hers creamy and pink.

And then he stroked a hand down her body. He explored slowly until his fingers slid through the dark triangle at her apex, rubbing along intimate folds. His other hand palmed one breast and then the other. His gaze flared and hitched as he devoured her reflection in the mirror.

And Augusta surrendered to this depravity, this sensual liberation. Blood thundered in her ears.

His member prodded Augusta from behind, and she spread her feet wider.

"Look at us," he said again. But she already was. She was looking at him, his body wrapped around her from behind, his hands stroking, prodding.

Claiming.

Bending forward now, Augusta kept her eyes locked with his.

"Mine." His eyes narrowed as he nudged his tip inside, retreated, and then slid deeper.

"Mine," he vowed again, shoving himself deeper.

Augusta bit her lip to keep from crying out.

Because she was his—she always had been. Just as he was her destiny.

"So wet. *Ah, hell.*" Desire contorted his expression. It was raw, an expression of pain and relief. He increased the pace and the pressure, his length stroking her inside while his hands plucked and pinched and rubbed her belly, her breasts, her sex where they joined.

His thrusts took on more dominance and while her insides vibrated, her arms began shaking from holding herself up. As he grew larger, she braced herself, meeting him fully, aching, irrationally wanting him inside her forever.

At some point, her arms collapsed and she dropped her face to rest on the table. Her nerves exploded, a deep cry tore through her.

Rowan let out a guttural growl and then gave a mighty

push, tearing himself from her body. Her cheek resting on the wooden surface of her vanity, Augusta vaguely felt the heat of his seed as he spent on her bare back.

Even in this state, his words drifted through her thoughts.

"I'll never do to a child what my father did to me. I put you in danger once, Augusta. I'll never do that again."

She squeezed her eyes together as though that would shut the words out even as Rowan collapsed forward as well, his hands bracketing hers, resting a good deal of his weight along her back. Their breaths synchronized, and at least a full minute passed before either spoke.

"My God, Augusta." It was Rowan who broke the silence.

"What?" she murmured, perfectly content to remain like this all night. Satiated.

Surrounded by him.

"Just that." He chuckled. "My God."

MISS PRIMM AND PROPER?

*a*ugusta awoke late the next morning, and when she reached across the bed, discovered it empty.

Neither had accomplished much sleeping throughout the night, and with work to accomplish, Augusta realized she'd pay for the lack of sleep. But Rowan was already up and about.

She sighed. He was a revelation indeed.

Augusta rolled over, and the unfamiliar tenderness reminded her that it had been worth it. There was a raw sensation between her thighs and sore muscles and aches in other intimate areas.

How many times had they made love? Each time she began dozing off, Rowan would wake her, pulling her on top of him, turning her to face him, or away from him, and her body came alert each time.

"Tea," she murmured. "I need a strong cup of tea."

And as though he'd been waiting for her command, the door to her room opened and Rowan sauntered in.

Cup and saucer in hand, he whipped the drapes open with the other and then crossed back to her.

"What time is it?" Augusta pushed herself to sit up, belatedly clutching the sheet to her chest.

It was one thing to bare oneself while in the throes of passion, quite another to do so while taking tea.

He chuckled, no doubt reading her thoughts. "Nearly noon," he answered. But before she could express dismay, he held up a hand. "Everything's quiet and the alternative shift came on as planned." He carefully transferred the saucer to her and then lowered himself to sit on the edge beside her. "Now, here. Drink."

Nothing about him gave away that he suffered from lack of sleep. He was fully dressed in his usual work clothes, which consisted of a shirt, sturdy breeches, and his by-now-familiar woolen jacket. She recalled how he'd dressed in Mayfair while participating in the Season.

He'd tied his black silky curls at the base of his neck and been fitted with the latest fashion.

She had found him handsome then, but dressed to work as he was now, his strength, power, and vitality were on full display.

And she suddenly felt unusually feminine. She also felt weak and dependent. Neither condition was something she'd welcomed in a very long time.

The events of the night hovered in the air. Her chamber no longer felt prim and proper. The sheets were twisted into a tangled mass, her hair was in disarray, and the hint of a musky aroma had the ability to make her blush.

Because here she sat beside her lover, drinking tea as though this was all perfectly normal.

She blew on the steaming liquid and, finding it too hot to drink, set it on the night table. "I have work to do, Rowan." But her words lacked the tone she'd intended.

Because he was Rowan.

And because…

217

Everything was, in fact, different now. But did that mean anything had changed?

He rose and crossed to stare out the window.

"I'm not losing you again."

Augusta jerked her head up to stare at him. How could he sound so confident? Her heart swelled even as an army of doubts assaulted her. And yet he was no longer the untried young man she'd fallen for in London. He was an established gentleman who'd experienced great success in a harsh world. He was a man of his word, a man who knew what he wanted.

"I—"

"We've lost too much time already. We're intelligent people, Augusta. If we want to find a way to be together, we will."

Some of what he was saying made perfect sense. Because she was a grown woman. And she realized something she ought to have comprehended a long time ago.

They were stronger together than either could be individually. If they were both willing to compromise...

But he had his buildings, and she, the school to consider.

And *Ivy.*

There would always be Ivy. *I need to tell him.*

She had had her night alone with him, with nothing to wedge them apart. Now, perhaps, was as good a time as any.

"Rowan." She cleared her throat. "I have something—there is something I need to—" she began, but her words were cut off by the distant rumble of an approaching carriage outside. She closed her mouth, half relieved at the interruption but also frustrated.

Rowan was already off the bed. "Get dressed. I'll see who it is."

He disappeared, and Augusta cursed beneath her breath. The school was to appear empty. A visitor could scare their villain away. They had less than one week to lure the vandal.

Rushing about the room, she quickly washed and dressed.

She was just tying her half boots when Rowan reappeared at the door.

"It's my brother."

"Addison?"

"And his wife. Likely, Fiona wished to return early."

No. No, no, no! This could ruin everything. She didn't even try hiding her panic, but Rowan looked calm.

He placed his hands on her shoulders and squeezed. " Breathe, Augusta. You can do this. *We* can do this."

His strength flowed through her and her heart returned to its normal pace.

"Yes," she agreed. "We can."

"Good girl. Now, invite them inside and I'll join you in a few minutes," he said, urging her toward the corridor. "After that, take the ladies into the dining room for tea. That way I can speak privately with Addison."

"Lemonade," Augusta said, remembering the jar Jenny had left in the larder. "And after, we'll send them to the dower house at Longbow Castle. Victoria can keep them occupied."

"See. Everything's under control."

She almost rolled her eyes at his use of her favorite word. Because she'd lost control a long time ago.

Rowan winked, and after one last meaningful glance, they went their separate ways.

Rowan allowed Augusta a few minutes to bid their guests to enter before he slipped around to the front and knocked on the front door. When she opened it, he made as little of a spectacle as he could, keeping his voice low.

Augusta put on a performance as well, inviting him in, exclaiming that some very special visitors had just arrived as she led him to the parlor.

His brother, looking as polished as ever, jumped up to greet him, taking his hand, but then also pulling Rowan into a firm but short embrace. The duchess rose as well, as did Fiona's little friend, Miss Annesley.

Fiona flew across the room, however, blond curls bouncing, illustrating all the exuberance of a young girl who was not quite yet a lady.

"You didn't come to the house party," she accused. "So I convinced Addison and Collette that we must come to you instead. Miss Primm won't mind, will you? That Ivy and I are here early. We can help with preparations. But where is everyone?"

"Manners, Fiona." Addison sent the very feminine whirlwind a meaningful glance. "Remember where you are." But then he turned back to Rowan. "We went to the castle first and one of your men said you might be here." Unspoken questions lurked in Rowan's younger brother's eyes.

"We missed you this summer, Row," the duchess added, pushing up onto her toes and pressing a chaste kiss to his cheek. When she stepped back, she turned to Augusta. "You're looking lovely, Miss Primm. But it is certainly quiet around here. We expected the school to be busy with a last-minute frenzy to launch the new term."

Rowan's gaze locked with Augusta's. He needed to get his brother alone. They certainly couldn't reveal their plans to Fiona and her young friend.

Already, despite doing their best to keep the scheme a secret, by necessity, too many people were in the know.

"Your Grace," Augusta addressed the duchess. "What a pleasant surprise this is." At the duchess's nod, Augusta kept right on talking. "Jenny's away for a few days—you do remember Jenny, don't you? Miss Wolcott is in London and the other teachers are in the village." Rowan couldn't remember any time when he'd heard her ramble. She was nervous.

And then he forcibly bit back an unlikely grin when he realized she'd missed a button while dressing in such a hurry.

"Won't you ladies join me in the kitchen?" She'd taken the duchess by the arm. "This summer's been unusually warm, and I imagine you must be parched from your travels."

"Do you have any lemonade?" the two younger girls asked in unison, looking all too eager to explore their headmistress's private abode.

Addison's duchess laughed. "These two girls have spent the entire summer in one another's pockets. They might as well be sisters by now. They dress alike, are constantly giggling, and have even taken on each other's mannerisms."

Their little friendship hadn't changed, then. Rowan nodded, trying not to appear overly impatient.

But Augusta stilled, focusing on Miss Annesley. With one hand on the girl's shoulder, she brushed a stray lock of black hair away from her face. "I thought your parents were collecting you in July. Did they decide to extend their holiday on the Continent?"

The duchess winced, but it was Addison who answered.

"That was our understanding." He frowned. "But Mr. and Mrs. Annesley must have changed their plans. I imagine their letter was lost in the post." He schooled his features. "I expect we'll hear word of their whereabouts any day."

"No doubt it's waiting for us at home this very minute," the duchess added.

But watching Augusta address the young lady, a buzzing stilled him—an inexplicable dissonance.

Augusta—as *Miss Primm*—encouraged her students, she reprimanded them, and she provided stability to those who needed it. But not once could he remember her ever treating any of them with such... tender affection.

Fiona's little friend, Miss Annesley, lifted her chin, her hands clasped at her waist. "Mother sent her last letter from

Florence. She assured me they were having a splendid time." She certainly was a serious little thing. "But that was in June, and I haven't heard anything since." The girl looked more disappointed than upset, her blue eyes bright and dry, her back straight. An unexpected wave of awareness washed over him.

Something familiar that he couldn't place.

The girl's composure remained intact, even with all attention on her. Rowan found himself watching Fiona's young friend curiously, despite his urgent need to speak with Addison.

For her sake, he hoped Mr. and Mrs. Annesley hadn't met with trouble.

Augusta exhaled slowly, squeezing the girl's shoulder. "It's not as though they've never extended their holidays in the past, is it?" She straightened and then awkwardly smoothed her skirt. She extended a hand. "Would you ladies care for some biscuits with your lemonade? Your Grace?"

Enticed by the promise of drinks and sweet treats, the younger girls seemed eager enough to see more of their headmistress's home. Fiona and her friend, no longer children but not yet adults, skipped behind Augusta and the duchess as they exited the parlor.

Glancing over her shoulder, the duchess raised her brows toward her husband, but then allowed herself to be dragged away by Augusta. "I'd be delighted," her voice carried from down the corridor. "And do call me Collette."

Rowan remembered that the duchess had worked for Augusta a few years before. Augusta had, in fact, sacked her.

Once their voices faded away, Rowan shrugged off an odd feeling and then turned to his brother.

"Fiona said you were smitten with her, but I refused to believe it."

"Smitten?"

"With Augusta Primm," Addison said. "I was young when

222

you met her, but not so young that I don't remember you chasing after her. Nor will I ever forget your condition the night she jilted you."

"I—" Rowan scrubbed a hand down his face. "I don't have time to get into this now. The thing is… You need to take the duchess, Fiona, and Miss Annesley somewhere else now. They aren't safe here." A ghostly sensation whispered down his spine, but he didn't have time to analyze it.

Speaking in low, somber tones, Rowan explained the calamities of the past year to his brother.

But as he stared into Addison's blue eyes, a suspicion planted itself in his brain. The possibility twisted his gut, and he barely made it through his conversation.

It was an outlandish idea, wasn't it? And how had he missed it before?

And yet… the twisting tightened.

"You needn't be formal with me." The duchess smiled with what seemed like effortless warmth as she sipped her tea. The younger woman had her blond hair in a simple knot, and she wore discreetly fashionable clothing. She was very pretty, but it was her spirit that set her apart.

No wonder Bedwell had scooped her up, despite her having been born illegitimately.

Augusta glanced to the opposite end of the table where the two bosom friends carried on a conversation of their own, and then fixed her attention on the duchess again.

Distracted as the other two were, Augusta's apology should be private enough for her purposes.

"Then you needn't call me Miss Primm." Augusta shifted in her chair. The duchess, formerly Miss Collette Jones, was a very forgiving person. The fact that Augusta had never asked outright for forgiveness weighed heavily on her conscience as she sat across from the other woman.

A qualified teacher whom she'd sacked in a most heartless manner.

Despite feeling like a different person, Augusta was still the woman who'd caved to threats made by a handful of parents nearly two years ago.

But she would take responsibility for the actions she'd taken to protect the school.

And as she faced dear, sweet Collette today, Augusta's mistakes became crystal clear.

Augusta inhaled a shaky breath.

"I owe you an apology, Collette, and it's long overdue." When Collette looked as though she was going to wave it away, Augusta held up a hand. "You came here to teach in good faith. You needed a place to establish yourself—a place where you could belong, and even after such a short time teaching here, I knew you were going to be a favorite."

"I did enjoy it." Collette stared at her hands, biting her lower lip as though she was holding something back.

"It wasn't fair for me to terminate your employment, and although circumstances ended up working out for you, I'd like to say that if I could go back, I would handle things differently."

Ultimately, the school's reputation ought to have spoken for itself. Augusta had only employed the most excellent teachers, and her graduating students entered the world armed and refined to lead meaningful lives.

She should not have sent Priscilla to address Allison Meadowbrook's mess. Chloe would never have fallen into her predicament, which had led to Adelaide's circumstances. And she ought to have talked Beatrice out of going to London with Lord Sexton...

Augusta's poise nearly collapsed under the weight of her

poor choices. She'd lost sight of her purpose, of what had truly satisfied her in the first years of operating the school.

And now she'd backed herself into a situation where she would have to place her students under the control of ladies she wasn't wholly comfortable with.

Understanding flooded her, along with a hefty dose of shame. Each time she'd felt threatened, she'd pushed those closest to her away. Should she have shared her burden instead? If they'd bonded together, would they have already defeated these threats?

Rowan had told her more than once that she didn't need to do everything alone. Even now, he was doing everything he could to help her.

As were others... dozens of others.

What would it be like to go on sharing her responsibilities? She couldn't control everything, no matter how badly she wanted to—no matter how hard she tried.

She reached across the table and took Collette's hand in hers. "I am so very, very sorry. I knew how badly you needed the position, and instead of making the school a place of refuge for you, I gave in to ridiculous fears. I don't expect you to forgive me. Really—"

"Oh, Miss Primm, of course I forgive you." Collette squeezed Augusta's hand in return. "And truth be told, I wouldn't have it any other way." She leaned forward. "Addison and I are expecting. Not until next spring, so we haven't shared the news, but if I don't tell anyone, I think I might burst!"

For reasons she didn't fully understand, Augusta's eyes filled with tears.

"So you are... happy?"

"I am so very, very happy." But then Collette glanced toward the end of the table as though making sure their conversation remained private. "Addison told me you knew Rowan years ago, that the two of you had grown quite attached at one time."

"Yes," Augusta admitted reluctantly.

This sharing of one's emotions might be better embarked upon with very small steps.

"And now, you are here with him alone," Collette added. She then flicked a glance to just below Augusta's neck. "And you, er, missed several buttons on your gown. I wouldn't have mentioned anything, but there's a... love bite peeking through."

A love bite?

From when Rowan...

Augusta's heart stopped, and then she glanced down and did her best to discreetly right her bodice. "I wasn't expecting anyone—" she began. "I never sleep in—and Rowan, er, Mr. Stewart—" But how did one explain away what Collette had so easily identified as a love bite?

Collette's eyes danced with mirth, and Augusta inhaled a sharp gasp, then they both burst out laughing.

When she was finally able to bring herself under control, Augusta leaned forward. "I've never before... Please—"

"It shall remain between the two of us." Collette swept a glance toward her young sister-in-law and Ivy. "But I'm not as certain that your dishevelment escaped the notice of those two."

Panic was Augusta's initial reaction, and then... resignation.

A relieved sort of resignation.

Because although gossip could do a good deal of harm, these days Augusta had far more challenging problems to address.

The school, Rowan... and...

She turned serious. "Will you keep me informed as to Ivy's parents' whereabouts? They can be disorganized at times, but they are good people. And it's not like them to go so long without writing to her."

Collette's eyes clouded. "I will, of course I will."

Just then, Rowan appeared in the doorway, followed by the

duke. Both of them looked far more serious than they had before they'd gone off alone together.

But Rowan also looked… perplexed. As though he couldn't quite work out a puzzle.

"Collette, girls." The duke strolled around the table and placed his hands on the back of his wife's chair. "There's been a change in plans." He turned to speak to his younger sister. "I know you wanted to spend time here before the term starts, but we're going to travel on to London instead."

"But you said—" Fiona began, but the look her brother shot her was enough to silence her protests.

"Certain events are at play, Fi."

"What about Ivy?"

"Of course, Ivy will accompany us. Until her parents return, she stays with us." He then clapped his hands. "Come along now. Thank Miss Primm and let's be moving along."

Obviously confused, but moving swiftly, the small party of guests was back in their carriage and on the road in less than ten minutes.

Augusta sighed from where she stood on her front step. Overwhelmed by what she'd realized about herself, she kept silent as she watched the coach disappear.

Rowan stood just inside, behind her.

And when she finally pivoted, a smile on her face, she found herself looking into agonized, hurt, and even accusing eyes.

"Why didn't you tell me?"

THE TRUTH

"*T*-t-tell you?" But the look in his eyes was too much to bear.

Augusta's heart dropped. *He knows.*

It would have been so much better if he'd learned the truth first from her. Oh, why hadn't she told him before?

He'd noticed. It was the only explanation. He'd seen the two girls sitting together. Even with their different coloring, the similarities in some of their features were uncanny. Augusta grappled for the words to explain even as he unceremoniously pulled her inside and closed the door.

Looking exhausted, he scrubbed a hand down his face. "Don't do this, Augusta. I thought we were past this... keeping secrets."

"We are." Augusta refused to pretend even a second longer. She'd grown accustomed to protecting this secret. It had been hers and hers alone. She'd believed that telling a single soul would bring the world crashing down. Even now...

But he deserved to know—despite her aunt's warning and her father's threats. Not telling him had been below her. She should have trusted him before, and she already regretted not realizing that.

"I didn't tell you because…" She closed her eyes, at a loss for words for one of the first times in her life. Had she been afraid? Ashamed?

"You knowing… won't change anything. It cannot change anything." She summoned the image of Ivy's dear face. "I know how you feel about the circumstances surrounding your own birth… I didn't want to hurt you." Her reasons sounded weak in her own ears as she said them aloud. But that being the case… "It wasn't my secret to share. I made promises…"

He scoffed, pacing down the foyer and then back.

"But I was going to. After… last night. I knew I had to tell you. If we were going to… If anything could come of this, I knew I couldn't keep it from you any longer." Her throat thickened. "I knew I couldn't keep *her* from you any longer."

How had she been so ignorant about so many things?

He finally pinned his stare on her. "I'm not imagining it, then, am I? At first, I thought I must be going insane. But she has your build, my brother's eyes, and her skin is nearly as light as yours, but I saw glimpses of my mother."

He turned and strode along the corridor again, and then, coming to a halt, slammed a fist into the wall. Augusta jumped at the sound, wincing when she saw the crack he left there.

"God damn it, Augusta!" he hissed. "What else haven't you told me?"

She'd never seen him like this. Frustrated, angry, and… filled with despair. She'd never seen him out of control.

He made another pass and this time, she caught at his arm. Seeing blood on his knuckles, she, nonetheless, kept her reprimands to herself.

Now was not the time.

"Come sit down," she all but begged him. "I'll tell you everything. But…" She swallowed around the huge lump suddenly lodged in her throat. "You knowing cannot change anything. You must understand that. Because her well-being comes first. Not yours or mine, but hers." When he refused to budge, she gave a harder tug. "Please, Rowan?"

His eyes somewhat dazed, he nodded and allowed her to lead him into the parlor and over to the settee. He sat, and she lowered herself beside him.

"She's mine," he said, almost as though saying it out loud would help him to believe it. "Since the day I realized I was different, I've cursed my father for siring me, for allowing me to be born a bastard, and all along..."

"But it is not the same." Augusta shook her head. "We'd planned to marry. We were young... And then my father..." But she had not gone to Rowan after. And he'd not come to her.

Even after hearing her whereabouts, he hadn't chosen to come to her. He'd chosen to go on with his life without her.

Until this year.

How many times had she made excuses for their separation? Would his learning about Ivy be the unsurmountable wedge that would ultimately keep them apart forever?

He'd spent years believing she'd betrayed him. It would not take much for him to believe it again.

But she'd done the only thing she could do. She wouldn't change it even if she could.

He stiffened and turned to face her. "You could have come to me. Once you had the school, you could have come to me." His voice was void of emotion.

You never came to me! But instead of going there, she exhaled. "It wasn't that simple." It never was.

So she would explain. She would tell him everything. Augusta would tell him anything he wanted to know, regardless of her pride. Regardless of the contract she'd signed, he would have the truth.

"Please, Rowan. Just listen," she all but begged.

"You have my attention." He stared across the room almost as though she wasn't sitting there beside him.

Augusta inhaled. She would begin... at the beginning.

"My aunt suspected my condition about a month after I arrived at her estate. I attributed my loss of appetite, my tiredness, to... a broken heart. But Aunt Lucy knew. And once it was confirmed, she began making plans right away." Augusta couldn't stop her voice from shaking as she shared the memory she'd kept to herself for nearly two decades. As an adult now, she realized it had been the most vulnerable time of her life.

"My aunt sent for a midwife who, of course, reported to my father. *Everything* was reported to my father. But my aunt understood him. She understood what mattered to him. And my giving birth out of wedlock was the very worst thing I could do. So she convinced me to promise we could keep it a secret. You, as much as anyone, must understand that appearances, above all else, were what mattered to my father. Aunt Lucy promised him that she would keep me out of sight until after the babe was delivered.

"It was Aunt Lucy, of course, who set up the arrangement with the Annesleys. She assured me they were good people. They couldn't have their own child and could provide Ivy with a comfortable life—a normal life. It was all very hush-hush.

"They would never know who birthed her, and I was never to know the name of the people who would be her parents."

Rowan sat quietly, listening, absorbing what she'd had a lifetime to come to terms with.

"She was born December twenty-seventh." A vice squeezed Augusta's chest at the memory. "I never got to hold her. She was whisked away less than ten seconds after they cut the cord. I remember feeling frantic to see her. My aunt later told me I was hysterical. In order to keep me from hurting myself, I was dosed with laudanum. I don't remember much of the weeks that followed. I wasn't myself for at least a fortnight. I wasn't... anyone."

"You never held her?" This seemed to jar him and he jerked his head to meet her gaze.

Augusta dipped her chin, remembering. "My aunt insisted it was for the best. I didn't know her name or where she'd been taken to. She just disappeared." Augusta stared, unseeing, at the floor.

She hadn't cared if she lived or died but the drugs kept her from doing much of anything. Once free of the fog, she'd considered taking her own life. But that would have been the coward's way out. It likely would have pleased her father—and that was the very last thing she wanted to do. "I... I needed to find something to live for again."

"The school."

"Yes." *The school.* "Pouring myself into it... saved me." Augusta cleared her throat. "And then, the most miraculous thing happened."

She forced a wobbly smile, brushing at her eyes. "Seven years later, a very kind couple showed up at the school to enroll their daughter. Even if I hadn't recognized you in her, I would have known. When they completed the paperwork and presented her certificate of birth, my suspicions were confirmed. Ivy Annesley was born on the same date that I gave birth to our daughter. The witness's signature was a name I recognized well. It was the name of the midwife who tended me." Millicent Smith: a name Augusta could never forget.

Rowan still listened. Was he in shock?

"So, you see," Augusta forced herself to go on. "I was given this incredible gift. The gift of watching my daughter, of seeing her almost every day. I've seen her grow from a girl into a lovely young woman, taken part in shaping her character... of..."

"Of loving her," Rowan filled in.

"Yes." Augusta closed her eyes. "My aunt passed away a few years ago, and I never got the chance to ask if she was the one who suggested they send her here. For all I know, it was nothing more than a coincidence. But I could never tell a soul. If questions about Ivy's parentage ever got out, she would be the one to suffer. Yes, my reputation would be tarnished, and the school's. I don't know what the Annesleys would have done if they'd realized who I was. No doubt, they'd send her elsewhere. But most important of all, I needed to protect Ivy. She's lived a normal life. I didn't want to ruin it for her."

He nodded, but his expression was shuttered. Because he'd not had the same opportunity that she had.

He'd missed out.

And Rowan Stewart was not the sort of man who would ever willingly abandon his child.

"I know you feel betrayed, but I..." She pressed her fingertips against her forehead and then dropped them into her lap. "I couldn't tell you."

Please, please, please understand.

But he didn't speak and Augusta's throat thickened with emotion. She'd taken years to recover after losing him before. There would be no recovering this time. She would have loved and lost a second time.

"Please, say something." Her voice came out little more than a whisper.

He dipped his chin, such a subtle movement she wondered if she had imagined it.

And then he lifted his gaze to meet hers. "I—" He shook his head. "I need time."

And then he rose.

Augusta burst off the settee as well, clutching her hands together to keep herself from holding on to him. "You are leaving?"

"I'm not leaving." He exhaled. Of course. What was he feeling? She doubted that even he knew.

He scrubbed a hand down his face. "I need to meet with the men who've been keeping watch. You've had a lifetime to come to terms with this. I just—I need to be somewhere else. I can't..." He stiffened. "I can't be here right now."

He was not leaving, he'd said. Augusta consoled herself with those words.

But then he walked out of the parlor—out of her apartment...

She dropped onto the settee and buried her face in her hands.

Was he also walking out of her life?

THE AFTERMATH

*N*umb, Rowan had little to no awareness that he'd marched away from the school until he was nearly halfway down the road to the village. Where did he think he was going?

He promptly spun around and began marching back, the three-story building that represented Augusta's lifelong dream looming in the distance.

But had the school really been her dream? Or had it merely been a means to an end? An occupation she took because she had no other options. Likely, it had somehow been both.

Augusta's explanation of Miss Annesley—*of Ivy*—made perfect sense. Of course it did. And yet, Rowan struggled to accept it. She'd given birth to his daughter and he'd been kept in the dark for all this time. He wanted to howl at the injustice of it. The last thing in the world he'd ever knowingly allow was for his own child to be born a bastard.

Red rimmed his thoughts. Anger. Panic. Regret. And in the midst of all of it, some glimmer that fought for understanding.

His gaze landed on one of the trees where he'd posted a watchman the day before.

Of all the days she could have told him, he'd had to learn of his daughter's existence on this one.

My daughter.

One of his knees buckled, and he barely caught himself before he went sprawling.

My daughter!

No, not his—not in any of the ways that mattered. He'd not provided for her, nor had he done anything to shape her character. All he'd given her was his blood.

The girl's face came to mind easily. She'd come around with Fiona often enough. He'd looked right through her. Otherwise, he surely would have noticed. Wouldn't he?

By God, he'd barely looked at the girl. Fiona's exuberance and vivaciousness tended to drown out the presence of those around her. But…

He ought to have noticed…

A flock of birds lifted off a tree, taking flight in unison, and Rowan took a moment to study his surroundings.

He had important details to track today. He needed to meet with each of the watchmen he'd put in place, and he damned well shouldn't be walking out in the open like this.

He would talk to Augusta later tonight.

This fury, this betrayal burning up inside him wasn't logical. Because she was right. The well-being of their daughter usurped everything else. And yet…

Rowan jogged until he was hidden by the trees and then made his way to the nearest watch station. Set in the brush, this vantage point provided unobstructed views of everyone who came and went while keeping the guard well out of sight.

Rhys rose from his position when he realized who was approaching.

"Nothing unusual last night?" Rowan asked, crouching down. He was amazed his voice sounded so normal.

Rhys narrowed his eyes. "You look like hell this morning.

Does that have anything to do with your brother showing up out of nowhere?" he observed.

"You could say that." But Rowan didn't expound. He didn't keep much from Rhys, but he wasn't willing to share Augusta's secret with anyone. In fact, she was right. The girl was better off not knowing. She was better off existing behind the secret.

Rowan shook his head. "It's been quiet? Other than Bedwell's coach?"

"Giles fell ill," said Rhys. One of his more trusted workers. "He was assigned the first floor, but a man can't be of much help with his head buried in a chamber pot. I didn't want his post unmanned, so I let Primm's brother take the shift."

"Rosewood?"

"No, the younger one. Lord Noah."

The change in plans nettled Rowan. He hadn't decided he trusted the younger man, but Rhys was right in that they needed every pair of eyes they could get keeping watch.

The young lordling would have to suffice for today. "Does Giles need a doctor?" he asked.

"The doc's not in the area. But Giles insists he must have eaten something bad. Promised he'd be up and about later this evening."

"Good." Rowan glanced around and rose but kept his head low. "We have to end this. That bastard is out there somewhere and we're damned well going to catch him," he muttered.

"I, for one, would like to get back to work on the castle."

"Agreed." But there was more to it. If the plan failed, Augusta couldn't open the school. And if she couldn't reopen the school...

With this morning's revelation in mind, Rowan imagined the circumstances from Augusta's perspective. And suddenly, her fierce determination to keep the school open made even greater sense.

The coming year would be Ivy's last as a student. It very

possibly would be Augusta's last opportunity to take part in their daughter's life.

No wonder she's been so desperate. He'd thought it was the school that mattered to her more than anything else, when it had represented a far greater need—the need to know their child.

He recalled how, in the midst of their frenzy earlier that morning, she'd taken the time to touch the girl's hair, to comfort her. Rowan's chest grew tight. Having Ivy as a student, although a blessing, or a gift as she'd said, could not have been easy.

Rowan forced himself to focus on his surroundings, his mind very much distracted by what he'd initially believed to have been a betrayal.

Augusta had said she kept Ivy's existence from him because she didn't want to *hurt* him. Because those secrets must remain secrets. Miss Annesley had lived a relatively normal life. Upending that wasn't an option.

Definitely not an option.

But Augusta had seemed confused. *Of course she had been confused!*

He needed to talk with her again. She'd done what she believed was best.

He couldn't be thinking about all this now. He needed to be attentive to the school and the grounds surrounding it.

Using the trees for cover as long as possible, Rowan then dashed across to the stables, where his man's report was similar to the one Rhys provided.

Inside the school, he located Lord Noah in the designated spot.

Sleeping.

The lordling required more than one nudge to awaken. "Do you think you'll see anything if you're napping?"

Lord Noah blinked rapidly, adjusting his position. "Just

resting my eyes. Won't happen again." He stretched with a yawn, looking utterly unconcerned.

In that moment, Rowan would have liked to toss the man out on his arse.

But the man was Augusta's brother. "The safety of the school means the world to your sister. I wouldn't think you'd want to let her down."

"Of course I won't." The younger man gingerly rose to take his position. "I only want the best for her."

Partially satisfied that he'd made his point, Rowan stalked about to the other stations as discreetly as possible. And as he did so, Augusta's words worked their way through his thick skull.

He might have been beaten to within an inch of his life, but it was she who had been the victim in all of this. She'd been just a little older than Fiona was now, robbed of her freedom.

By God, she'd been naught more than a child.

Pregnant with a child.

Augusta had not only carried their daughter, but she'd also suffered through childbirth.

And had her torn from her arms.

Women died giving birth. If things had gone wrong, he never would have known. Rowan half-stumbled, because the thought of a world without Augusta Primm was a devastating one.

Thank God she'd delivered the baby safely. She'd had her aunt for support.

While he'd gallivanted around building meaningless monuments.

The realization nearly had him kicking himself. She'd done her best and, by God, she'd succeeded beyond imagination.

What could she have said if she'd come to him? If she'd even been able to find him? She had been running a damn school, for God's sake. Did he expect she'd take weeks off, traveling around the country in search of him?

And what could he have done? *What would I have done?*

With a suddenly urgent need to reassure her—to throw himself at her mercy for everything she'd done and for all that he'd failed to do—Rowan marched around the back of the school where he'd slip in through the kitchen entrance.

First, he was going to kiss her senseless. Then he'd tell her how proud he was of her, and that... he loved her. He'd always loved her.

And last, but not least, he was going to convince her to marry him.

Because he wasn't losing her again.

He unlocked the door, but as he pushed it open, he was met with silence.

Before he could do any of those things, he needed to find her.

LITTLE BROTHERS

*A*ugusta didn't know how long she remained sitting in the parlor in the wake of Rowan's departure. She was either oddly calm or understandably numb.

She accepted that Rowan needed time to himself. He wasn't going to do anything irrational. He was too levelheaded and responsible for that. And he loved her, didn't he?

He hadn't said as much, but... She blinked and rose from the settee. Sitting here and berating herself for not telling him before accomplished nothing.

All she could do was give him time to work these new revelations out. Because he would.

He had to!

Allowing herself a few minutes to repair herself—to ensure her dress was buttoned up properly and that any of those love bites Collette mentioned were hidden—Augusta then went to the one place where she always found peace.

The domicile where the scent of wood, paper, and ink permeated her senses—the one retreat where she would find her balance.

Her office.

Exhaling a trembling sigh, she settled in behind her desk and opened the drawer that contained her files. Focusing, however, was not as easy as usual.

Will he come back? Will he forgive me?

Before she could start on one of her lists, Noah appeared in her doorway. And for once, she welcomed the distraction.

"You look tired today." He waggled his brows, familiar blue eyes twinkling as he took the chair across from her. "Did you stay awake all night with… one of your books?" He winked.

His lack of solemnity came as no surprise. Noah could jest about practically anything. He would tease, but there was no way he'd have any idea as to what truly had kept her from getting much sleep.

"I do love to read…" she answered vaguely, but then narrowed her gaze on him. "What are you doing here? Did Piers send you?" It had been decided the school would remain as empty as possible. "Has something happened?"

"In case you haven't noticed, I'm a grown man, Auggie. I'm not Piers's errand boy." Noah's mouth twisted into a grimace. But then he began fidgeting with the lace on his sleeve. "I have found something that might be of interest, however, and I want you to take a look at it."

"Has something else been damaged?" How would that be possible?

"Not exactly." He didn't meet her eyes. And rather than explain, he rose. "Just come with me and see."

Having accomplished very little, Augusta had no doubt she'd be too distracted to focus on work until Rowan returned —until she could see his face, recognize the affection in his eyes, and know he forgave her.

So, with only a moment of hesitation, she conceded.

"Just tell me, Noah, did you find more damage?" she asked, keeping her voice low as she followed him into the corridor.

"Something like that. Just come."

"This isn't really the time for games, Noah." A shiver ran through her for no reason. "Should we send for Piers?" She wished Rowan were about. Because if new damages had appeared, the plan had already failed.

"No, no, that won't be necessary." Noah persisted in being vague, and Augusta's curiosity grew. He led her to the center of the building, toward the large closet that led to the cellar. Rowan had made good use of it while working on the repairs.

Noah opened the door and indicated she go inside first. "You'll definitely want to see this."

"The cellar?" Augusta's steps stuttered. She hated going down there!

"Afraid?" Because, of course, Noah would have remembered her abhorrence for dark, creepy spaces.

"It's not my favorite place," she admitted, entering regardless. "Are there problems with the joists again?" She craned her neck to meet her brother's eyes and then stilled.

Noah had a strange look on his face. The door to the stairs leading to the foundation was propped open, and just as she went to brace a hand on the frame, he closed the closet door behind them.

"Leave that open, Noah."

She frowned when, rather than doing as she asked, he stepped toward her.

"You really ought to have just come home. I cannot imagine how Father allowed you to keep this ridiculous place open as long as you have."

"What are you talking about?" She turned to face him, her back to the stairwell.

"It's over, Augusta," he said. "We've had enough."

"Who's had enough?" Augusta frowned. "And what, exactly, is over?

What was Noah up to now?

"All of it," he said. But it had to be some sort of joke.

Noah was her sweet, charming, easy-going younger brother, so when he reached out and gave her a hard shove, she did nothing to protect herself.

"Noah!" She reached a hand for him to take, trusting that he would help her.

He stepped back, evading her grasp. This no longer felt like a joke at all; in fact, it felt more like a nightmare. Augusta's hands slid along the door frame in vain, and she could not prevent herself from falling backward.

Her whimper was one of anguished disbelief as she toppled down the stairs, the railing eluding her as she tumbled head over heels. Her palms slid along the wood, stinging, lacking the strength to stop her momentum. Pain shot through her back, her thighs, and then an even sharper stabbing as her arm struck the wall.

She grew disoriented with each glancing blow while half-somersaulting down the steps. This wasn't happening! This could not be happening!

Would she live?

She thought of Rowan. Of his dear, loving eyes. Of his indulgent smiles.

She should have told him everything the first day he'd arrived at the school. She should have listened to him and invited him into her life sooner. They had wasted so much time.

And most of all, she should have told him she loved him.

And then the world turned black.

AFTER THIRTY FRUITLESS minutes looking for Augusta, a pit of dread developed in Rowan's stomach. He'd thought she might have gone walking, but none of the watchmen had seen her outside. Not one had caught even a glimpse of her, despite the entire perimeter having been secured.

Increasingly frantic that he'd already wasted too much precious time, he sent the third-floor watchman to see if she'd somehow slipped past all of them and made the short journey to the dower house at Longbow Castle.

Lady Rosewood was her friend, and she'd relied on her more than once.

Rowan never should have stormed out the way he did. She'd asked him if he was leaving—if he was going to abandon her—and he'd heard the fear in her voice.

All this after the night they'd spent together—a night he'd gladly repeat over and over again.

She'd gradually opened up to him, and then today, when he'd given her no choice, she'd told him everything. Would she have told him eventually?

He'd felt betrayed—blindsided.

He'd felt like she'd lied to him again. But she hadn't lied to him the first time. What the devil had he been thinking?

He wished she could have told him about Ivy sooner, but she had had good reason to remain silent about all of it. And she'd been confused. Who wouldn't have been?

She would be upset. *Of course she would be upset.*

Rowan planted his feet in the shadow of this bloody school and wracked his brain for where she might be. He would know if she'd gone, wouldn't he?

He would find her. He refused to entertain the alternative.

But whereas he'd initially believed his inability to locate her had been due to an unfortunate misunderstanding, his senses now screamed otherwise. She'd not been in her office earlier, the first place where he'd sought her out.

That was where she should be.

But someone had been trying to harm the school—to harm

her. Her disappearing the moment he turned his back was not a coincidence. Imagining otherwise was nothing more than wishful thinking. He inhaled and forced himself to analyze what he knew.

Her office had been unlocked but empty. She never left it unlocked—not since last spring.

Hoping he'd simply missed her at every turn, he jogged up the entrance of the school again and, hearing a sound from the direction of her office, breathed a sigh of relief as he strode toward the door.

Only… it wasn't Augusta.

Her brother, Lord Noah, sat behind her desk, his hand clutching a file and looking almost smug. When he caught sight of Rowan, he reschooled his expression to one of concern.

"Stewart…" Lord Noah quickly slammed the drawer shut.

"What are you doing?" Rowan demanded. This man was Augusta's brother, but no one rifled through Augusta's desk.

Lord Noah reclined in her chair and brushed back an errant lock of hair. "I thought she may have left some clue as to where she'd gone." He flicked a worried glance toward the drawer, and Rowan couldn't help but identify the keys hanging out of the lock as Augusta's personal set.

"Where'd you get those?"

The man's gaze skittered around the room. "Oh, the keys? They were here when I sat down."

Rowan hadn't inspected the desk when he'd come by earlier, but he damn well knew Augusta wouldn't have left them hanging there.

She was a detailed person—and diligent.

"Why would you think to look in her files?" Rowan asked through clenched teeth.

Lord Noah was one wrong word away from being shaken senseless. Rowan didn't have time for games.

He needed to find her, and a nagging inner voice taunted

that the man seated behind her desk knew precisely where she was.

Her brother, not meeting Rowan's stare, tossed one of the files onto the surface of Augusta's desk. "These are the enrollment files, including directions to their homes." And then he pointed to one of Augusta's lists and read aloud, *"Send notice that the autumn term has been canceled until further notice. Perhaps she's gone to post them?"*

The notion, although weak, had a smidge of merit. Rowan had to consider it.

If she'd feared Rowan was going to abandon her, would she abandon their plan and go ahead with delaying the autumn term?

The notion that she was posting those letters was possible, if not probable.

He jerked his chin toward the second half of the task which was written boldly and underlined: *If necessary.* Her plan had been to wait until the end of the week.

But after he'd confronted her over Ivy, had she changed her mind?

Lord Noah's eyes shifted to the door, and then back to stare at Rowan. "Why don't I go into the village and ask around?" He rose, hesitating behind Augusta's desk and looking anxious for the first time. Of course, he was worried about his sister. Rowan would trust the man.

For now.

Because Augusta might have gone into the village. One of the watchmen might have fallen asleep, or simply not been paying attention when she'd walked off of the school grounds.

The sounds of horses racing up the road to the school and then coming to a halt caught his attention. Outside the window, Rosewood had already dismounted his horse, and he wasn't alone. Lord Sexton, Rhys, and a handful of other men accompanied the earl.

Rowan ought to feel a sense of relief that help had arrived, but there was none. He wouldn't feel anything until he'd located Augusta.

Safe and sound.

If anything were to happen to her... He clenched his fists.

"Very well," he addressed Augusta's brother. "But don't waste too much time there. Go to the inn and the mercantile, and if she isn't there, put out word for assistance with a search. And then return here."

"Of course." Rowan didn't wait for the man to be on his way, but rushed to meet the new arrivals on the front steps of the school.

A PRISONER IN HER OWN SCHOOL

The throbbing at the back of her head woke her up. Augusta moaned, and when she tried shifting her position, cold dampness seeped through her gown even as the scent of rank dirt filled her nostrils. She was in the cellar, in the dark, with no way of protecting herself from the cobwebs, spiders, and rodents.

And Noah.

She wished she'd imagined it, and yet she knew she had not. Her own brother had turned against her.

She opened her eyes but was met with darkness. When she tried to call out, all she managed was a muffled grunt. Her chest squeezed tight when she realized a cloth was tied around her mouth. Terrified, she sucked air in through her nostrils. It was ominously familiar.

Don't panic. Don't panic. She did her best to stay calm even as she recalled the last thing she remembered.

How could Noah, of all her family members, do this to her?

"*It's over,*" he had said. He'd pushed her!

The steps were steep, and she had thought she was going to die. She hadn't, of course, but…

She had not died.

Noah wouldn't kill her, would he? Of course not!

And yet, he'd *pushed her* down the stairs, not bothering to care for her injuries.

She wiggled again and stabbing pain shot up her right arm. Otherwise—she moved her hips, legs, and feet—all seemingly functioning and intact.

Her head ached terribly, though, and she'd likely broken her arm.

Her wrists were bound, and it felt as though she'd been tied to one of the foundation supports.

She was inside the school, though. Rowan and his men would be near.

She needed to make some sort of noise. She needed to get someone's attention—someone who was not Noah.

Was he working alone?

He'd told her that *we've* had enough. He meant her family, of course. Did Liam know? Did her mother? So many questions raced through her mind as she realized how dire her circumstances might be. But panicking would only make things worse. She needed to gather information and formulate a plan.

She closed her eyes and tried to recall what the cellar had looked like when she'd last come down with Rowan...

Rowan, who had been upset when he'd left her earlier. But he would come back.

He didn't come after you before... a traitorous voice reminded her.

But this was different. The two of them were smarter now, more mature.

Something wet rolled down her cheek. Not blood—tears.

Crying wasn't going to get her out of here. The trouble was, as she imagined the empty space surrounding her, she didn't know anything else that would, either.

~

"HAVE YOU FOUND HER YET?" Rosewood did, in fact, possess all the necessary concern one would expect of a loving brother.

Rowan shook his head. "I have the watchmen searching everywhere, but no one's seen her since earlier this morning." He scrubbed a hand down his face. "Your brother's going into the village, but I can't imagine she could have made it down the road undetected." And then he turned to Lord Sexton, nodding his chin in a brisk greeting.

"A proper search is in order." Sexton's voice carried the authority of a person who knew precisely what he was doing. "We need to organize the coordinates of where Miss Primm might be into smaller sections. Once that's done, we'll assign two people to search each one. I need paper. We need a base for the teams to report to."

"Her office." Rowan didn't wait for the others to agree. Sexton was correct. Sending searchers out without a plan could waste precious time. Already, his own efforts seemed chaotic and directionless. They'd obviously been ineffective.

In less than seven minutes, the marquess had drawn up a map and assigned teams of two, who were promptly dismissed to conduct very detailed searches of the entire school and her residence, as well as the grounds and the forest in the vicinity.

Even knowing they were doing everything possible to find her, guilt twisted Rowan's gut. This was the one thing he'd promised himself he wouldn't do—leave her alone and vulnerable.

What if she was already miles away? A racing coach could very well be on the way to London or Scotland or Wales, for God's sake.

Sexton, who was now seated behind Primm's desk, met Rowan's eyes.

"Tell me everything that happened leading up to her disappearance," he said.

Even knowing the detective was an expert in this area, Rowan couldn't help but think this was a waste of time.

When Rowan didn't move, the marquess added, "Together we need to go over the facts in case we're missing something." And then, "Trust me, Stewart. You never know which detail is the one that matters."

THE ACCOMPLICE

The sound of the door being unlocked was the first indication Augusta hadn't been left here alone to die. But along with relief, icy fear tiptoed down her spine.

The creaking of the door opening was followed by heavy footsteps, and then lighter ones lagging behind. The glow of a candle confirmed that the heavier footsteps belonged to her brother, but she was shocked at the face illuminated by a second light. Although perhaps she ought not to be.

Miss Agatha Black.

One look at the woman's expression and Augusta knew she hadn't come down here to help. No, in fact, Miss Black looked rather smug.

"Close the door behind you," Noah instructed the gloating teacher. He then turned back to Augusta. "Decided to join the living again, I see. I must admit, thought I'd gone too far there for a few minutes." He winced. Was that because he would mourn her death or because Liam wanted her brought home alive? At this point, Augusta had no idea what to believe.

Having been unconscious, Augusta had no idea how long she'd been down here. But his words brought new tears to her eyes. Noah had suspected she'd been seriously injured and done nothing to help her.

She'd known her family had control issues, but she'd never guessed her brothers would go to such extremes. Apparently, she had underestimated the influence her father had had on those who remained at home.

BUT THE REALIZATION did nothing to help her present circumstances.

He dropped to his haunches, holding the taper toward her face.

Augusta stared back into eyes she'd trusted, she'd loved... a person she would have died for, if necessary. Noah had always been one of her favorites...

"Why?" She managed the muffled syllable around the cloth in her mouth.

"Why? You have to ask why?" Noah looked quite comfortable, balancing on the balls of his feet and dangling one hand between his knees. "You always thought you were so much better than the rest of us—both you and Piers. Even when we were children, you knowingly broke many of Father's rules. He betrothed you to a bloody duke, Auggie, and you threw it back in his face by getting involved with Bedwell's bastard—a Barbadian, no less!"

Augusta suppressed the need to defend Rowan Stewart to Noah or anyone. Rowan was a thousand times the man her brother was. Anyone who failed to realize that was a fool.

As was, she realized, her brother.

She frowned and shifted her shoulders, even though doing so made her head hurt even more.

"Untie me," she mumbled through the coarse fabric. She was the older sister, used to her instructions being followed.

But Noah shook his head. "I'm afraid I can't do that, Auggie.

And I'd rather not have to hurt you again, so don't try anything stupid. It's time you come home and fall in line with the rest of us. You're the daughter of a marquess. You need to start acting like one."

When she'd spoken, the gag had loosened slightly, but she wasn't about to alert either him or Miss Black.

Noah paused at the sounds of footsteps indicative of half an army marching around overhead, and then pointed up. "We need to wait for the school to clear out and then get you into the carriage I have waiting down the road."

Augusta simply stared at her brother. If there was a carriage, Rowan would find it.

If he didn't find her down here first.

Which he will!

But she didn't want Noah to believe either could happen. She wanted him to let down his guard. Overconfidence had always been one of his weaknesses.

"DoesLeemnobodis?" She deliberately muffled the words from behind the cloth. Liam *must* be behind this. She couldn't believe Noah would come up with something so despicable on his own.

More tears stung the backs of her eyes. But Liam too? She'd understood her father's resentment, she'd been born a girl, after all. But when had her brothers turned their hearts against her? All she'd ever wanted was her freedom.

And Rowan. She'd wanted Rowan.

"Does Liam know?" Noah comprehended her muffled question. "It was his idea. Idiot Piers. He might very well be the rightful heir, but he doesn't know anything about running the marquessate. Of course, Liam knows, as does Father."

"And Mother?"

"Not Mother, nor Theodore. But they do as they're told. They know their place." He scowled. "Unlike you and Piers."

"Youdonwannado this?" Augusta wanted to keep Noah talking.

Noah stared at the ground for a moment and then exhaled.

"I adored you when we were younger, remember? You were the one to read to me, to listen to me when everyone else dismissed me as the spare to the spare. God, Auggie, you could do no wrong.

"Right up until we went to London for your season. And then one day, while hiding under the table in your chamber, what do I hear you telling your maid? That you were going to run away with Mr. *Rowan Stewart*—that you were going to betray our family—make fools of us by jilting the Duke of Malum. You were going to sneak away—not even bother saying goodbye. This is no one's fault but your own, Auggie. You betrayed us first."

This particular information came as a surprise to Augusta. All this time, she'd thought it was Martha who'd told her parents. And it had been... Noah?

"You were lucky Father allowed you to run this farce of a school for as long as you did—poisoning the minds of innocent young women—teaching subjects unfit for proper ladies. Likely, Father was already losing his faculties." He laughed. "Did you really think we didn't know everything?" He grinned at how clever they all had been. "Mr. and Mrs. Driver, I'll have you know, have proven inordinately helpful. You'd be surprised what people will do for a handful of extra coin."

Augusta shot her gaze to Miss Black, and Noah grinned. "We got lucky when you finally got rid of those teachers you hired. Gave us the perfect opportunity to supply the agency with more suitable teachers."

"Except for Pepperspring," Miss Black inserted, rolling her eyes. "That woman has no business being a teacher."

"Well, three out of four was good enough." Noah seemed

inordinately satisfied with himself. "Regardless, you won't be needing them now."

"Whynot?" Augusta wasn't sure she wanted to hear the answer to this question. But all her troubles were beginning to make sense. Although some had been coincidental, many had likely been orchestrated by the long arm of her family.

"Because the running of the school will no longer be your concern." Noah pushed to his feet and stretched. "But enough for now. Miss Black here is going to keep you company so you don't do anything stupid."

Augusta had no doubt that Noah was going to go upstairs and do his level best to convince them she'd left willingly—but no one would believe him. Everyone in the entire village knew the level of her dedication.

Those thoughts, however, diminished in significance when her brother handed a small pistol into Agatha Black's eager hands.

"Don't try anything, Augusta. Remember, we know everything. Even your little romp with Bedwell's bastard last night—something Liam will not be pleased to hear about."

But Augusta no longer cared about that. She was a grown woman. She'd not apologize for her personal affairs. And she wasn't giving up—not this time.

Where are you, Rowan?

Noah continued. "You're finally going to realize that you aren't in control—that you never were in the first place."

And then, brushing dirt off his pants, Augusta's sweet younger brother pushed to his full height and climbed the stairs, leaving her alone with this cold-tempered woman.

Rowan would see through him. Rowan would figure this out.

He has to.

THOSE DETAILS

*R*owan rubbed the back of his neck and then paced the length of the room again. He and Sexton had rehashed the attacks on the school, from the first damages to the foundation, to the fire, and the rock that had been thrown through the window, as well as everything that could possibly be considered suspicious in between.

He'd finished by explaining his brother's visit earlier that morning, and although he'd mentioned that he and Augusta had had a disagreement, he'd kept the events of the previous night to himself, along with Augusta's secret.

After going over the most insignificant of details provided by the watchmen and coming up with nothing, Sexton began opening Augusta's desk drawers.

Which reminded Rowan.

"I caught Lord Noah going through those earlier." Something bothered him, though. Noah had withdrawn the student lists but still been interested in the drawer's contents.

Rowan strode behind the desk, crouched down, and reopened the one her brother had been interested in. Lord Noah had kept his hand on one of them. An older one. Rowan ran his fingertips along the files and then recognized it immediately.

She hadn't labeled it, which was highly unlike Augusta, and once he opened it, he realized why.

The papers inside were stained by age. It was the title to the school, along with a receipt showing it had been paid in full.

"Noah Primm was interested in the title to the school," Rowan said, his mind racing. What the devil would he want with her school?

Unless that had been the purpose all along—for Augusta's family to relieve her of the one thing that mattered to her—the one thing that allowed her to be free of them.

"They want Lady Augusta back home where she can't embarrass them any longer," Sexton said. Obviously, the man had paid attention while visiting Starbridge Abbey. "Where's the blighter now?"

Rowan burst to his feet. "I sent him into the village to look for her earlier. He should be back by now."

"When was this?" The marquess frowned.

"At the precise time you and Rosewood arrived. I didn't see him actually ride away." Was it possible he'd gone on foot?

"But the roads are being watched," Sexton announced. "I'll send one of the men into the village."

Rowan was shaking his head. *What was he missing?*

Throughout this meeting, Rowan had felt half-compelled to take to the road in search of Augusta. He'd felt certain she'd been taken by her family, but this time to Starbridge Abbey. But that had not been possible. Somebody would have seen something! He would have known.

He rubbed his chin and then peered down at the sketch of the school with the search areas marked off across the desk.

It wasn't quite right.

So far, no one had found anything helpful—not in the kitchens, her residence, any of the classrooms, or the stables.

They hadn't heard back yet from the teams searching the woods.

"I need to think," he muttered.

Rowan couldn't spend another minute doing what felt like nothing in this office. He excused himself and exited to the foyer where he could move around.

And as he passed one of the classrooms, the answer suddenly became obvious.

When the vandal had first gone to work, he'd hidden out and done his damage *underneath* the school.

The blueprints they'd been looking at hadn't included the cellar!

Rowan didn't wait but sprinted toward the closet that hid the door to the space beneath the first floor. She *had* to be there. It was the only thing that made sense.

Standing at the threshold, however, Rowan paused. If this was where they were keeping her, he needed to catch them by surprise. Which meant he couldn't be accompanied by a thundering mob.

Furthermore, time was running out.

Rowan clenched his fists.

Exhaling a slow breath, he didn't make a sound as he very slowly opened the door and left it wide open behind him.

The glow of candlelight flickering from below proved he must be right. He briefly considered alerting Sexton before discarding the idea. Augusta was so close, he couldn't stand the thought of leaving her vulnerable and alone for another second, not if he could help it.

He eased onto each step one at a time, hoping none of them would creak under his weight.

But when he was nearly halfway down, he froze, and then his blood turned to ice. It was obvious Augusta was injured.

Dried blood caked one side of her dear face. She was bound and gagged, tied to one of the supports, looking far too broken where she sat on the ground. Rowan only allowed himself a moment to drink in the sight of the only woman he'd ever loved because she was not alone. One of the newly hired teachers, Miss Agatha Black, was sitting on a chair not six feet from where Augusta slumped.

Pointing a double-barrel Flintlock directly at Augusta's head.

Such a weapon was heavier than the smaller pistols a woman might favor. His heart skipped a beat as he watched the barrel waver. The teacher's hand was shaking, and her finger slipped ominously along the trigger.

He took another step, but this time, the old wood betrayed him, giving his presence away.

Miss Black snapped around, but aside from the narrowing of her eyes, she didn't look all that surprised. Apparently, Augusta had hired a cold-hearted bitch. When this was over, he was going to have to take her to task for this.

"Careful, now," Rowan said, keeping his voice deceptively calm as he gestured toward the weapon. "Those things have a tendency to backfire."

"Stay back," the woman ordered. "Or our dear Miss Primm gets a bullet between the eyes."

"Lord Noah hired you, I presume." Rowan allowed a deceptive smile to creep across his mouth. "Fancy yourself something of a double agent, eh?" He oh, so slowly lowered himself to the next step.

"I suggest you stop where you are, Mr. Stewart. Lord Noah will be returning shortly, and he'll have you taken into custody. Miss Primm only *thinks* this school belongs to her, but the rightful owner is Lord Starbridge."

"The marquess?" Rowan asked. "Why would you be interested in helping the likes of him? Do you think he'll protect you from hanging from the gallows? Once you've served your purpose, he'll abandon you without a second thought. You're nothing to him."

"I may be nothing to him." Miss Black smirked. "But he cares even less about this school. All that matters to the nobs are their reputations—something dear Miss Primm here has dragged through the mud long enough."

"You think aristocrats don't care about money?" Rowan made a scoffing sound. "Because, trust me, this school is worth a good deal."

"Which makes my efforts worth the risk. In return for my help, Lord Noah has promised to hand the deed over to *me—to me!*"

Rowan had managed to progress down two more steps. "And he might if it actually belonged to him."

"What could you possibly know?" Miss Black's confidence was yet to waver. "Lord Noah is the son of a marquess and you are nothing but a bastard. He's sickened that his sister would lie with the likes of you, but that's over now. Her time ignoring her duty to her family is over. They've had enough. And there is nothing anyone can do to stop them. They are nobility."

"But you have been lied to." Rowan kept his gaze locked on the woman holding Augusta's life in her hand. He couldn't afford to take his eyes off her. "Marquess or not, he cannot give you something he doesn't own."

A few more steps and he could use his own body to protect Augusta if necessary.

Poor, dear Augusta, who'd been sitting on the damp ground for most of the day.

"You're wrong!" Miss Black spat, but doubt had entered her eyes. "Lord Noah has told me everything—Miss Primm only *thinks* the school is hers. In truth, it belongs to her father. And as soon as he returns her to Starbridge Abbey, where a lady like her belongs, he's going to sign ownership over to me."

"Fairy tales," Rowan said.

Agatha Black shook her head. "It will be mine. And then it can be run properly—teaching these impressionable females how to be suitable wives. Science? Math?" She chortled. "The subjects Miss Primm has in place here have done nothing but taint perfectly proper young ladies with ridiculous ideas."

Rowan flicked his glance to Augusta, whose gaze flicked downward. "Peezetakedisoff," Augusta begged in a muffled voice.

Keeping his attention on Miss Black, Rowan held both hands up, trying to appear as unthreatening as possible.

"Miss Primm can explain better than I." He stepped onto the ground. "I'm going to remove the cloth from her mouth and perhaps," Rowan all but cooed, "She has something even better to offer."

"She has nothing to offer." Miss Black narrowed her gaze, but she didn't demand that he halt his progress. The pistol wavered slightly away from Augusta—in Rowan's direction.

Holding his palms out, Rowan crept slowly toward where Augusta sat.

Augusta's gaze shot between Miss Black and back to him.

"Just hear her out," he said. "She is not an unreasonable woman."

He crouched down and loosened the cloth. Augusta gasped and then twisted her head, sending him a terrified stare.

Rowan kept his breath even as his fingertips discreetly stroked along her jaw. Sweet, plump lips he'd kissed that morning were now cracked and dry. The skin on her cheeks and jaw had been rubbed raw. Rowan dismissed any relief he felt to be touching her.

Because she wasn't safe yet.

When he spoke, he addressed the newly-hired teacher rather than this precious woman before him.

"Miss Primm understands the duplicity her father is capable

of better than anyone." Rowan glanced toward the top of the stairs. "And her brothers as well."

"Miss Black…" Augusta's voice came out hoarse-sounding. "May I call you Agatha?"

With suspicious eyes, Miss Black stared daggers at Augusta. But then she dipped her chin.

"My father doesn't hold the deed. I have it. And my solicitor has a copy in his custody as well. So, you see—"

"Why should I trust you? I've heard about how you fired all those teachers that came before us. I imagine they trusted you once as well." She pointed the pistol directly at Augusta once again.

"But we are just women, and we need to stick together, you and I."

"We're nothing alike!" Miss Black argued. "I'm the daughter of a tradesman, and your father is a marquess! While I've had to scrap and save to achieve my place in life, you walked away from yours. You had a life the rest of us only ever dream of, and you squandered it for this mockery of a school. You are nothing more than an ungrateful fool, Miss Primm." She said Augusta's name as though it were sour in her mouth.

Augusta's eyes were wide as Miss Black rambled on.

"Miss Primm's Private Seminary for the Education of Ladies! What a joke that is. When I get my hands on it, it shall be a finishing school. Lord Noah will return you to your family home where, once and for all, you will cease to be an embarrassment to them—to all of England, for that matter."

Augusta licked her lips but before she could speak again, another voice floated down from the steps. "You ought to listen to her, Auggie."

Lord Noah was in possession of an identical gun—likely the second half of a fine set. Rowan met the man's gaze and braced himself.

He should have brought reinforcements after all.

But Lord Noah had to realize that the ranks upstairs were about to close around him.

"I'm not an embarrassment!" Augusta, most unfortunately, chose that moment to demand her brother's attention. "And you can't keep me locked up. This isn't the Middle Ages, you know."

She'd caused her brother to turn his pistol from Rowan to herself. Two pistols now, that might as well be directed at Rowan's own heart.

"In that case, perhaps I should do what Father should have done the first time you disobeyed him," Lord Noah said.

He then stretched his arm toward his sister, finger ready on the trigger.

But as he began squeezing it, Rowan lurched forward.

A loud explosion echoed off the walls, followed by pain shooting through his thigh.

Pain meant that the bullet had missed Augusta.

A second shot, sent off by Miss Black, whizzed by Rowan's ear and presumably wedged itself into the wall.

Thank God. For once he'd succeeded at protecting her. But it wasn't over yet.

Rowan watched as Lord Noah stared at his own hand. The gun's action had caught the man right between his thumb and fingers and the oozing blood seemed to have paralyzed him. The sound of gunshots would have alerted Sexton. Rowan only hoped help arrived before it was too late.

But until then, Rowan would buy a few more seconds.

"Hurts when your plans backfire, doesn't it?" he asked, ignoring the weakness entering his own body. "I hope they don't have to amputate. Infection, you know."

Lord Noah's eyes widened as he studied the insignificant wound.

Swaying, Rowan reached his hand out to the support to keep from falling as he considered his own condition.

Bright crimson would be seeping onto his trousers. As more blood escaped his body, the color would darken to a deep scarlet—practically black.

Footsteps thundered overhead, and Rowan heard the door opening upstairs. They were too late for him, but that didn't matter.

A torrent of footsteps rumbled down the steps, and after a brief scuffle, two more gunshots sounded.

"Rowan!" Augusta's voice caught just as Rowan turned to reassure her. Bloodied and bruised, Augusta Primm was the most beautiful sight in the world. *My love.*

Time ceased to exist as he held her gaze. Gray eyes, overcome with emotion, stared back at him. A single tear escaped and rolled down her cheek.

"Don't cry," he said.

"I'm so sorry. For everything. I'm so sorry."

"I know. And you did what was best."

Another tear escaped. "I never meant—"

"I know. I know, love. You did everything right." Rowan would be sure she knew. "And I'm so damn proud of you."

Her response was a choked sob. And then she flicked her stare to his leg. "You're hurt!"

He should have untied her. Why hadn't he untied her? His brain felt fuzzy and his eyelids suddenly heavy.

"I'm fine," he said.

But he wasn't. He'd been shot. He moved to take a step but his leg refused to hold his weight, and he dropped onto the ground beside her. But he was relieved. For the first time in his life, he'd protected the person he loved.

All he'd regret was that he would be denied a life of loving her.

Within a matter of seconds, dozens of candles illuminated the dark cellar while Sexton, Rosewood, Rhys, and a handful of other familiar faces arrived. Rhys addressed Rowan's leg, and Rosewood went about freeing Augusta.

"It was Noah, damn it," the earl cursed. "My fault... should have seen this coming..."

ROWAN'S HEAD rested in Augusta's lap.

He was soaked in blood now, and his leg had gone oddly numb, but all Rowan cared about was the woman cradling him.

"I love you." Her mouth formed the words he'd ached for but he couldn't hear them over the booming sound of his own heartbeat.

"Love you," he managed, wishing he could catch the tears rolling down her cheeks. "Forever."

She nodded. "Always, I've loved you forever."

His old friend cinched a belt around the wound and that blessed numbness fled, replaced with burning pain.

But it was only pain. And because of it, Augusta was alive.

"You're not going to die on me, do you hear that, Rowan Stewart?" she cried as she bent over him, pressing kisses along his face, in his hair. "We've waited too long for you to die on me now, do you hear me?"

Rowan reached up and touched her cheek. Each breath was a struggle, but he forced himself to speak. "You were worth it, Augusta. You were worth every second."

Chaos ensued around them, and Rowan tugged her face down to his mouth.

"Every damn second." Was this his goodbye to her?

He couldn't know for sure. And then she slipped away as darkness engulfed him.

WAITING

"*L*et go, Auggie." Piers all but pried Augusta off of Rowan, who'd gone still, lifeless.

She feared she'd never hold him again.

"He's just passed out." Piers did his best to reassure her, but Augusta was terrified.

She'd just found him again. Was this to be the end?

Rowan had been shot. He'd thrown himself in front of her.

She focused on Piers's voice. It was all she had.

"Mr. Rhys has stopped the bleeding. Let go now, Auggie. They're going to take him to your spare bedchamber so the bullet can be removed."

Of course. Piers was right.

But letting go, and then watching as three men carried Rowan away from her, she'd never felt more helpless in her entire life. "I should boil some water," she said. "I have a medical supply box…" But her limbs were weak from being tied up and her legs nearly gave out beneath her. She would have fallen if not for her brother's support.

"Let's get you out of this damned cellar. You're injured as

well—and freezing. What good will you be to him if you fall ill?"

Augusta vaguely realized that Piers was right, especially when she had no choice but to depend on him to help her climb out of her prison. She ignored the pain in her arm and forced all her energy on moving one foot and then the other. And as she climbed out of the darkness, she vowed that if she never went down to the cellar again, that would be too soon.

"Where is he?" Augusta's voice trembled. *He cannot die!*

"He's being cared for now. Mr. Rhys seems quite proficient," Beatrice answered, placing an arm around Augusta's waist while Victoria took over for Piers. "Oh, your head's bleeding."

It didn't matter. Augusta spent every ounce of her spirit willing Rowan to live.

To heal.

She could not lose him now!

She wanted to see his dear face—to hold his hand. "Then I'll go to him," Augusta murmured.

"And you will." Victoria practically shoved Augusta into her chamber. "But first, let's get you changed."

Augusta dropped her gaze to her gown, one of her prettier ones, actually, which was now soaked through with Rowan's blood.

"He has to live…"

"And he will, Primm." Victoria's voice sounded as though she spoke from far away. "We'll take you in there as soon as he's out of danger."

Exhaustion struck and Augusta nodded.

She couldn't speak. She couldn't cry.

She ought to ask about Noah… and Miss Black, both of whom had also been shot when her rescuers had arrived, but she couldn't bring herself to care. Her gaze landed on the large bed she'd shared with Rowan the night before. Had that only been last night? Was one of the best nights of her life to be followed immediately by the worst?

Having accompanied Augusta to her chamber, Victoria dabbed at the gash on her head while Beatrice paced the room. "Good heavens, but this is deep, Primm. No wonder you've so much blood on you."

"It isn't mine," Augusta said. She didn't even flinch.

Rowan couldn't die! He could not! Augusta was whole and well. All because Rowan had thrown himself in front of her.

She would know if his soul left the earth. For years, she'd lived a life apart from him, able to go on knowing he was somewhere, working, eating, sleeping—knowing he was somewhere in the world, building magnificent structures, existing under the same sky, staring at the same stars.

I would feel the absence of his spirit!

Victoria went to assist Augusta out of her gown but froze instead. "You hurt your wrist. Oh, Primm. You should have said something."

Augusta glanced down. It was swollen and bruised.

She'd forgotten. "I landed on it when I fell down the stairs…" When she'd been pushed. By her own brother. "Noah…" She blinked. How could he? Would it ever seem real to her?

And he'd said Liam had known. Had they really paid off the Drivers?

"She's in shock," Beatrice announced. "Who wouldn't be?"

"To think that it was her own family!" Victoria spoke in hushed tones.

Although it didn't matter who knew. Such a scandal was sure to get out eventually. And that didn't matter either.

All that mattered was Rowan. Augusta turned her head toward the door. "Will you check on him? Please? I need to know."

"On Lord Noah?"

"On Rowan—Mr. Stewart."

"I'm sure we would have heard if…" Beatrice began but then shook her head. "I'll go now. I'm sure he's going to be just fine, but give me a moment. I'll return shortly." And then she rushed out the door, seeming to understand Augusta's fear.

Augusta had also heard someone mention chasing down the Duke of Bedwell's coach. Because he was next of kin…

Dear God… Rowan could not die. He absolutely could not die!

Victoria was handling Augusta tenderly, sliding off her gown and gently lowering a night rail over her head, when Beatrice returned.

"The doctor isn't here yet, but Mr. Stewart is awake," she announced. "I believe they are getting him drunk…"

"That would be to take away the pain," Victoria explained.

In the absence of Dr. McBride, who, as was often the case, was off visiting patients in another village, Piers and Rowan's foreman, Mr. Rhys, tended to the bullet wound. They lacked formal training but were likely more familiar with this sort of injury than the country doctor would be anyhow.

Victoria pressed the linen to Augusta's head.

"Piers knows what he's doing," she said. "He told me he removed bullets from two of his colleagues while traveling on the Continent. And remember, he showed me how to clean and sew a wound? Your Mr. Stewart is in excellent hands."

Augusta wanted to be comforted by her sister-in-law's words, but she wasn't fool enough not to realize that the worst could come later—if infection set in.

"He is *your* Mr. Stewart, is he not?" Beatrice asked gently while coaxing Augusta across the room. "Come sit so I can brush these knots out of your hair."

Victoria hovered. "How dare Lord Noah leave you down there all alone? I'd shoot the bastard myself if Mr. Rhys hadn't."

"It was not Piers who shot Noah, then." Augusta felt an odd

sort of relief to learn this detail. Because, for all his evil deeds, Noah was their brother. "I'm glad. Even though Noah…" Augusta didn't know how to describe what her younger brother had done. "Piers would have hated himself."

"Piers shot Miss Black. Neither had a choice, it seemed," Victoria offered.

"Sexton says their injuries are minor. And that both of their testimonies match up with all the other evidence." Beatrice began brushing the ends of Augusta's hair. "They've been taken upstairs to the teachers' quarters, and will be tended to once the doctor arrives."

"Lord Sexton is here?" Augusta belatedly realized that Beatrice had returned as well. "You're back from London!"

Beatrice met Augusta's gaze in the mirror. "Oh, yes! We arrived late last night! Sexton won his vote, and…" Beatrice blushed. "We've married!"

"But… the engagement wasn't supposed to be real…"

A loud wailing groan interrupted the momentary distraction.

Rowan. In pain. But if he was in pain, at least he was alive.

"I need to go to him." Augusta tried to rise, but Victoria pressed down on her shoulder.

"You'll only get in the way. He won't want you to see him like this."

Beatrice nodded. "Lord Rosewood must be removing the bullet now. Once it's out, he'll clean the wound and stitch it up. After that…"

"We can only wait," Augusta finished for her.

"And you need stitches as well." Victoria turned rather stern. "Your arm could very well be broken, and the cut on your head is still bleeding!" She clucked her tongue. "If that Dr. McBride isn't back by then, Piers will take care of you."

In an odd shift of roles, Augusta did as Victoria ordered. And oddly enough, she didn't mind.

Beatrice pulled a stool from across the room to sit beside her. "Mr. Stewart is the one, is he not? The one you loved?"

Augusta's initial reaction was to deny it. But she was tired of hiding. She was tired of pretending and working constantly to maintain everything around her. A person could do everything right and have all their efforts still be for naught.

And whereas she'd imagined running the school successfully was her dream, she realized dreams could change.

She had changed.

"Yes. He is the one," she answered. And she felt a giant sense of relief to admit it.

But she was tired. So very tired.

"Then he simply must get better," Beatrice said. "He'll be up and about in no time at all."

"Because he can't..." Augusta gulped. "He can't..."

"He won't." Both Victoria and Beatrice spoke in unison.

A few minutes later, Dr. McBride finally arrived. He was ushered in and promptly announced that, although Augusta's arm was sprained, it was not broken. He closed the cut on her head with a few stitches and promised that it, too, would heal.

He ordered rest.

But when he suggested laudanum, Augusta adamantly refused. She would only lie down for a short while, and as soon as he was able, she would go to Rowan's side.

Because that, she realized, was precisely where she belonged.

THE TALK

*R*owan's initial awareness was of pain—pain reminiscent of the days spent convalescing following the beating he'd taken years before.

But it was different. He was not alone.

Augusta was there with him—cooling his brow and crooning words of encouragement. Her comforting words had him initially wondering if he had indeed been killed by the gunshot.

"Drink this for me, love," she whispered in his ear. "My poor, dear sweetheart." Warm lips pressed against his forehead, followed by a cool cloth. On the edge of consciousness, he felt her small hand in his.

There were other moments, times when he was burning up, when she sounded stern—far more the Miss Primm he'd come to know over the past year. "You have to get well, Rowan. I refuse to lose you again." She'd practically poured spoonfuls of liquid down his throat, giving him no choice but to swallow bitter tonics...

But she was always there. Even in his restless sleep, her

presence wound itself around him. And knowing he wasn't alone meant everything.

It provided him with constant hope. It strengthened his will.

Day and night blended into one another, a series of episodes that consisted of unbearable heat followed by violent chills wracking his body.

She remained by his side. And with her there, giving up was not a choice.

He had something to fight for.

But it was exhausting. And he knew great relief when calm finally swept through him. The calm that follows hours of endless agony, resulting in healing sleep—a sleep so deep that when he awoke, it was as though he was returning to earth.

Opening his eyes, he only vaguely recognized the room. He was in Augusta's house, and slumped asleep in the chair beside him was Augusta herself.

Half her hair had escaped what must once have been a tight chignon, her spectacles rested on the table beside her, and her gown was wrinkled and gathered around her knees, exposing smooth calves and rather delicate ankles.

She'd never looked more beautiful to him.

He reached out a hand, just enough to touch her arm, and she immediately stiffened and turned. "Rowan!" She pressed a hand to his face. "It's gone. Your fever. Thank God!"

And then she did something he'd never seen her do before.

Augusta Primm burst into tears. Not the delicate kind one could hide, but violent, shaking sobs.

Raising her hands to her cheeks, she leaned forward and buried her face in the sheets covering his chest.

"I thought—I thought—"

"Shh…" Rowan placed a heavy hand on her head, stroking her hair even as the events leading to his injury came back to him. He'd thought he'd lost her. And then he'd been shot. The wound, he realized, must have putrefied. That would explain the hallucinations—the burning and subsequent chills. He had not dreamed that she'd been here with him.

"I'm fine, love. I'm not going anywhere." His voice sounded scratchy and dry. After a few minutes, her sobs came farther and farther apart. Even after she was all cried out, however, she rested there, not even trying to hide the sniffles that followed.

"You're all done in," he soothed. He hated that he'd scared her. God, he'd been terrified when he'd imagined he'd lost her.

"I was so worried." The sheets muffled her voice.

"I know." But he hadn't met his end after all. "I felt the same." His mouth went dry, remembering how he'd felt when he'd seen a gun pointed at her. "My poor Augusta."

When she tried sitting up, Rowan wasn't prepared to let go. Unfortunately, in his weakened state, he was no match for her.

"What would I have done without you?" he asked. Not only in the dark hours of his fever, but for all time... He didn't want a future that didn't include her.

She clasped his hands in hers. "You'll never know. Not if I have anything to say about it."

He had not imagined her words of love.

"I love you, Augusta," he said. Fatigue already washed over him again. But he would have his say. "I always have—always will. Are you going to marry me? Or must I spend another year schooling you?"

"*Schooling me?*"

"Convincing you," he amended.

She squeezed his hands. "Of course I'll marry you, you foolish, foolish man."

"I'll build you a manor fit for a queen. There's a piece of land I've been looking at just north of here, or I could build our home on school grounds. Whatever you want—"

She touched a fingertip to his lips. And then pressed a

gentle kiss there. "We don't need to figure this out now. You're out of the woods, thank God, but you mustn't overdo it."

Rowan closed his eyes, but nothing could erase his smile. "Augusta Primm is going to marry me."

"Augusta Primm is going to marry Rowan Stewart." She laughed. "And nothing in the world will keep me from doing so this time."

Rowan exhaled. "And you love me…?"

"With all my heart." She kissed him again. "But I need you to rest now, love. I need you healthy and whole."

She'd moved to sit on the edge of the bed and snuggled up beside him. Rowan sighed when he felt her hand cover his heart.

She would rest beside him. He exhaled and covered her hand with his.

Finally, she was where she belonged.

Finally.

IF THE DECISION had been up to Rowan, he'd have insisted on getting out of bed the following day, but Augusta was the most stubborn woman he'd ever known and, for the first time, he became acquainted with the iron will with which she'd ruled the school.

But he was not complaining. And truth be told, the bullet wound was going to take more than a few days to heal. So, with no choice but to recover, for the most part, he sat back and allowed her to coddle him.

With help from Jenny, her housekeeper, Augusta waited on him hand and foot, insisting he drink and eat and rest, and when she sensed he was tiring from any of the plentiful visitors who came about, she shooed them away without so much as an apology.

She wasn't cowed by any of them, not even Addison, who, along with his entourage, had been tracked down and were staying at the inn.

Another frequent visitor was Lord Sexton, and Rowan was happy to provide necessary details required to tighten up the case. Rather than turn Lord Noah and Miss Black over to the local magistrate, Sexton, as the Director of the Society for the Advancement of Ingenuity, could try the case in a special court. The ability to press charges against the aristocracy was part of why the marquess had fought so hard for his position.

Which put Lords Liam and Noah in a small cell in Newgate Prison while they awaited trial. It was doubtful they'd be hanged, but Lord Sexton had assured both Augusta and Lord Rosewood that they'd not be allowed the typical leniency granted to members of the aristocracy.

They would pay for their crimes.

Miss Black, for her part, faced a lifetime in prison, but Augusta had written a letter asking to spare the woman's life. Despite the former teacher's duplicity, Augusta felt sorry for her.

But once all that was settled, and with no additional details to keep his mind busy, Rowan quickly grew bored enduring forced bedrest. Knowing his own body, he finally put his foot down, literally and figuratively.

It was time he got moving again.

With the use of a cane smuggled in by Addison, Rowan took to wandering about the chamber at first, washing up and dressing himself.

With those tasks mastered, he ventured out and around Augusta's small residence, making his way to the parlor. The day after that, he trekked all the way to her office.

He wasn't at all surprised when, catching sight of him, she frowned.

But although she reprimanded him vehemently, she jumped up, crossed to his side, and wound her arms around his neck.

"You're in big trouble, Mr. Stewart," she said, but then she pressed her lips to his.

"I was missing you," Rowan admitted. "And I've missed making myself useful." With one arm draped around her shoulders and the other hand on the handle of his cane, he hobbled over to sit down.

Because although he was well on the mend, the fatigue from his long walk was very real and *very maddening.*

Dash and damn.

With concern on her brow, but not as much as usual, Augusta assured herself that he was comfortable and then returned to her desk to face him. "You don't need to be useful all the time, Rowan." She leaned forward, and without consciously doing so, the two of them were holding hands across her desk.

"I don't?" He cocked a brow. Rowan had spent more time in her company over the past week than he had in a lifetime, and he hated that he wasn't at his best. Physical weakness wasn't something he endured easily.

Her expression warmed, however, and holding his gaze, she shook her head. "I just need you to be… you." Her cheeks flushed. "As long as you are mine."

Ignoring the dull throbbing in his thigh, Rowan pushed up, leaned across the desk, and claimed her mouth with his, drawing the kiss out longer than he'd intended until she touched the side of his face.

"Your leg is aching, isn't it?" she murmured.

It was throbbing. "Some," he admitted, but so was his cock. Torn, he half-groaned. He was willing to endure a little pain to make love to her again, but knowing this woman, she'd require a good deal of convincing that he was fully recovered.

Augusta released his hands so he could sit back in the chair and then relaxed into her own. Her flushed cheeks and shining eyes showed she ached for him as well.

But Rowan had searched her out for a reason. "I'm tired of sleeping alone," he said. "One advantage to having a duke for a brother..." Rowan reached into his jacket. "Is the ease with which he can obtain a special license."

Augusta's mouth fell open. Rowan rose and moved around her desk, contemplating how he would get back up after dropping onto—

"Don't you dare drop down on one knee." She turned to face him. "Or I might have to rethink my answer."

"Too late," Rowan growled as his knee hit the floor.

She stared down at him, shaking her head but with a dazzling smile. "When? When can I become your wife?"

"Today? Tomorrow if we can't pin down the rector? Unless you want an elaborate celebration—"

"Tomorrow."

"You won't mind sharing your chamber with a husband? Until he can build you a proper house?"

"I don't mind sharing at all. In fact, I insist upon it." But then she frowned. "But what of you? Will you mind sharing your wife with a school full of girls?

"Only if you'll share your burdens. You don't have to manage all of it alone." And as his wife, she'd never have to worry over finances again. Of course, she'd refuse his money at first, but he'd... convince her.

Rowan forced himself off the floor, trying not to groan. Perhaps that hadn't been his best idea.

But when he took her in his arms, he decided otherwise.

Augusta sighed. "That sounds... absolutely perfect."

"You will always be their Miss Primm. But when you aren't Miss Primm, you'll be mine."

"I'll be Mrs. Stewart."

"I like the sound of that," he said.

Augusta buried her face in his neck. "So do I, my love, so do I."

EPILOGUE

*D*espite all the troubles that had besieged the school, the term had been a success.

It had been delayed, true, but with help from Collette, Beatrice, and Victoria, as well as a good deal of understanding from their respective husbands, not a single class had been canceled and Augusta had felt satisfied that each student had been presented with powerful opportunities to learn and grow.

But most importantly, the staff and students had been safe. The campaign launched by her brother Liam had failed. The culprits had been caught and punished.

Except for the Marquess of Starbridge, who had been been deemed unfit to face charges. Physically, he was fit for a man his age; mentally, he existed in a world of his own making.

Piers and Augusta had decided against having him sent to Bedlam, and instead hired all new staff to work at Starbridge Abbey. Round-the-clock guards were charged with keeping the old marquess in check—guards who reported to the rightful heir, rather than the raving madman.

And keeping to his original decision, Piers refused to consider moving back to Starbridge Abbey. Just before Christmas, he'd moved their mother and younger brother, both of who'd been horrified to learn what had transpired, to live with him in the dower house at Longbow Castle.

Without having to deal with protecting the school, Rowan and his team had accomplished an unprecedented amount of work over the autumn months. Victoria and Piers were excited to celebrate the holidays in the wing that was completed and refurnished.

And Rowan had worked indeed, but each night, he'd returned to the school, to Augusta's bed. With years to make up for, the newlywed couple took full advantage of living as man and wife.

There had been only one shadow to darken the past few months.

Ivy Annesley's parents had never made it back from the Continent. Shortly after the term began, word had arrived that they'd perished along with forty-three other souls when their ship capsized off the coast of Calais.

Addison and Collette had offered to take her in and given her the choice of taking the term off, but she had refused. The somber young woman insisted she'd prefer to return to her studies.

And watching her, Augusta could not help but see some of herself in the girl's mental fortitude.

And Rowan's.

But even with the girl's steely determination, she'd suffered bouts of despair. Augusta had ached for her daughter, her own flesh and blood, knowing that no one could ever replace the people who'd raised her.

Augusta and Rowan had done their best to provide the necessary comfort Ivy needed when she'd been ready to receive it.

She'd even accepted their invitation to spend the holidays with them rather than go home with Fiona.

They'd spent Christmas Eve with Piers, Victoria, Augusta's mother, and her youngest brother, and Augusta couldn't remember enjoying herself more.

She had Rowan at her side—her best friend, her lover, her husband.

Together, they spent Christmas with their daughter.

And following several very long, very emotional discussions, they'd decided to tell Ivy the truth. And in an act of sheer optimism, they'd decided to do it on her birthday.

"Are you sure you want to do this?" Rowan hugged Augusta from behind. Christmas had been two days ago and all the students had gone home but for one.

Which was why Augusta found herself shaking as she stared into Rowan's eyes in the looking glass, even with his arms encircling her.

With the other girls gone, Ivy had taken up temporary residence in their extra bedchamber. Augusta had insisted.

Over the term, and more so over the holidays, Ivy's mood could go from laughing and smiling one moment to that faraway sadness the next.

Rowan and Augusta had agreed Ivy would fare better knowing she was not alone, and that it was best she know the truth.

"We don't want to keep her waiting," Rowan whispered, his mouth near Augusta's ear. Dinner had been ready for nearly half an hour. "Although, she's likely got her nose in a book."

Augusta nodded. "You're sure?"

"One can never be sure." He kissed the shell of her ear. "But I think it's for the best. No one need know but Ivy. And from there, we'll simply provide what she needs."

"Yes," Augusta agreed. They had discussed this many, many times. The very last thing in the world they wanted was to hurt her.

And on that note, Rowan turned her to face him. They'd

faced many storms, both apart from one another and together. After a reassuring embrace, Rowan took Augusta's hand and strolled out of the bedchamber toward the parlor. They would face this one together.

Just as Rowan predicted, Ivy sat waiting in the parlor with a book in her lap. "You'll need spectacles if you read too much in the dark." Augusta did her best to keep the nerves from making her sound shrill.

Rowan meandered around the room, lighting the other sconces. As calm as he seemed, Augusta knew he was nervous as well.

Ivy lifted her gaze from her book and sat up straight. "You said you wanted to talk to me about something before we went in for dinner? You said I shouldn't be worried, but I do hope you don't have bad news." Ivy had a tendency toward caution. And who could blame her?

"Oh, no!" Augusta crossed to sit beside her daughter. "At least, I hope you don't see it as bad news."

With all the candles lit now, Rowan had nothing to do but take the seat facing them.

The only sign of his nervousness was the slight wrinkle between his eyes.

Augusta had thought her words through a thousand times, but she'd never quite been satisfied with any of them. Sitting with her daughter now, she decided to start at the beginning.

"A very long time ago, before you were born, I fell in love with Mr. Stewart." Augusta met Rowan's encouraging stare and then continued, "We'd agreed to marry. I loved him very much. But... my parents didn't approve of the match and I was sent away."

"But you found one another again." Ivy glanced between the two of them, looking a little confused but also pleased.

"Yes. Oh, but so much happened in the time we were apart." Augusta reached out and took Ivy by the hand. "Before we were separated, we, well, the two of us anticipated our vows." Heat spread up Augusta's neck. This wasn't something one ever expected to discuss with a young girl.

But Augusta had determined that Ivy would know the truth.

"On the twenty-seventh day of December, of the year one thousand, eight hundred and fifteen, I gave birth to a baby girl. My aunt had found a couple who wanted a daughter more than anything but couldn't have one on their own." Augusta blinked back tears. Because this particular part of the story never failed to break her heart. "I was never told their names, and they were never told the identity of the mother."

Ivy was not a dimwitted girl. She glanced between Rowan and Augusta. "That couple was my parents?" She did not pull her hand away from Augusta, but she remained still, motionless.

"Yes," Rowan answered and then cleared his throat.

"And you," Ivy stared at Augusta, "birthed me." She turned back to Rowan. "I am that child?"

Both Augusta and Rowan nodded and for the next minute, the only sound in the room was the ticking of the clock.

And then Ivy narrowed her eyes thoughtfully. "I wondered. Because Mother and Father were both fair-skinned, with light hair." And Ivy's skin was a beautiful golden color. "And I over-heard bits and pieces of conversations that didn't make sense."

"So you are not shocked?" Augusta asked.

"No." And then Ivy glanced up. "Did they know it was you? Did you know when I started attending school here?"

"No one did." But Augusta explained how she had learned, and why she kept quiet. "And once I realized, I decided it was best to keep the information to myself. It wouldn't have been fair to disrupt your life, and I didn't want to lose the opportunity of... watching you grow up."

Rowan was leaning forward, resting his arms on his knees, and watching Ivy with concerned eyes. "But with your parents gone, we decided you should know. What you choose to do with the knowledge is your decision and your decision alone. Regardless, Ivy, you aren't alone in this world. You will never be alone again."

"I guess I never was." Ivy blinked and turned to Augusta. "That must have been horrible for you."

"Not being able to tell you was one of the most painful things I've ever experienced. But you grew into such a wonderful young lady. Your parents gave you the life that I could not. When they brought you to my school, it was the best gift I could ever ask for."

"They were good parents. I miss them." Ivy's lips trembled.

"They loved you," Augusta said. Watching Ivy go home at the end of each term would have been impossible if she hadn't believed this.

"Yes." Ivy fell silent again.

"It's a lot to take in, we realize." Augusta's heart ached for the young woman beside her. Had they made a mistake in telling her? But before any more doubts could set in, Ivy turned to Augusta with a smile.

"You are my mother," she said.

"Yes."

Then she turned to Rowan. "And you are my father."

"Yes," he answered.

"It's going to take some getting used to, and I'll continue to call you Miss Primm and Mr. Stewart," Ivy said. But then she surprised them both when she rose. "But I cannot help but think it's one of the best presents a girl could receive on her birthday."

"You are not... upset?" Augusta asked.

Ivy pondered the question before answering. "Not in a bad way. And it hardly seems real. But I... trust both of you. I'm sure I'll think of questions later, once I've had a chance to think it all over. But for now..."

"Yes?"

"I'm just hungry. Did Jenny really make a cake for my birthday?"

"She did!" Augusta laughed in relief, and Rowan took her hand as they followed their daughter in to dinner.

And although time had stolen a good deal of the past, the future stretched out in front of them with a lifetime of promise.

Because dreams did, in fact, come true. Sometimes, however, one needed to change them along the way.

And there was nothing wrong with that.

—The End—

THANK you for Reading **Schooled by the Bastard**. Check out Annabelle's next series **Rakes of Rotten Row!** Book one is **Hanover Square Spare.**

You can also purchase the entire Miss Primm's series for **50% off, direct from Annabelle.**

The Earl of Standish couldn't have a worse name. He's not in good standing anywhere, but with luck and the right bride, that should all change...

As the Duke of Crossing's overlooked daughter, Lady Marigold Hathaway's prospects are limited, at best. So when Lord Standish comes to her with a shocking proposition, she can't help but consider it.

Complete Seven Book Series!

Direct from Author

Miss Primm's Secret School
for Budding Bluestockings

When everyone has always wanted her older sister, why would this handsome earl suddenly want her? And does it matter, seeing as she was halfway to falling in love with him anyway?

Hanover Square Spare was initially titled, Earl of Standish, and was published on Jan.3, 2023, in Wicked Earls Forever. This edition includes exclusive bonus content and is book 1 of Annabelle Anders' series, Rakes of Rotten Row.

Hanover Square Spare

Here is your free sneak peek!

CHAPTER 1 - HANOVER SQUARE SPARE

TWO HEADLINES

*R*eed Rutherford, the Earl of Standish now, stepped into the foyer of the club he'd only heard of before: *The Domus Emporium*—a discreet gentlemen's club set just outside of Mayfair.

Inhaling, Reed detected the scent that was uniquely male and uniquely noble—a subtle blend of cigar smoke, scotch, and expensive colognes he'd always associated with his uncle.

Until recently, he'd only heard of the club from his less-than-upstanding male relatives—now, all dead. A disturbing wave of emptiness washed over him, but he ignored it and took in his surroundings. The understated luxury consisted of gleaming mahogany tables and furnishings upholstered with either leather or forest-green velvet. Two or three dozen candles burned overhead, secured in an understated chandelier dangling from the high ceiling.

A few ladies mingled amongst them, dressed in finery and jewels that would put any duchess to shame. It was the intelligence in their eyes, however, that truly set them apart from ladies of the *ton*.

That and the fact that they made their living providing all manner of sexual favors.

As Reed picked his way between the felt-covered tables, patrons gradually became aware of his presence, and the low murmurs fell silent. Sharp eyes followed him, and an oppressive hush settled upon the room.

But he would not be cowed, and he narrowed his gaze when an annoying voice cut through the tension.

"What have we here, fellows, but the new Earl of Standish?" The Marquess of Pittsguard, or "Pitt" as he was known, lifted a snifter in Reed's direction. The seams on the balding lord's jacket strained against the padding in his shoulders, and if the shirt points on his collar were any higher, they'd likely put the man's eyes out.

Reed kept his expression bland. He was not fool enough to see the toast for anything other than the mockery intended.

"How lucky for you, *Standish*," a second voice leered. "I can only dream that the seven blokes standing between myself and my great uncle's title would vanish as conveniently as yours have." Mr. Marshall, one of the younger gentlemen present, raised his glass as well. His hooded eyes and wobbling stance revealed that although it was barely noon, he was already deep into his cups.

Glancing around, Reed realized most of them were in a similar condition.

Likely, they'd been at it all night.

Reed, of course, was stone-cold sober. Despite his new waistcoat, shining Hessians, and perfectly tied cravat, he wasn't one of them.

"Indeed," he addressed Marshall, the word dripping in sarcasm, "but not everyone can be so lucky." Fists clenched at his sides, he was prepared to make the next heckler pay.

Luck—a ridiculous word to describe the tragedy his family had experienced over the past month.

Reed hated being the subject of attention. He far preferred holing up in Rutherford Place, the century-old Standish Mayfair townhouse discreetly set back from the street across from Hanover Square. He'd prefer to be anywhere else, actually, sorting out estate accounts, or even addressing the abundance of vowels he'd inherited along with the title.

And that was precisely what he'd be doing if not for the urgent message he'd received from his long-time trusted friend, Jasper Perry, the Baron of Westcott. Considered to be something of a philanderer, some referred to West as the Piccadilly Player. *Ludicrous.* Reed pinched his mouth flat. All it had taken were a few dubious accusations from a scorned debutante's mama and the nickname had stuck.

Which was only one of the reasons Reed had avoided Mayfair as long as he had.

Reed searched the room, eager to find the fellow and learn what could possibly merit such urgency.

Having *benefitted* from the recent demise of his uncle, cousin, older brother, and father, he'd suspected there would be rumors. Any man in his situation would find himself under intense speculation and scrutiny.

Damn, damn, and double damn.

Because, despite four healthy male relatives having stood between himself and the title, Reed was Standish now—as in *Lord Standish.*

As in, the *bloody Earl of Standish.* Something he'd never wished for or wanted.

All four men had perished in the fire that had consumed the hunting cabin at Searidge Manor, his uncle's estate.

Hell, now it was *his* estate.

And although the cause of death listed on their certificates was accurate, it was but a small part of the story.

Only a handful of people comprehended the vices practiced by the recently deceased—and how those depravities had come into play. They'd all been incoherent—out of their heads from the combination of opium and alcohol they favored. Even less had heard his uncle's recent ramblings of ending it all—of escaping this world permanently. Had it been an accident? If just one of them had been even partly conscious, the fire could have been extinguished.

At the very least, they could have escaped and lived to tempt fate some other time in the future.

Reed refused to mourn them. Hell, he hadn't time to mourn them—what with fielding the massive debts they'd left behind.

Debts beyond comprehension. Disgruntled tenants. Unpaid vendors. Gambling vowels.

Not to mention the care of his mother and three sisters. His uncle's wife had departed the estate the day following the funeral, announcing she'd rather live with her sister than remain at Seabridge Manor another day. For which Reed had been grateful.

One less burden for him to bear.

Because his mother and sisters had been left distraught in the wake of the tragedy. His mother had cared about her husband and loved Randal, her oldest son. Reed's sisters had looked to the two men for security, until recently.

But for the most part, they had been left reeling by the loss of their father and eldest brother.

Reed clenched and then unclenched his fists. He could not dwell on them now. He had far more pressing issues to sort out.

Blasted issues none of them had considered before acting so recklessly.

The most urgent of which was this unsavory scandal. By revealing as few details of the fire as possible, by declining any further investigation that might expose his uncle's dark comments, Reed himself had fallen under suspicion.

And ridicule.

And a few legal challenges.

But it was best this way. He'd bury the unsavory circumstances of their deaths right along with them. No one need ever suspect the worst.

Caroline, Melanie, and Josephine's innocent faces came to mind. The rumors about Reed's part in all of it would die down and then he could go about salvaging his sisters' futures. If anything else got out, the poor girls would forever live as pariahs.

"Rutherford." A friendly face appeared, loosening the vise that had begun to tighten around Reed's chest. Westcott and Reed had been in the same level at Eton and, together, had fought off more than one bully. "Right on time." West jerked his head toward a darkened corner near the back of the room. Upon closer inspection, Reed could see a set of heavy velvet drapes hanging there, likely concealing a back entrance.

Reed exhaled.

Not at all reluctant to absent himself from dubious happenings around the gaming tables, Reed shook the hand West offered and followed him away from the main area.

"Good to see you," he said. Relieved as he was, Reed was still keenly aware that West had refused to share with him the purpose of this meeting. The continued secrecy only further fueled his curiosity.

"Likewise, my friend." West glanced over his shoulder with a warm smile. The baron hadn't changed much in the past few years. He was still slim and broad-shouldered, one of the rare noblemen never to have worn padding. He had hair that alternately appeared light brown and dark blond, and hazel eyes, making the man something of a chameleon.

Stepping through the heavy curtains, Reed followed West up a spiraling staircase to a carpeted foyer. On one side, a wall, on the other, a gleaming railing that overlooked the main floor of the club. West marched to the end of the foyer, and knocked on the heavy wooden door. Without waiting for an answer, he pushed it open and gestured for Reed to precede him inside.

Knowing the Duke of Malum owned the club, Reed immediately guessed this to be the infamous duke's personal office. Hints of cigar smoke blended with lemon oil, mahogany, leather, and an unrecognizable spice. On one side of the office, a massive desk. On the other, a comfortably arranged seating area where hot coals burned in the adjacent hearth.

As Reed perused the faces of the occupants, the hairs on the back of his neck stood up.

Despite having kept mostly absent from society, he had, however, kept abreast of happenings via the newspapers. He'd seen the caricatures and recognized all but one of the gentlemen lounging there—a handful of the most powerful men in all of England.

And not one of them appeared welcoming. What the hell was West up to?

His old friend gestured toward two of them. "Standish, you know Helton and Winterhope." Maxwell Black, the Earl of Helton, lived year-round in London and had recently entered the London Gazette. The man's black hair was unkempt and he looked not to have shaved in two or three days. Nonetheless, intelligent green eyes met Reed's from behind a pair of spectacles.

With the earl having taken permanent residence in London, Reed wondered at the condition of the man's country estate. Had he simply abandoned it?

"Helton," Reed leaned forward, noting ink stains on the man's hand as he shook it.

He then turned to Benjamin St. Lancaster, the Marquess of Winterhope and owner of England's finest stables, Hope Downs. With neatly trimmed brown hair and sideburns, the man's flamboyant suit fit him like a glove, and his cravat was tied perfectly. Winterhope's appearance contrasted sharply with that of the earl's.

"You're looking nobbish," Winterhope observed. The comment came as no surprise to Reed, but even having been dressed in the latest finery—by his dead cousin's valet—he'd yet to feel comfortable in his new position.

And damned if he ever would.

Before Reed could respond, West gestured toward the seedier-looking of the other two gentlemen. Although the hulking fellow appeared relaxed, with one booted foot resting on his knee, the man's eyes burned with a cunning intensity. "Mr. Beckworth," West introduced the man without further explanation.

And none was needed. Reed had heard of Leopold Beckworth. The man, known to be ruthless and calculating, likely controlled half the commerce that took place on the docks. When they shook hands, Reed found Beckworth's grip to be firm, his hands, scarred and rugged.

"And, of course, Malum."

Whereas Beckworth was rumored to rule over the darker money that came into England, word was that Malum controlled a good deal of the legitimate wealth. As well as most of what existed in-between.

Despite Malum's status and resources, most of the *ton* publicly shunned him. Behind closed doors, however, England's revered nobility proved their hypocrisy by patronizing the emporium on a regular basis.

All that aside, Reed was dubiously honored to find himself in the company of such men. And suddenly wary as hell.

Sighing internally, Reed resigned himself to yet more trouble. Had he inherited yet further debt, the kind that put him in trouble with the underbelly of society? He wouldn't exactly be surprised if that was the case. He turned to Westcott with a raised brow, and his friend chuckled.

"Have a seat." West shook a wayward lock of hair out of his eyes, crossed his feet, and slouched against the wall. "You're wondering why I asked you here."

Not fooled by West's friendly manner, Reed remained standing. "I'll admit to some curiosity," he conceded.

Helton leaned forward. "I'll skip the small talk, Rutherford—"

"Standish," Malum grunted, not looking up.

"Standish... Damn. Never thought I'd see the day," West inserted. "Anyhow, good to see you and all that, but I've asked you here because of the latest rumors."

"Rumors?" Reed cocked a brow. How many times had the two of them mocked some rumor or another?

West winced. "Unfortunately, yes. Talk that you murdered your predecessors is... gaining traction." Reed's friend's tone turned serious. "You need to put them down."

Reed frowned. "But they are only rumors."

"Rumors alleging murder," West pointed out. Before Reed could emphatically declare his innocence, West held up a hand. "I know they're false, but in society, even the most unfounded of suspicions take on a life of their own."

His friend, *the Piccadilly Player*, ought to know.

"Innocent or not, you're going to need help, Standish." Winterhope folded his arms across his chest, looking far too serious. "And if these dangerous rumors aren't subdued, the authorities will have no choice but to get involved."

Reed clutched his hands behind his back, stunned by this conversation.

"That's why you sent for me?" A moment ago, he would have laughed at this. But this powerful group of gentlemen most definitely were not laughing. And West had never been one to exaggerate or worry needlessly over anything.

Quite the opposite, actually.

"You need to put them to rest. Something you can't accomplish while hiding away at Rutherford Place." His old friend's tone remained somber.

"I thought peers were above accountability," Reed argued. Having managed both his father's and uncles' affairs for nearly a decade, he'd seen crime go unpunished often enough.

"But yours are unique circumstances," Winterhope said. "Because this crime, in particular, is against another peer—or in your case, peers."

"You could be thrown in Newgate," West said, "If these aren't squashed before the Season begins."

"The Season always complicates matters. There are more mouths to speculate. More ears to perk up to the gossip." Winterhope shrugged. "In general, more fuel."

The Season? But the first event of the Season was less than a fortnight away. *Bloody hell.*

"Surely it will die down as soon as some footman runs off with one of the new debutantes?" he offered.

"But we're talking about murder, Reed." West's voice was firm. "You simply cannot leave this to chance."

"And that's why West here asked for us to step in," Winterhope said. "Have a seat." He gestured toward a plush, high-backed chair.

"You'll want to take a look at this." Unsmiling, the Earl of Helton tossed a newspaper onto the small table in front of him.

Reed gingerly lowered himself onto the offered seat and shifted his gaze to the newspaper—which was, oddly enough, dated three days in the future. But it was the headline that sent his heart plummeting.

Tragic accident or murder—or worse?

"It's on everyone's minds. The public will demand a thorough investigation. It's impossible for me to ignore such a prominent scandal," Helton said. "But Westcott here says you were chums in school—mentioned that you'd helped him out a time or two. So, I'm willing to hold off. If you can change the narrative, give me something even more interesting by..." He glanced over to the fireplace, where a large clock sat upon the mantel. "Midnight Tuesday, I'll print this instead."

He tossed out a second paper.

"Standish marries the Duke of Crossings' daughter?" Reed asked. "But she was my cousin's fiancée." A bark of ironic laughter escaped. Even given an entire year, he doubted he could make the headline true.

As her fiancé's cousin, Reed had been introduced to Lady Gardenia Hathaway and even attended the house party to celebrate her and Rupert's betrothal. But it had been well known that he was there as a courtesy, and worked for his family as the estate manager. The duke's beautiful daughter had been polite enough but otherwise dismissive.

In truth, she'd been raised to be a duchess. Her mother had, in fact, made it clear that she'd considered even Rupert, heir to an earl, to be beneath her daughter. If not for Reed's uncle's dealings with the Duke of Crossings, the betrothal would never have come about.

"But you are Standish now," West pointed out.

Reed stared across the room at Helton, earl and publisher. "Couldn't you simply water down the first version?"

"No." Helton didn't even think about it. "Not if I'm going to make this paper profitable. But if you provide me with something to distract them..." He shrugged.

Reed swallowed, imagining a noose being dropped around his neck.

In exchange for one story, Helton wanted another. And it would have to be marriage. An exclusive announcement of a mere engagement to Crossings' daughter, while interesting, couldn't replace the drama of the first headline.

The first story was by far more damning. Words such as suicide, arson, murder, and even treason were all mentioned. The article would erase any hope he had for securing his sisters' futures. And if he did end up in Newgate, they'd be left to fend for themselves.

Newgate.

The word pinged around his brain and sweat snaked down his spine as he imagined walls closing in around him.

"You certainly are thorough." He grimaced.

"Not me," Helton said. "My reporters."

Reed shifted his attention to the second headline and exhaled. "You'll kill the first story if I convince Crossings' daughter to marry me before you go to print Tuesday night." Today was Sunday, and the day was already half over. So he'd have less than three days. The only way he saw himself succeeding in this demand was if he kidnapped the chit.

And that scenario had the potential to bring his standing even lower.

"It would hardly be worthy of the front page if you observed proper mourning first," Helton spoke around the cheroot in his mouth.

Reed shifted his gaze to West and then around the room before allowing it to land on Helton. He couldn't technically call this blackmail, but his arm might as well be twisting right out of the socket.

"Why?" Reed asked. "Why even give me a choice?"

Westcott's grimace turned into a deep frown. "Back at school, you came to my aid more than once. I'd do more if I could. But the rumors need to be squashed. I wouldn't have requested this meeting if it wasn't dire."

If the truth behind the fire were made public, his sisters could say goodbye to the possibility of landing proper husbands. Caroline, the eldest and most independent, would no doubt manage, but Melanie had always wanted a family, and Josephine had grown up with stars in her eyes. She was too young to have them extinguished.

And Reed... well, he wasn't sure how long he could survive being locked up in Newgate.

Contemplating the aftermath of the fire objectively, even Reed comprehended how the circumstances were damning.

But they were just that—circumstances.

Westcott reached into his pocket and pulled out a folded slip of parchment. "We've acquired a special license for you. Send word once you've secured her agreement and we'll make arrangements for a ceremony at St. George's on Tuesday evening—that way, I'll send word to Helton before he puts the paper to bed."

The location was simple enough—just across the square from Rutherford Place. But getting a bride there. That was a near impossibility.

Reed shook his head, imagining his cousin's former fiancée—the diamond of the Season, in fact. With her perfect figure, golden hair, and crystal blue eyes, Lady Gardenia could have anyone she wanted. "She'll never agree to it." She had a reputation for being her father's puppet, dancing to his tune, obeying the duke's every command. "There has to be another way."

"Nothing as newsworthy," Helton said. "Crossings' chit has been said to have the character of an angel. If she marries you, that's as good of a declaration of your innocence as you can hope for."

"You are Standish." The Duke of Malum pinned his gaze on Reed.

Ten minutes later, Reed marched past the towering cathedral on his way back to Rutherford Place on Hanover Square, one of the premier addresses in Mayfair.

Where he, Reed Rutherford, was lord of the manor now—a manor tended to by servants his uncle had employed. This was madness.

He rubbed the back of his neck.

But if he was going to bring honor back to the title and pave the way for his sisters' futures, he needed legitimacy.

If he wanted to maintain his freedom, he needed to squash all speculation. He wanted to be angry with Helton, but the blasted publisher was, in fact, offering him a bone.

Reed had no choice but to convince the duke's daughter to marry him.

CHECK out Annabelle's next series **Rakes of Rotten Row!** Book one is **Hanover Square Spare.**

You can also purchase the entire Miss Primm's series for **50% off, direct from Annabelle.**

Be notified when I have a new release or sale by subscribing to my newsletter: **https://www. annabelleanders.com/news letter-subscribe**

Miss Primm's Secret School for Budding Bluestockings

THE RAKES OF ROTTEN ROW

Hanover Square Spare

The Earl of Standish

Piccadilly Player

Westcott's story

Fleet Street Scoundrel

Maxwell Black's story

Pall Mall Peer

Winterhope's story

Bond Street Bachelor

Mr. Beckworth's story

Regent Street Rogue

The Duke of Malum's Story

Other Popular Series by Annabelle Anders

Devilish Debutantes

The Regency Cocky Gents

Miss Primm's Secret School for Budding Bluestockings

And more!

Learn about all of Annabelle's books at

https://www.annabelleanders.com

MISS PRIMM'S SECRET SCHOOL FOR BUDDING BLUESTOCKINGS

Trapped With the Duke

Miss Colette Jones

Educated by the Earl

Miss Victoria Shipley

Pretending to be a Debutante

Lady Priscilla

Rescued by the Rake

Miss Chloe Fortune

Advising the Viscount

Miss Addy

Make Believe With the Marquess

Beatrice Wolcott

Schooled by the Bastard

Miss Primm

ABOUT THE AUTHOR

Married to the same man for over 25 years, I am a mother to three children and two Miniature Wiener dogs.

After owning a business and experiencing considerable success, my husband and I got caught in the financial crisis and lost everything in 2008; our business, our home, even our car.

At this point, I put my B.A. in Poly Sci to use and took work as a waitress and bartender (Insert irony). Unwilling to give up on a professional life, I simultaneously went back to college and obtained a degree in EnergyManagement.

And then the energy market dropped off.

And then my dog died.

I can only be grateful for this series of unfortunate events, for, with nothing to lose and completely demoralized, I sat down and began to write the romance novels which had until then, existed only my imagination. After publishing over twenty novels now, with one having been nominated for RWA's Distinguished ™RITA Award in 2019, I am happy to tell you that I have finally found my place in life.

Thank you so much for being a part of my journey!

Be notified when I have a new release or sale by subscribing to my newsletter: **https://www.annabelleanders.com/news letter-subscribe**

www.annabelleanders.com

GET A FREE BOOK

Sign up for the news letter and download a book from Annabelle,

For **FREE!**

Sign up at **www.annabelleanders.com**

Printed in Dunstable, United Kingdom